SHADOW MOVES

A MILITARY SPACE OPERA TALE

P. R. ADAMS

PROMETHEAN TALES

SHADOW MOVES

Copyright © 2018 P R Adams

Illustration © Tom Edwards
TomEdwardsDesign.com

❀ Created with Vellum

ALSO BY P. R. ADAMS

For updates on new releases and news on other series, visit my website and sign up for my mailing list at:

http://www.p-r-adams.com

The War in Shadow

Shadow Moves

Shadow Play

Shadow Strike

Shadow Talk

Shadow Pawn (2020)

Books in the On The Brink Universe

The Stefan Mendoza Trilogy

Into Twilight

Gone Dark

End State

The Rimes Trilogy

Momentary Stasis

Transition of Order

Awakening to Judgment

The ERF Series

Turning Point

Valley of Death

Jungle Dark

Chariot Bright

Dawn Fire

The Lancers Series

Deep Descent

Deadly Game

Dire Straits

The Burning Sands Trilogy

Beneath Burning Sands

Across Burning Sands

Beyond Burning Sands

Books in The Chain Series

The Chain: Shattered

The Journey Home

Rock of Salvation

From the Depths

Ever Shining

DEDICATION

For all those lost as a result of the Gulf of Tonkin Resolution.

1

SHEETS WHISPERED AS LIEUTENANT COMMANDER FAITH BENSON PULLED herself closer to Sergeant Clive Halliwell. It wasn't as if there was much room to separate the two on her fold-out bunk, but when she'd nodded off, she'd gone onto her left side and he onto his right. So there was a gap. A little one.

She pressed herself against his warm back, trembling at the feel of his powerful muscles against her flesh. His breathing had become hypnotic to her the last few days, his scent something she could bathe in. Looking into his dark eyes when he was above her, the way his stare became so intense, the way his skin wrinkled around the nub on his nose where it'd been broken in boarding action a few years back.

What would it be like, just the two of them living together? No obligations. No one telling them how to live. No chance of something pulling them apart.

Even in a small cabin like hers—the second largest aboard the *Pandora* —she was content. Having to squeeze between the fold-out furniture when he was in the cabin didn't bother her. It meant forced intimacy. And what memorabilia would he add to the shelves lining her room? Not much. He never paid any attention to her silly trinkets, and she'd seen the cabins he and his Marines lived in. They lived as light as she did. Lighter.

A simple life held a lot of appeal, actually.

But a simple life together was stupid. This was just animal attraction. It was her body telling her that now was the time, and he was the one.

Just basic reproductive nonsense trying to manage how she lived her life.

She knew better, though. She'd screwed up and fallen for him. His arms around her, his lips on hers…it was something she looked forward to as much as the dream of attaining a ship of her own to command, a ship better than the dump she was serving on now.

An alarm chimed, and the cabin lights powered on hesitantly.

Halliwell growled and his head came up from the pillow. He came around like that, as if he were reliving something terrible in the seconds before wakefulness. Then he realized where he was, twisted around, and smiled at her.

They shared a morning breath kiss, and it didn't bother her at all. What more could better confirm her fears?

"Want another go-round?" His voice was raspy.

"You need to get out of Officer Country before someone spots you."

She rolled over him, taking pleasure in the way his hands caressed her. When she powered on a wall display and brought up the security camera interface, he stood behind her, kissing her shoulder. Who else on the ship was even tall enough to do that? It used to bother her, being tall. Not with him.

"The passageway's clear. Go." But she didn't want him to.

He pulled on his underwear. "I've been thinking."

"Dangerous. Don't do it."

He snorted. "Yeah. Look. Seriously. Thinking. We get back to Station-42, I push for my separation paperwork. They can't delay it any longer."

It hurt hearing him talk about leaving, but he'd already been forced to extend an extra stint. "They won't delay it again."

"Right. And that's another three months. I take all that extra money they owe me, I head back to Muresi. I work the local trade routes. Cargo handler. Crew chief. Hired security. Whatever. Three months later, you resign. We buy our own ship, a short hauler at first—something good enough for intra-system work—and we start a trader business."

"Hauling cargo? In a little rust bucket?" Her knees wobbled at the idea.

"To start, sure. And we won't have anyone bossing us around."

"Every job has a boss. What you're describing, your boss is the bank."

"But if you know what you're doing, you grow the business."

"Until you can afford a bigger rust bucket?"

He tapped a finger against his temple. "I've got vision."

"So I see." She confirmed the passageway was clear again. "Go."

He popped the hatch, winked at her, then darted out.

She settled onto the bed, running fingers over the last of his heat. Would it be just another fit of self-destruction if she resigned her commission to become a pilot on some junker that tooled around in his home system? Would it be just another poke in her mother's eye? Had going to the Academy really been that, or was it just another one of her digs?

Benson sighed. "Hard to self-sabotage when you've got a mother who makes a career out of sabotaging you."

She closed the bunk against the bulkhead and snatched her underwear from the floor where it had fallen. His desperate tugs and yanks had stretched out the elastic, almost ruining them. She'd need to print out more soon.

As she searched through her drawers for her workout gear, an annoying voice in the back of her head said she was getting too old for this.

Passion? Heat?

That was for irresponsible kids. She'd had plenty of time for it back on Kedraal and never pursued it.

Too busy trying to impress her mother, the great and important Representative Sargota Zhanya.

At least that's how Sargota saw herself.

The reality was, of course, different. Outside the home, Sargota still went by Benson, even though she had nothing but contempt for her absent husband. And her importance as just another lower chamber minister in the government?

Benson shoved those thought aside and headed for the fitness cabin.

Lights flickered when the hatch opened. It was chilly inside, which was fine with her. She didn't like working up a big sweat, and today she needed to work cardio.

She lowered a treadmill platform from the bulkhead and climbed on. The machine identified the program she was supposed to do and hummed to life.

The walls turned reflective, and she got a look at herself: disheveled brown hair pulled back in a ponytail for the workout, jade eyes, full lips that were a little pale, like her flesh.

And a puffy face.

How did she start to fall apart so fast? She was thirty-one, but everything seemed to be failing for her. Even while watching her diet, she'd developed a small paunch. Slight. Just a hint of a curve. But it was a paunch. And her breasts had started to sag.

It was being stuck on a ship like the *Pandora*. She was a distinguished graduate from the Kedraalian Republic Naval Academy. She should've had a fleet assignment by now. A tour on a flagship. *Something*.

In her mind, she called the *Pandora* a rust bucket, but today the term brought a smile to her lips. She'd used that term to describe Halliwell's business venture idea, but the term fit the *Pandora* as well. The ship was old and worn, and something was always breaking down.

The bitterness built as she jogged, and before she knew it, her cheeks were red.

She looked terrible. How did she hope to keep someone like Halliwell interested—?

The hatch opened, and Petty Officer Brianna Stiles stepped through. Centimeters shorter, with golden brown skin that glowed and stretched taut over perfect proportions, shapely lips that always seemed split in a smile. She made the same T-shirt and shorts ensemble look like a fashion statement. "Morning, Commander."

"It's eighteen hundred."

"Way I see it, ma'am, it's space." She pulled a strength-building resistance bench out from the bulkhead just short of the treadmill. "We get to say what time it is."

Stiles had been the focus of attention since coming aboard at their last stop, and she knew it. And ate it up.

Benson felt just hideous being in the same cabin with the younger woman.

Did I ever look that young and vibrant and...perfect?

The resistance system whispered as the petty officer pulled down on the overhead bar. "You been at it a while, ma'am?"

Fifteen minutes short of an hour. Benson wasn't sure she could make the rest. "I—"

Her comm device chimed. It was Commander Martinez's tone. She accepted. "What's up?"

"I need you on the bridge."

Blunt. He was always blunt. "I'm not due for turnover—"

"Commander Benson, I need you on the bridge." He had that edge now.

"Give me a few minutes."

He disconnected without further guidance.

Stiles's deep breathing stopped as she released the overhead bar. "Everything okay?"

"No. I don't think so."

"I'll close the treadmill up, ma'am."

"Thanks."

Benson hurried back to her cabin, grabbed fresh clothes, her personal bag, and a towel, then slipped into the Officers' Country head. Leave it to the Navy to carry on traditions like naming a bathroom the "head."

She toweled off on the way to her cabin and zipped her flight suit up as she made her way to the bridge.

An alarm shrieked as she reached for the hatch access panel; she froze for a second.

Then the alarm was silenced.

She opened the hatch.

Martinez leaned against the overhead systems, one hand wrapped around a stabilizing bar as he stood over Petty Officer Kohn. The younger man was hunched over a bank of displays on the port side of the cramped bridge space, thick brown hair mussed.

The commander was short, lanky, with an angular face that was most obviously manifested in his sharp nose. He liked to compensate for his height by getting in people's space and by looming over them.

He ran fingers through the black hair that curved back in a widow's peak. "Then what the hell happened, Chuck?"

Kohn, who was himself gangly and long, shook his head. "I—" He tapped at the clunky console keys, keys that had long ago been worn down so much that the ruggedized plastic had no labels, and many of the heavily used keys had a melted look to them. "I don't know."

"You damned well better figure it out." Martinez turned and waved her forward with his free hand.

"What is it?" She ducked on her way through the maze of overhanging systems and panels.

Kohn's dark eyes closed. "It doesn't make sense, ma'am."

Martinez pointed to the plate of glass that covered the front of the bridge where it protruded over the lower deck. "Notice anything?"

There were just distant stars and the black of space. Nothing—

"Oh." She squeezed past him and leaned against the back of the pilot chair she used when running the second shift.

Everything was crisp, clear, bright. The twinkle of distant stars wasn't distorted.

"We came out of Fold Space?"

Martinez squeezed into the secondary pilot seat to her right and slid it forward. His hands darted across the various panels and consoles, fingers flipping switches and tapping buttons. "Thrown out."

To her left, Kohn licked his lips. "Can't be thrown out, sir."

"You have a better way of describing this, Petty Officer?"

Kohn's head sank lower.

Data scrolled across the displays of the pilot station: coordinates, trajectories, readouts from engines and sensors. None of the information looked right.

She pulled her chair back, dropped in, then slid it forward. "Where are we?"

"Well—" Martinez tapped a few more commands, then leaned over to her console and punched a button. "I can tell you where we're not."

The sensor readouts populated her screen, showing the Kedraalian sector and their course, which should have taken them to the remote planet Baregis. According to the readouts, they were light years off-course.

Hundreds of light years.

It...wasn't possible.

The hatch opened, and a bleary-eyed, short man entered. His soft cheeks were unshaven; his blond hair was as mussed up as the petty officer's. The short man sneered and glanced past Kohn. The look wiped out what could almost be described as a pampered attractiveness. "Something wrong?"

Martinez waved for Kohn to give up his seat. "Wrong is an understatement, Mr. Parkinson. Perhaps you can make sense of what we're seeing. Petty Officer Kohn apparently can't."

Kohn shoved his seat back, head down, lips trembling. "It was a power surge."

"Please?" Parkinson held a silencing finger up until he was seated at the console. "Leave it to me."

Loathing burned in Kohn's slitted eyes as he glared at the back of Parkinson's head. "There was—"

"Zuh!" Parkinson shook his finger without looking back.

Kohn turned away while the shorter man tapped at the keys with a confidence and finesse that truly was remarkable.

The way Martinez showed his favoritism and let some of the crew run roughshod over the others had never sat well with Benson. It was a dysfunctional crew, certainly, but some consistency and some level of order was the best way to ensure cohesion.

Parkinson exhaled through his nose loudly. "All right." He twisted his chair around to face the commander, stubby thumb rubbing at a stain on his flight suit. "We're not in Fold Space, and we're hundreds of light years off course. Right so far?"

Martinez nodded.

Parkinson pointed to the view screen. "And that's the DMZ."

Another nod while Benson crossed her arms over her chest. The drama was feeding Parkinson's ego.

"Fold Space drive is offline after failure." Parkinson rubbed the side of his nose. "So are several other systems."

Kohn looked at Benson and mouthed, "Power surge."

She nodded enough for him to see.

Martinez seemed absorbed in Parkinson's little show. "Any ideas?"

Parkinson rubbed his hands, bent forward, then pinched his bottom lip between his index fingers. Again, all dramatic. "Power surge."

Kohn rolled his eyes. "I said—"

Martinez turned back to his console. "Let it go, Chuck."

The young man's shoulders slumped.

Benson couldn't take it anymore. "Petty Officer Kohn, you said this wasn't possible earlier."

"Yes, ma'am. It shouldn't be. But a power surge is the only explanation. All these systems are related."

"Related in what—"

Martinez cleared his throat. "Let's pipe it down, okay? Chief Parkinson, this power surge shouldn't be possible?"

The tension that had crept into the engineering chief's body during Benson's exchange with Kohn slipped away once it became clear the focus of attention had returned squarely to Parkinson again. "No. *Impossible*, actually. The redundancies at the hardware and software level..." He waved at the console. "But it's there. The data doesn't lie."

Benson shook her head. "Wait. I'm sorry I'm being so slow, but I'm hearing words that make no sense. If something is impossible, then it couldn't happen."

Parkinson stretched his arms over his head and yawned. "*Technically* impossible."

"I'm not seeing the difference. We have redundancies built in. Safeguards. That makes it impossible."

"Technically."

Martinez glanced at her, lips compressed and pale. "Any safeguard can be overcome with enough skill."

Parkinson pointed at Martinez. "Bingo."

Kohn's eyes widened and his jaw dropped. "That's—"

"Sabotage." Benson shivered. "You're saying someone committed sabotage."

Martinez studied the console between them. "It's the best explanation."

Sabotage! "But…who?"

2

SOMETHING CLATTERED INSIDE THE MAINTENANCE BAY SUBFLOOR, followed almost immediately by a bang against the floor, followed by a gasp.

Benson knelt beside the open panel and squinted into the crawlspace. A white light seemed to suck the color from the dull, gray equipment lining the secure sub-compartment walls. Beneath the scuffed-up floor, another light flickered in the cramped space, revealing the bent legs of a dark blue flight suit. "Petty Officer Kohn?"

"I'm fine." The bent legs straightened. "The wrench slipped off the bolt."

"All right."

Chief Parkinson pressed his face into an open palm. "You're not going to find anything inside that access panel."

Benson ground a knuckle into her chin and stared into the distance. "This is the auxiliary access juncture, isn't it, Mr. Parkinson?"

"Assuming Kohn's in the right place—"

Kohn's voice boomed from below. "Screw you!"

Benson shook her head. "Same team, guys."

Parkinson smirked. "Assuming Kohn's in the right place, yes, it is the auxiliary access juncture. However, this section of the maintenance bay is off-limits to anyone but Kohn and me, and we're logged every time we come in, which is only for critical work." He pointed at a video camera above the hatch that opened onto the main section of the engineering bay. "That camera and the one over the engineering bay hatch logs everything. Anything triggers it, there's a security alert. You, me, and the captain would get notified the second someone opens that hatch. Oh, and by the way, only the three of us have the security code."

"Any other means of accessing this compartment?"

He stomped on the floor panels. "Sealed off all the way around. You'd have to take a torch to the plates. Unless you came in through the hull."

Another scrape of metal preceded a hiss from the open panel.

Benson nodded toward a workstation-mounted terminal in the corner across from the entry hatch. "Maybe you could check the logs to be sure nothing kept the alarms from triggering."

Parkinson threw up his hands. Rather than argue further, though, he thumbed the terminal to life and tapped through the interface. "To be clear, this isn't possible."

"So you said." Benson leaned against a bulkhead. "What's even more troubling than it being impossible, though, is that we should be dead."

Parkinson's back stiffened. "That *is* the bigger problem, now isn't it."

"Fold Space has a tendency to be extremely un—" She grunted as something cool and slimy touched the skin of her back, then twisted around. The reflection of a clear gel on the section of bulkhead she'd leaned against caught her eye. "—forgiving about drift."

"Well, what matters is that we *did* survive." He bent forward and focused on the terminal.

"So long as no one detects that we're here, maybe we can maintain that good luck." She poked around on a shelf until she found a towel and wiped her back, but there was no getting the slimy stuff off completely. Her flight suit was ruined, and she'd need to toss the T-shirt as well.

The engineer squinted at the terminal. "Which border are we closer to, the Azoren or Gulmar?"

"Azoren, but we're pretty close to both."

"Well, I guess luck can only go so far. If half the things I've heard about the Azoren are true—"

"Focus on the task." Benson shivered. She didn't need anyone getting drawn off into worries about tall tales about Azoren atrocities, least of all her. There hadn't been a run-in with the Azoren or Gulmar in decades, not since the War of Separation, really.

Parkinson screwed his face up into a curious half-smile. "What are you—?"

She wiped the clear grease glob from the wall. "Some sort of gel."

"Ah. Well, it *is* the maintenance bay. Probably silicone. It never breaks down. We use it for everything, especially on an old rust bucket like the *Pandora*."

"You find anything?" She glanced over his shoulder.

"No." He scrolled up and down in the text file. "Except..."

"What?"

He tapped the screen. "Well, I never really thought of this, but there's a gap."

"A gap?" Benson leaned in closer. Numbers, text—it took her a second to recognize date and timestamps. "That's nearly two hours from...three months ago?"

"Nearly. When we docked at Persephone Station. We switched over to station power for the—"

"Transformer replacement. Right." She'd almost forgotten about that. "Took on Petty Officer Stiles and Private Lopez."

"And that restricted cargo for Outpost 27." One of his eyebrows arched. "Wasn't that when Sergeant Halliwell was planning to separate?"

"It was." And the military had mistreated him yet again, forcing him to extend his enlistment "for the good of the Kedraalian Republic military." They weren't at war with anyone, so the obscure clause used to keep him in just seemed petty, especially now.

"So, there *is* a gap." Parkinson frowned.

"And the cameras?"

"Would have been offline."

"But we had people down here while the work was being done, right?"

"Me. Well, and the captain took his turn, too."

"And there was no way anyone could have gotten in past you?"

"No."

How could someone have gotten in, then? She dropped to a knee over the open floor panel. "Petty Officer Kohn, anything?"

"The bolts are working free now. They're really old and rusty but doing pretty good." Kohn sighed. "Shouldn't be long."

Parkinson chuckled. "Could've used some of that silicone."

"Someone must've at some point."

"Oh."

The intercom mounted next to the entry hatch squealed, followed a second later by Martinez's voice. "Faith?"

Benson groaned inwardly at Martinez's complete lack of concern for protocol. She wasn't a ridiculous stickler for it herself, but there was no way someone in his position should have been so dismissive of the basics.

After a quick inspection of the bulkhead for even a hint of grease, she pressed the button. "This is Benson. Go ahead, Commander."

"I need you and Will to meet me in the galley."

"I'm sorry, did you say the galley?"

"All hands. You can leave Chuck there if he's still working."

"Gee, thanks." Kohn's muttering was barely audible from the crawlspace.

Benson caught the smug look on Parkinson's face that said he knew what was going on. He and Martinez had a dangerously friendly relationship, and that just exacerbated the problems between Kohn and his supervisor.

Benson bent closer to the intercom. "Shouldn't we be focused on getting the systems operational?"

"No. We need to understand what happened; otherwise, it might happen again."

"Snapshotting the systems would allow us to troubleshoot it later, when we have time."

"We have time *now*, and we need to figure this out. A copy of system memory won't—"

"Snapshots are perfect for this sort of troubleshooting. We put it all in offline storage and let the experts tear it apart later. We need to get the hell out of the DMZ."

"Faith…" Martinez's voice took on the cool tone he favored when she'd gone too far. "I'm going to need you to calm down, okay?"

The smirk on Parkinson's face spread into a smile. She wanted to punch him so badly at that moment.

"I am calm."

"You sound hysterical."

Centered, she told herself. Stay centered. Why was it always that if she challenged someone, she was being "hysterical"? "Commander Martinez, I'm calmly telling you that this is a bad call. We could start a war here."

"And I'm telling you to drop it. Toe the line. That's an order."

Heat shot into her cheeks. "I hope you know what you're doing."

"I know exactly what I'm doing. Come to the galley. Now."

Parkinson stayed a meter behind her the whole way, wisely keeping any commentary to himself. The other members of the crew were packed into the small galley, most of them seated around the two tables. The white flight suits of the medical team occupied one end of the forward table, and the olive drab of the Marine flight suits occupied the rest of the table. Dark blue and black flight suit—the crew proper—occupied the other table. Benson returned the warm smile of Dr. Gaines—Eve when no one else was around. Her full cheeks seemed to be a little darker than their normal pale brown, and Benson instantly caught the reason why.

Between Gaines and Petty Officer Stiles sat Commander Dietrich, the head of the small medical staff. His head was bowed so that his thinning, curly brown hair was pointed at Benson. The dextrous fingers of one of the best surgeons alive rubbed his pockmarked cheeks. It all said one thing: His eternally weary, brown eyes would be bloodshot, and there would be alcohol on his breath.

How could someone so capable be so self-destructive?

Martinez waved Benson to a spot just behind him. "All right, we've got everyone here, so let's get started."

Stiles raised a hand. "Commander? What about Petty Officer Kohn?"

It was delivered in such a sweet, innocent voice that Martinez couldn't possibly make any sort of challenge out of it.

And he didn't. "He's still working in the maintenance bay. What matters right now, though, is what we're all facing." He clapped his hands together. "Let's cover that, okay? I'm sure you've already heard that we suffered a Fold Drive malfunction and we drifted into the DMZ. We're a skosh closer to Azoren space than Gulmar, so—"

Dietrich's head came up. "So we can die in a couple horrible ways." Bleary-eyed. Slurred words.

Martinez looked ready to flip. "Commander Dietrich—"

Gaines stood, brushing back a stubborn wave of graying black hair. "I'm sorry, Commander. It's my fault. Ernie took an extra shift for me this morning. I should've been there for him today."

Dietrich shook his head. "Shifts don't matter if the Azoren get hold of us!"

Gaines put her hands on his shoulders. "Let me get him to his cabin. Please. He won't be any more trouble."

Martinez put on a patient smile that was anything but. "Please review the video of the meeting when you're done."

Halliwell hurried across to help Gaines get Dietrich to his feet and to the hatch, then returned to his seat. Parkinson made a point of theatrically shaking his head, and he shared a pained look with Martinez.

Brilliant surgeon or not, Dietrich was burning through his support.

Martinez rubbed his hands together. "Okay, back to the status. So we're trying to troubleshoot our systems so that we know the right step to take next."

Halliwell raised a hand and cleared his throat when Martinez didn't acknowledge. "Commander, why would we stay in the DMZ?"

"Well, Sergeant, we don't intend to *stay* here."

Parkinson chuckled, and Benson imagined the joy of just slugging him.

Halliwell shot her a confused look. The question in his eyes was obvious: *What's going on here?* "Shouldn't we be making full speed for—"

"Sergeant Halliwell—" There was no missing the heat in Martinez's voice. "—if you feel your long years as a Marine qualify you to make—"

Halliwell took a step forward. "I've been around long enough to know when someone's fucking up—"

Martinez jabbed a finger at Halliwell. "You are out of line, Sergeant!"

"For pointing out that you're making the wrong call? Putting your people in unnecessary danger *again*?"

"Don't you bring up matters you're in no position to understand, you hear me?"

Benson closed her eyes and planted her feet. Her stomach flipped. Halliwell was swinging a torch in a room full of methane. She wanted to stop him, to whisper in his ear to let it go, but there was nothing she could do. He'd been pushed—by the military, by Martinez's sloppy decisions, decisions that had cost lives.

Cloth whispered over plastic seats, and it sounded like a little scuffle kicked up. "Clive! Clive!"

It was Corporal Grier, Halliwell's second. She and Private Lopez were wrapped around Halliwell, their boots anchored to the deck and their shoulders planted in their boss's chest. Grier was a good few centimeters shorter than Halliwell but was built like a rock. That was good, because Lopez was a skinny kid. Together, they were barely enough to keep the sergeant in place.

Benson hurried over, able to help now that someone else had already intervened.

The olive color of Grier's cheeks was red from the sudden exertion. She had driven her face into Halliwell's chest so that her hook nose was bent sideways a bit. "Clive. Listen. Let it go. Just let it go. You're not bringing them back, okay?"

Lopez's narrow features were rigid with shock, and his dark eyes seemed unfocused as he turned to Benson. "Commander?"

Martinez was still shouting behind her, spitting out nonsensical half-sentences that mostly drowned out Parkinson's half-hearted calming words.

Madness.

Benson nodded, trying to appear reassuring. "Sergeant Halliwell, that's enough." She put some steel into her voice.

That got his attention—he stiffened. The calm that she'd always found so reassuring settled into his eyes.

And that calm seemed to trigger a little bit of sanity in Martinez.

He quit yelling. It sounded like his boots scraped across the floor.

Parkinson chuckled nervously. "All right. Okay. That was fun. Right?"

Halliwell smoothed the fabric of his flight suit. "I'm okay."

When Benson turned back to Martinez, he brushed at his own uniform, then turned away, hands raised to signal he was under control. But the fury that had been in his eyes before turning, the quaver in his voice when he was shouting gibberish—he had truly lost control there for a minute. The medical team had apparently seen it, but Lieutenant Clark had kept them calmly seated. Despite being wispy and pale, he often filled in for Gaines when she wasn't around, providing stability for the medical team when stress levels rose.

The captain kept his back to everyone for a bit, shoulders hunched. His and Halliwell's heavy breathing were the only sound anyone could hear in a room full of people holding their breath.

How could things become so broken? They were dead in space in the DMZ within a couple days' jump of their deadliest enemies, people who had once sworn to retake the worlds that had driven them away after years of fierce battle, and Martinez was wasting time worrying about the particulars of how the *Pandora* had gotten there?

Halliwell was right to challenge it as another reckless decision, and everyone agreed. It was clear in their eyes.

She squeezed the sergeant's shoulder and whispered, "Let me deal with this."

"I've got two Marines in cold sleep because of him and that idiot engineer of his." Halliwell's voice was as cold as the chemicals keeping his people in stasis. "He's irresponsible, and if it means getting him stripped of his command, I'll testify."

Martinez finally turned, the color now gone from his cheeks. He smiled again, sniffled, then sighed. "All right. All right. We've got a lot to do if we're going to get things moving again."

Parkinson's head bobbed quickly. "We're working on it."

The reassurance seemed to calm Martinez even more. "Let's get to our stations, then. Um, cooperate with Chief Parkinson if he needs you. And keep your eyes—"

A klaxon roared.

It wasn't the systems failure alert from before, which was somewhat reassuring. The sound was more familiar, a sound that normally brought dread with it.

Martinez spun around and pressed a button to silence the alarm, then another to activate the intercom. "Chuck, what's going on?"

His jaw muscles bulged as the seconds dragged by.

Finally, Kohn's voice was there. "It's not me, Commander. That's a real signal."

Martinez's eyes locked on Benson. "Get to your stations, people."

She hurried out after the captain, leaving the others gathered into little groups. "An SOS?"

"That's what it sounded like." His boots rang on the stairs up to the top deck.

"In the DMZ?"

"Somewhere."

It would have to be close by. The systems wouldn't trigger for an SOS that was too old for them to respond to. The hatch to the bridge hissed open as they approached, and Benson once more ducked through the maze of overhead systems until they were at their pilot chairs. Their fingers flew across the consoles, bringing up sensors, communications, and data searches. They needed to locate the origin of the signal, the type of ship, the exact message embedded, the timestamp.

Martinez's eyes darted left and right. "SOS all right. Not one of ours."

"Shit." Benson stared at the display of the sensor system. "I've got a location."

He turned. "Where?"

"Deeper in the DMZ."

3

DATA SCROLLED ACROSS BENSON'S MAIN DISPLAY, A DULL AMBER ON charcoal gray. That was the best the old system could manage. On a normal shift, the scuffs and flickers bruising the console were just a part of the worn charm that made *Pandora* home. It was like the seat she was in—almost a perfect fit after years of repeated use. It carried her scent, and the scent of dozens of first officers before her over the ship's decades of service. Like the metal and plastic of the console, the screen was scratched and battered. She had to squint to pick out some details. But no amount of squinting was going to bring the data into any sort of meaningful clarity.

Somewhere, about fifty thousand kilometers beyond their current position, a ship had suddenly started broadcasting an SOS.

In the heart of the DMZ, even closer to Azoren space.

Where no ships should be. And somehow, there were two, counting the *Pandora*.

Benson ran a thumb around the rim of her drink container, which held the cool, bittersweet stimulant drink she favored when starting her shift. To her right, Martinez leaned back in his seat, eyes closed.

"This is the RSS *Pandora*, location sixty-two thousand kilometers rimward into the DMZ on the Kedraalian side of the line bordering

Azoren space. We've suffered a Fold Drive malfunction and have now received an SOS from a ship deeper inside the DMZ, on the Azoren side of the line."

He had been repeating the message for several minutes, trying to get it just right before sending it to the closest Republic relay station via a directional Fold Space transmitter. And even with that, it would be days before the closest resource could possibly respond.

They would need to be gone long before then.

And Martinez was setting a ridiculous requirement that they have the problem sorted before they went anywhere, which meant studying the assorted system and audit logs.

For what?

Kohn was right: This was impossible. There was no way the system could miss that they were drifting while in fold space. A micronic drift could be enough to lead to disaster, and because of that the monitoring had multiple redundancies built into it for safety. With a Fold Space drive like the *Pandora* had—one of the only things going for it—the fold achieved was in the range of millions. If you drifted millimeters at full power, the system adjusted immediately, and if it couldn't, it alarmed.

It was that simple.

After all, those millimeters in Fold Space could equate to kilometers in normal space, which could in theory have the ship unfolding into someone else's planned unfolding space. Or if the drift was bad enough, the ship could unfold into a star or planet. Space might be vast and mostly empty, but you had to have your math down perfect if you wanted to travel out of dimension, where distances were vastly compressed.

Which looped her back to the start: How had this not been detected?

"We are now preparing to head into the DMZ on a rescue mission to see if anyone aboard this endangered ship can be saved. Commander Leonard Martinez out."

Benson's heart skipped a beat; her back pressed hard against the seat —he'd actually hit the transmit button! "What are you doing?"

He didn't look up from the console as he typed. "Our job. There's an SOS out there."

"In enemy space."

Martinez tapped his headset: *I'm busy.* "Will, I want the secure compartment sealed off. You and Chuck make sure systems are functioning and online." The captain stared through the thick glass into the depths of enemy space. "We launch in five minutes."

Five minutes? That was insane. Not even Martinez could be so reckless!

He put his headset on the console and massaged his forehead. "You have something to say?"

"Launch in five minutes, meaning what?"

"Meaning launch in five minutes. You losing the ability to comprehend now, Faith?"

He couldn't be thinking clearly. This was her shift, her call. "You've been on duty for fourteen hours. You need to rest."

"Are you questioning my authority, Lieutenant Commander Benson? Because an incident like this requires the ship's *captain* to make command decisions. So if you're going to challenge my—"

"Not yet."

"Good. Because we have a rescue operation waiting for us out there."

"On the Azoren side of the DMZ."

"Doesn't matter."

"The hell it doesn't; it's not a Kedraalian ship."

"We're SAR—search and rescue."

"For *Kedraalian* ships."

"For all ships."

"That could be an Azoren lure. We cross that line, we could give them grounds to start a war."

"Our charter and commission doesn't leave us a choice."

But it did. They could walk away. Nothing required a ship to risk certain destruction, and going into Azoren-claimed space was certain destruction.

The minutes passed with him scratching the beard that he normally kept immaculately trimmed. It had grown thicker than its usual fine, thin tracing from sideburn to chin, and she'd missed it. Was something distracting him? Perhaps it was the Marines he'd gotten killed on the *Elmayer* finally getting to him. Of course, thanks to their resuscitation systems, there was always a chance they could be resuscitated once the *Pandora* docked at a good enough facility to—

She twisted her head around. "Do the Azoren even use resuscitation systems?"

"The technology predates the War of Separation."

"But do they *use* it? If they really believe in this super-race nonsense, maybe—"

Martinez sighed. "We don't even know it's an Azoren ship."

"In Azoren space?"

The systems indicators flashed green on both consoles. They were operational.

Martinez grumbled beneath his breath and tapped the keys that activated the regular drives; the *Pandora* accelerated forward.

They were heading deeper into the DMZ, into Azoren space!

Dots danced in front of Benson's eyes. "We need to consult with higher-ranking officers. We can't just—"

"Lieutenant Commander Benson." Martinez turned his chair toward her. "This is my call."

"But you're putting lives at risk. A dozen people."

He leaned toward her. "My. Call."

She stared down at her console. Could she try to relieve him of command? Had he actually done anything that would justify an act like that? He hadn't technically violated any regulations, even with the *Elmayer* incident. He'd danced crazily close to irresponsible but stayed just this side of it. There was just too much latitude given to a ship's captain, especially on a ship like the *Pandora*.

But there were lives at stake. She should have had a say!

A strange tone accompanied an amber indicator on her console. Then another.

His console was getting them, too.

Her heart sank. "Sensor sweep?"

"We probably set off a thousand sensor buoys with the energy wash when we came out of Fold Space. Triggering a few more isn't going to change anything."

"But now we're clearly, actively moving deeper into the DMZ. Into

Azoren space. There's no way someone can reasonably claim we accidentally did this."

"We're saving lives, Faith."

"I certainly hope so."

The hatch opened, and Parkinson stepped through. He settled at the engineer station to her left. The earlier smug smile was gone. His face was now strained, his jaw set.

He tapped keys on his console, then swallowed loudly. "I can troubleshoot the Fold Space drive from here."

Martinez was leaning back in his chair, elbows on the arms, thumbs hooked under his chin. "That would be—?"

The hatch opened again, and Benson swung around. Gaines smiled, then made her way through the tight space. She was short enough that the overhang of systems wasn't a problem, but she was thick and wide in the hips. Brushing against chairs was inevitable. Once she was at the forward station, she leaned against the auxiliary console behind it.

"I saw the alert to the medical bay." She crossed her arms.

Martinez bowed his head. "Commander Dietrich should have responded."

"He's detoxing."

Benson caught the flash of color in Martinez's cheeks; she tried to appear calm. "This is becoming a problem."

The way Martinez rolled his eyes said she hadn't made the point hard enough.

Gaines twisted around to stare at Parkinson's back. "Will, could you give us a minute?"

Parkinson groaned and powered down his console, then stormed off the bridge.

The chunky doctor tugged at her lashes and brushed a few from her fingers. "No good can come from feeding the fire between those two."

Martinez arched an eyebrow. "Will's a professional."

Gaines smiled pleasantly. "I wanted to chat with the two of you earlier, when this was becoming a problem again for Ernie."

Benson could almost feel the tension rolling off Martinez. She wanted to suggest he follow Parkinson out, but this was the captain's mess. She could only do so much. "It's not that we don't have faith in you, Eve. It's—"

"I know." There was no breaking Gaines's spirit, not after everything life had dealt her. The smile grew stronger. "The timing of this emergency couldn't have been worse. This is the anniversary of Melissa's death."

Melissa. Dietrich's wife. As high profile a physicist as he was a surgeon. How they had ever expected a marriage to last was beyond understanding.

Like me thinking things can work out with Clive?

A bittersweet look washed over Gaines's face, and the smile faltered a little. "Losing someone you love in space is never easy. You just never can shake the feeling that maybe you could've made a difference somehow if you'd just been there."

It suddenly hit Benson: Gaines's partner had been on patrol somewhere near DMZ space when he'd disappeared some time ago. And then her kids' deaths… "How're you holding up?"

The humor returned to the doctor's brown eyes. "Well enough. I'll get Ernie cleaned up. Shouldn't be but a few more hours. If you two could just…give him a little slack. He was supposed to be on leave."

But all leaves had been canceled for the search-and-rescue crews for the same reason Halliwell's separation had been denied: a freeze due to shortages.

Benson cleared her throat. "We're probably going to need him if this ship turns out to have any survivors."

"I know."

"And Petty Officer Stiles? Is she going to be able to handle this?"

"She's going to do just fine. Her scores from training and her evaluations from her last assignment—everything points to someone more than capable." The warm smile seemed to grow even warmer, like a proud mother.

And Stiles's record did point to someone who should be capable. But Dietrich had a history of burning through nurses and med-techs. The stress of SAR life, with the long hours and the demands of trying to put people back together after explosions or emergency airlock accidents…it was a pressure cooker, even for the best. Stiles just seemed so young. And immature.

But with Gaines to make up for Dietrich's rough edges, maybe everything would be okay.

Martinez seemed to reach the same conclusion. "All right. Get him cleaned up, have Stiles get your kits together. We should be ready to board in—" He glanced down at his console. "—less than ninety minutes."

"We'll be ready." Gaines patted Benson on the shoulder, then squeezed back out.

Parkinson returned several minutes later, still stewing but keeping to himself while troubleshooting the Fold Drive.

Minutes counted down as they accelerated toward their target. The g-force was manageable, but it always produced a little bit of a headache for Benson. About forty minutes in, their own sensors finally chimed: They were picking up the target ship.

Martinez projected the initial sensor imagery on the view screen, which seemed to be enough to draw Parkinson out of his studying. He hunched down between their seats with a whistle.

Benson had the same reaction. The ship wasn't too much smaller than the *Pandora* and thankfully didn't have an obvious military configuration.

She fed the imagery into the identifier database. "When was the last time we got an update on Azoren military ship profiles?"

Parkinson snorted. "We haven't seen an Azoren ship in fifty years, right?"

Martinez cocked an eyebrow. "You sound skeptical."

"Well, we've had a lot of little incidents out here on the border, haven't we? Unless you believe it's all accidents."

"Space travel can be dangerous."

"Sure. But even if it's true, we haven't seen an Azoren warship in that long. That ship isn't going to show up in the database."

It didn't. Benson ran the scan again but got the same result. "It's not a known warship."

"Too small." Parkinson stroked the patch of whiskers under his lips. "Merchant. Smuggler."

Martinez squinted as another sensor sweep updated the image, revealing more details. "Look there. Along the starboard side. Is that a rupture? Close to stern."

"Yeah. Big one." Parkinson traced a finger along what looked like a substantial gash about three-quarters of the way back. "Weapons hit?"

"Maybe."

Benson waited for another sweep to provide more details. The vector control systems had reversed thrust, so they were decelerating now, but it felt like they were speeding toward something that should have been approached cautiously if at all.

She felt herself drawn to the hole in the ship. It was big, the sort of thing a heavy weapon would produce. "What's a merchant ship doing all the way out here?"

Parkinson chuckled nervously. "Yeah. Bad, bad place to be."

It was. "How long has it been powered down?"

"Too far out to guess that."

Martinez tapped a few keys. "Has to have been a while. There's no heat coming off of it, no sign of power. Probably days."

Benson squinted at the fourth sensor scan. "So how'd that SOS fire off?"

"I…I don't know. Luck?"

"There's been way too much luck today. We drift out here and survive, we pick up an SOS from a ship that's been dead in space for days…"

"Don't question luck." But the look on Martinez's face said he was, too.

He was nervous now, same as her, same as everyone else in the crew would be. It was in the set of his jaw and the way his fingers just hovered over the console, shaking.

What had he expected, a Kedraalian ship? They were on the Azoren side of the line!

Another sensor sweep provided greater detail, and the rupture in the hull took on an even stranger shape.

She pointed to the way the gash seemed more bent or warped. "That doesn't look right. A blaster bolt or laser would have melted the hull away. Particle beams wouldn't do that, either."

Parkinson grunted. Martinez just stared.

Benson shook her head. "We shouldn't be here. This ship, there's something odd about it. I mean something really odd."

Martinez put his headset on. "All hands, this is the captain. We'll be at the target in thirty-one minutes. I want the away team ready to go in twenty. I'll be leading the team. Corporal Grier, you and Private Lopez will be providing security. Petty Officer Kohn, you're with us."

He tossed the headset back down and licked his lips. Nerves.

Benson ran another check against the database of Azoren ships: nothing. "It's not registered."

Martinez nodded slowly.

"You can't go in there." She looked to Parkinson for support, but he returned to his station. She leaned closer to Martinez. "Lenny, this is just crazy. Don't."

He flashed a smile and pushed up from his chair. "We'll be in and out in an hour. Trust me."

"What the hell are we doing?"

He took a step past her, then stopped. "Following orders, Faith."

When he exited the bridge, she went back to studying the scans. She couldn't figure out what sort of orders Martinez was talking about, but she was sure they weren't any she'd ever heard of.

4

LIGHT MOVED GHOSTLY WHITE ACROSS THE GRAY METAL SKIN OF THE OTHER ship's hull. The things that caught Benson's attention immediately were the little details—the placement of antenna arrays in a fold that provided extra protection and concealment; the way the skin seemed to have no breaks or marring. It was a newer vessel, and it had a design behind it that didn't map well to the appearance of a simple merchant vessel.

Just forward of midship, Parkinson took the drone under the belly. It swung wide around a large bulge and headed aft again.

"Wait." Benson leaned closer to her console to get a better look at the display. "What's that bulge?"

The engineer shrugged. "Sensors."

"Midship?"

"Makes as much sense as a module fore and aft. Extended like that, you can compensate for your own shadow, especially if you have a matching module topside and farther aft."

"I didn't see one topside. Can you get a closer look at it?"

Parkinson pinched the bridge of his nose, annoyed. "Sure."

The drone headed back, lights sweeping over the protrusion in the hull.

"There." She pushed the image in on the viewscreen and highlighted a dark line. "See this?"

"Looks like a cover."

"Out of alignment enough to cause a shadow?"

"Happens all the time. As long as everything's airtight, you're good. There's no drag in space."

"But everything else has been flush. Not a single panel out of alignment by a centimeter. The ship looks like it rolled off the production line yesterday."

"So this cover took some damage." The irritation was in his voice now.

"Push in closer."

Light pierced through the shadow, revealing something inside.

"What the—" Parkinson squinted at his console.

The interior revealed through the cover was spacious.

Benson drilled down. "Do you have a smaller camera on that drone?"

"Sure, but it's tough to maneuver."

"Could you see if it can fit through that opening?"

"Yeah." Just like that, the irritation was gone as he was drawn into the puzzle himself.

The video shifted, taking on a narrower perspective that started within a protective sheath and then stretched out into the opening. A sliver of a shadow crept across the hidden cavity as the camera stalk extended.

Benson's connection to Martinez hissed, then his voice came through the headset loud and clear. "Umbilical connection established. Faith, any updates?"

He was going to be annoyed that they hadn't finished their fly-by of the damaged area, especially if they didn't have a good reason.

And she couldn't make out what was inside the bulge yet. "This is a new ship. And it's not a simple merchant vessel, either."

"How do you know that?"

"Well..." Couldn't the camera mechanism go any faster? "We've seen some things on the hull that just don't map to merchant vessels."

"Like what?"

"Like…the sensors."

"The sensors? We're getting ready to enter the airlock, and all you've got is a hunch about the sensors?"

"And…" She glanced at Parkinson for help, but he was focused on the camera controls. "Well, I think…"

"Faith, I can't have any surprises here." Martinez's voice grew soft. "Lives are on the line."

"Oh, shit." Parkinson froze the camera.

Benson turned. "What?"

"That's a gun!"

"Why would merchants have a gun hidden?"

"To deal with pirates."

The gun was big, turret mounted, with four barrels. From the look of it, it was a blaster. "A quad-mount light blaster turret on a merchant ship?"

"Um."

"If that cover is shielded, you could get up on other ships pretty easy, couldn't you, Chief?"

"Yeah."

"Up close, that would make the gun about as effective as medium blasters."

"It would." He slumped in his chair, defeated.

"So it's not likely a merchant ship weapon."

The hatch opened, and Halliwell stormed through, eyes slitted and shoulders hunched. She could imagine his inner dialogue: *I should be going across.*

Parkinson seemed a little flummoxed by the big Marine's presence but finally managed to get out, "No, not a merchant-class weapon, not for a ship that size, at least."

Halliwell slowed as he approached the front of the cabin, eyes now locked on the image of the weapon. He was confused but held any questions for the moment, instead leaning against the same console Gaines had earlier used for support.

Benson smiled just enough to signal that he was doing the right thing. "Commander Martinez, did you hear what Chief Parkinson said?"

"Yes." Martinez was even less enthusiastic now. "We'll proceed with caution, but I want a look at that hole in the hull. I'm getting ready to send our Marines over."

Our Marines. That didn't sit well with Halliwell. Not. At. All.

Parkinson nodded. "Yeah. Drone is on the way."

The camera pulled back out, then the view returned to the other camera as the drone skimmed along the hull, heading aft again. The engineer whistled as the tear in the hull came into view. With the drone's camera and finer control, they quickly had a better sense of the size and scale of the damage, with imagery from inside the ship and out.

Halliwell crossed his arms. "That's not a weapon hit."

The way the hull twisted and bloomed out, Benson agreed. "A blast from the inside."

"Yeah. You see the blackened sections in that compartment?" He leaned forward, one hand on her shoulder, the other tracing the scorching. "Fire. Lots of fire. Something may have been burning in there before the blast. A lot of external shots won't produce that."

Once again, Benson's sense of control faded, as if she were being drawn in by the wreck, floating. "You could almost fit through that hole without any risk to your environment suits."

"Almost. I'd never go near a jagged surface like that."

She'd heard stories of Marine zero-g training gone wrong. You always avoided unnecessary risk.

In the umbilical video feed, the harness was on its way back to the *Pandora* from the other ship's airlock. Benson sent that video and Martinez's camera feed to separate displays. "We're getting clean video from you and the umbilical."

Martinez repositioned inside the airlock. "All right. Airlock on the other ship is blown now. I'm heading across with Chuck. We'll stage the medical gear."

Halliwell tapped Benson on the shoulder. "This is off."

She muted and lowered her voice to match his. "Off? How?"

"How isn't it?"

It *was* off. *Everything* was wrong about it, but she needed to hear it from him. "But what? I mean, specifically, what's getting to you?"

"All of it. It just feels…" The Marine sighed. "Right after I made corporal, my platoon was part of this bizarre operation. It was supposed to be a pirate intervention in the Zulasse system. Six days, we were on gunships patrolling the system, constantly going from one area to another. Never saw a single pirate ship, but we saw other ships. Unmarked ships. Guys in black armor, no insignia."

"Directorate?"

"SAID? Maybe. Or GSA."

No one liked the Security and Intelligence Directorate, and Benson had never met anyone who would talk openly about the GSA—the Group for Strategic Assessment. They were both spook organizations, but at least the GSA was military. "Why would they be behind this?"

"Dunno. Can you get me a connection to Corporal Grier?"

Benson pulled a spare headset from under her console and handed that to Halliwell while connecting to his second. "Corporal Grier? Do you copy?"

"Loud and clear, Commander."

"Sergeant Halliwell wants a word with you."

Halliwell edged over to the pilot station Martinez normally used and brought up a display. "Show me what you're seeing, Toni."

Benson winced. If things had gotten so bad between Halliwell and Martinez that video feeds couldn't be trusted, there was a problem.

Benson turned back to Parkinson. "Best guess—what kind of ship do you think would have a little surprise like that in it? Pirate?"

He tugged on the patch of whiskers beneath his bottom lip. "Depends on which kind. It's not a huge advantage if you're just trying to get up on a merchant vessel. I mean, it's overkill."

"But if you're targeting something big and slow. Something that comes out of Fold Space and can't make a fast run to port."

"Yeah. But those ships have better armor and weapons than the small merchants a pirate normally goes after."

"So a privateer. Someone interested in specific targets? Choice targets?"

"You think these guys would run operations like that?"

"The Azoren?" It sounded a little far-fetched for a government supposedly overrun with war hawks. "Maybe it's Union. The Gulmar will do pretty much anything for money, right?"

Using proxies to raid enemy shipping lanes made sense for a government that favored companies fielding private security forces over maintaining a large standing military. Then again, perhaps the Azoren had changed after decades of isolation. That assumed they hadn't already wiped out the Gulmar and the other factions that had split off from the Kedraalian Republic.

If they had, how long would it be before they turned their attention back to the Republic that had driven them off?

"Faith?" It was Martinez. "I think we've got a cargo hold. Maybe it's a merchant after all."

His video revealed the other ship's airlock. Grier and Lopez were beyond the inner hatch, standing in a large, open compartment that flashlights couldn't fully reveal. The lights caught stairs and a catwalk, cargo straps and tools associated with cargo. But it wasn't big enough to be a meaningful merchant vessel cargo hold.

No atmosphere. No power. Dead in space. A big hole in the hull maybe caused by some sort of fire. That didn't bode well for survivors.

But she couldn't make out any fire damage in the big, open compartment or any other sort of damage for that matter. "You think they failed to seal everything off when the hull blew?"

Martinez pushed the medical equipment into the open space. "Maybe. It would've had to have crippled emergency systems."

"Maybe that's what was blown up."

"Yeah."

He popped open a panel on the bulkhead beside the inner hatch, revealing a familiar emergency interface. So after decades, some things hadn't changed. Even the language seemed to be the same. A couple switch flips, and the panel lit up.

"Power." Martinez grunted. "Batteries. That explains the SOS."

"Enough to be running their sensors?"

"No, but enough that they should've been able to seal everything off."

Benson sneaked a look at Grier's video feed. She was deeper into the cargo hold; she'd found a sealed hatch opposite the airlock.

Sealed.

There should've been an atmosphere. Even if it was unbreathable, there should've been *something*. What could have caused everything they were seeing? What made sense? Nothing.

They needed to get out of there. "Can you access their systems?"

"No way they'll have anything unprotected."

"Basic logs—life support, whatever. See if there's any record of what happened. If not, we need to go."

"We're not going anywhere until we've confirmed there aren't any survivors."

"No atmosphere? Everything powered down? A big hole in the ship?"

"We're checking it out, Faith."

"You've already done more than was reasonable, Lenny. We went into the DMZ!"

"Every signatory of the armistice accepted the laws of basic SOS responses. We're perfectly within our rights while meeting our obligations."

"Our obligations are to this crew, not this stupid—"

"Slow your roll, Faith."

"Slow my...?" Heat shot through Benson.

"You want to make command decisions, you'll have a chance to. Academy grads with your marks always do."

"What's that supposed to mean?"

"It means you'll have your turn, okay? But not right now. The *Pandora* isn't your ship."

Making it about her ambition was a cheap shot. She'd never hid her low regard for search-and-rescue, but she was an exceptional officer, and Martinez knew it. She should never have been assigned to his ship.

Halliwell was staring at her, lips compressed; he'd heard the exchange.

Grier's voice crackled through Halliwell's connection to her. "Commander Martinez? We've got a hatch here. What do we do?"

"Hold position, Corporal." Martinez helped Gaines and Stiles through the airlock, then cranked the outer hatch closed. He waved Lopez over to help get the rest of the medical gear inside, then the two of them cranked the inner hatch closed.

Grier patiently ran her flashlight along the bulkhead. "Clive, you seeing this?"

Halliwell pushed the microphone arm closer to his lips. "Your video's solid. You see any cargo in there yet?"

She edged along the bulkhead. Her light revealed plenty of braces and mounts for cargo cases, but not cargo. "Nothing."

"Pirates would've burned their way in, wouldn't they?"

"Or blown the cargo hatch, yeah." Grier drifted back to the hatch.

Martinez approached, his light faint on the sealed hatch. "Corporal Grier, you test that hatch yet?"

"No, sir."

Halliwell tapped the microphone tip, and the light along the arm switched from green to red; he was muted.

Benson did the same. "You see anything?"

"An empty cargo hold." Halliwell clenched his jaw tight. "What's the point of this? He should be able to get something off that emergency panel, right?"

"Apparently not."

Lopez joined Grier at the hatch, cranking it open while Martinez shone his light through the crack. It was sloppy work. He should have been on the crank with Lopez while Grier had her weapon at the ready.

Martinez liked doing unconventional things. Risky things.

With the hatch open, the video showed a passageway that cut right and ran straight before cutting left. No lights, still. No bodies. No indication of any sort of what had transpired.

Halliwell shook his head. "You said something about pirates?"

Benson nodded toward Parkinson, who was absorbed in piloting the drone along the rest of the hull. "He found a pretty impressive gun camouflaged to look like a sensor module."

"Why should we care about whether or not pirates survived an accident?"

"We probably shouldn't."

Gaines and Stiles were at the open hatch. They'd broken out the medical gear contained in the cases they'd pulled across, and each had pouches strapped around their legs and packs slung over their backs. Stiles had secured a light to the backpack straps.

It was the perfect time for Martinez to make the call to abandon the mission. The ship could be left to the Azoren or Gulmar to retrieve. *Someone* would be coming soon enough now that the SOS had somehow triggered.

Martinez had muted his connection to Benson; he now turned it back on. "Commander Benson?"

"Yes?" *Please tell me you've come to your senses and we're pulling out.*

"We're going to search for survivors. Two decks. The infirmary should be off the main passageway. We shouldn't be long."

Get out of there! "We're ready."

The timer showed they were already twenty-one minutes into his promised hour.

5

ONCE THROUGH THE INNER CARGO BAY HATCH, THE VIDEO FEED FROM Martinez and Grier became choppy and grainy. Benson immediately tensed—it was the *Elmayer* all over again. Halliwell didn't catch on for a few seconds, but when the significance of the change hit him, he straightened so fast that he banged his head on the overhanging equipment.

She grabbed his hand before he could key his mic. "Wait."

His eyes bugged out; his nostrils flared. "Wait?"

The realization was like electricity shooting through her, so she could only imagine what he was feeling. Grier was heading into strong radiation, the same way Martinez had sent Halliwell's other Marines into the same hazard.

Benson squeezed. "Let me talk to him."

"He's not listening to you."

"And if you say something, that'll get worse."

"What could be worse than getting more of my people killed?" His raised voice drew Parkinson out of his drone-induced fugue state.

Benson squeezed Halliwell's hand again. If it looked inappropriate, so be it. "Let me handle it."

The Marine sergeant glared at Parkinson. Nothing would ever repair the damage done to Halliwell's trust of Martinez for his irresponsible actions. Two Marines were dead, maybe forever, because of the decisions he'd made. And the engineer was just as much at fault. It was his poor evaluation of the risk of the situation that had led to the captain's ill-advised decisions.

She took a calming breath and keyed her mic. "Lenny, check your radiation counters."

Martinez hissed. "Dammit, Faith. Do not undermine—"

"Check your counter. Please."

The hiss dragged on, but Benson realized it was just an audio artifact.

Then Martinez's video feed froze.

No. He had stopped moving. "Hold up, everyone."

The others stopped.

Benson held her breath. The last thing they needed was for Martinez to feel like his authority was being challenged. He'd been prickly about that even before the incident. Since then, he'd been unbearably fragile. The slightest question became an attempt to usurp command.

"Okay." Martinez sighed. "We've got a minor elevation in radiation levels."

"Your video and audio started to degrade when you stepped out of the cargo hold. Maybe it's shielded better than the other areas."

"Sure." He swung around to look back the way he'd come. "And it tells us the source isn't in the cargo hold. That's good to know."

"But it also tells you something inside that ship is leaking radiation. Shielding has been compromised somewhere." Like where the hull had been blown out.

"All right, yeah. But it's not a lethal dosage. The suits can handle this."

"For a while. You said you'd wrap up in an hour. You're twenty-five minutes in."

"I see that." He was getting testy again. "Okay. We'll speed this up. Hold on."

Halliwell seemed to relax a little at that.

Then Martinez pushed past the others. "Listen up! We need to pick up the pace. We'll check the infirmary and bridge, see if we can find out where the crew is."

Grier's brow wrinkled as he squeezed past her. "Commander, I should be on point."

"Your complaint is noted, Corporal."

Halliwell rubbed his brow. "He's doing it again."

Martinez hopped down the passageway at a reckless pace, stopping long enough to tap on a barely noticeable hatch. "We should be able to get to the bridge through this stairwell. Private Lopez, if you'll take Dr. Gaines with you and confirm that, please."

Grier's video swept back and forth in the passageway, as if she were searching for something. "Commander, we don't—"

"Corporal, why don't you use some of that plentiful energy of yours to check that other passageway."

"Sir—?"

"It should get you aft. Maybe you can get us a better look at the damaged compartment."

"But—"

"You're our explosives expert. I'd like to know what caused that damage."

Halliwell slammed a fist into the console. "That son of a bitch!"

Parkinson almost jumped in his seat. "What the—?"

Benson muted her mic. "Sergeant Halliwell, if you'd please accompany me to the passageway?"

He glared at her with pain-filled eyes.

"Please."

The second the hatch sealed behind them, she grabbed a handful of Halliwell's flight suit and pushed him against the bulkhead. "Clive, listen to me."

His hand grabbed hers, as if he might push her away. He quickly let go. "He's going to get them killed."

"They're safe for the moment."

"He's not fit—"

She leaned into him, lips close to his. "Listen to me! You're causing more trouble than good. You blow up on him, you're not getting separation, you're going to prison. You understand?"

Halliwell slumped. "I can't let him kill Toni. She's the last of us."

He rubbed his chest—the chunk of shrapnel he had encased in synthetic quartz hanging from his neck. From Dramoran. It had nearly killed him. He would never be able to get past that. Who could? He and Grier had watched most of their battalion get turned into paste by friendly fire.

"Clive, we'll get her out of there. We'll get them all out of there. But doing that starts with you keeping your cool."

He swallowed. "I-I know."

The panic and fury were still in his eyes, but there was something more there—a rational look that approached calm. He was getting himself under control.

The passageway was clear, and they were outside the range of any cameras; she kissed him. "Work with me."

"Yeah." He bowed his head. "Sorry."

"Don't apologize. We're all feeling the stress right now."

"These are the last of my people. Lopez is just a kid."

Being excluded hurt. "They'll be okay."

The hatch opened, and Parkinson slipped out just as they pulled apart. His eyes were downcast. "Lost contact with Roddy when I tried to send him in for a better look at the hole."

Benson smoothed her flight suit. "Power?"

"I think it's the radiation." He tugged on his whiskers. "I'm going to send Sam over to do a retrieval."

"Won't he just encounter the same problem?"

"Not Sam. Better shielding, a more robust error-correction system."

Halliwell glared at the engineer's back as he headed past Benson and Martinez's living quarters, then out the hatch that would take him to the stairwell to the lower deck. "He cares more about his stupid robots than humans."

She pulled Halliwell through the bridge hatch.

Grier was already moving aft when Benson settled back in her seat, and there was no sign of Lopez and Gaines on Martinez's video. The team left palm-sized lights in its path. In the pale light, sections of passageways glowed flickering white.

Martinez stopped at one point to crank open a hatch. "Living space. Empty, but lived in."

His beam caught a small cabin with two bunks, dropped down, with disheveled sheets. Two emergency oxygen masks were still mounted just inside the hatch.

Martinez popped open a drawer at the foot of the bunk and pulled out underwear for the camera. "They weren't expecting whatever happened."

Halliwell pointed to the video feed coming in from Grier. The chop that had developed earlier was worse now. In the span of a few seconds, the video degraded to artifacts, then froze completely.

Benson muted her headset. "Have her check her radiation counter."

Muscles bulged the length of Halliwell's neck. "Toni. Hey. Can you hear me okay?"

"Yeah." Grier's audio dropped into a deep bass tone that skipped for a couple seconds. "What's up?"

"I need you to check your radiation counter for me, okay?"

The video froze, and the audio became a strange chirping noise, then Grier's voice replaced the noise. "—ello—do—"

Halliwell glared at Benson; he wanted Grier out of there. Now. "Toni." Halliwell's voice held a remarkable calm. "You're breaking up. Did you say you're in the yellow?"

"—ello—!"

An image came through the connection: She'd sent them her readout, which was scrambled, corrupted.

Halliwell muted his headset. "That's where the radiation's coming from. We need to pull her out!"

Benson ran her thumb along the rim of her fluid container. "How far is she from the hole?"

"She needs to—"

"She's safe for now. Have her run aft, then get back. The problem is only going to be if she lingers there."

He seemed to consider arguing more, then said, "Toni, get a look at that compartment that has the hole in it, then get back to the cargo bay. You hear me? Double time. Examine that hole, back to the cargo bay.

Double time. You owe us that strudel, remember? Thawing apples this week. Remember?"

The video froze, then it seemed to come back. When they had a stretch of almost-clean imagery, it was obvious Grier was moving faster.

Halliwell smiled. "She's really good in zero-g."

Benson took a sip of the stimulant. Her nerves were firing like crazy, so a stimulant was the last thing she needed, but the sweet coolness was welcome.

Martinez and Stiles were exiting what looked like a galley, the last of their light catching a table against the bulkhead next to the hatch. There was a tray with a stained fork and a dish caked with some sort of dried sauce or gravy in the video frame for just a second, then they were at the next hatch with the prying tool.

Martinez laughed nervously. "This should be it. Kind of running out of options."

Benson keyed her mic. "What's the radiation like?"

"Still in the green. Barely."

"Corporal Grier is in the yellow."

The video image spun around, catching a wide-eyed Stiles before locking onto the passageway behind her, as if Martinez thought he could just look back toward the *Pandora* and see Benson. "You've been talking to her?"

"I'm trying to keep track of what's going on, Lenny."

"Dammit!" He shook his head, and both video feeds died.

Halliwell pulled his headset off. "What the hell is he doing?"

"I—" None of the connections worked: audio, video, the encrypted laser running outside the umbilical frame. Benson couldn't even get simple text through. "He shut comms down. All of it."

And then it was back. At least Martinez's connection was back. "All right. Here's how it goes from here on out, Lieutenant Commander Benson. You work through me. You understand? All communication goes through me. No more working behind my back."

"I wasn't working behind—"

"Drop it. I've got everyone headed to our position. You have any questions, I'll relay them. That assumes they're appropriate."

He finished prying the hatch open, and their lights reflected off stainless steel light fixtures suspended from the ceiling and carts loaded down with rusted surgical tools.

The infirmary.

It was a small cabin with three beds. Two held gory corpses; the third was stained with dark blood.

The surgical tools weren't rusty but blood-coated.

Stiles squeezed past Martinez and hurried to the beds. The audio of their connection bled through Martinez's microphone. She confirmed two corpses but couldn't find an obvious cause of death. Something must have caught her eye, because she twisted around.

"Third corpse." Stiles's voice was calm. She pushed off from the beds and disappeared behind what had appeared in the poor lighting to maybe be a small antechamber.

Martinez pushed into the room. "Two dead here. Um, Petty Officer Stiles found a third." His voice shook.

He turned, and his video revealed Lopez in the hatch. Gaines was behind him, still in the passageway.

More half-heard chatter over Martinez's hot mic.

The bridge was intact, no sign of any damage, no survivors or corpses up there.

Martinez sent Lopez to help Stiles. "Um. Some updates—Corporal Grier said the damage to the compartment and that hole were definitely caused by an explosion. A bomb. It looks like the reactor shielding—" He spun around. "Go ahead."

Lopez's voice sounded far away, but there was just enough to make out that he was requesting the captain's presence.

"Hold on." Martinez drifted over to the area where Lopez and Stiles had gone.

The third corpse seemed less bloody than the other two. It wore dark gray coveralls with a few bloodstains and tears, but everything otherwise looked fine. Stiles seemed to be focused on examining the head. What had Lopez's interest was something on the floor. Benson realized what it was before the corporal ran a flashlight along the floor, tracking the path for Martinez.

She leaned forward. "Lenny? Commander Martinez?"

Martinez was either absorbed by what Lopez was saying or the communications system was having problems again.

Halliwell studied her through squinted eyes. "What?"

"That glistening in the flashlight—see it?"

"Yeah. Water?"

"No." Benson keyed her mic again. Lopez was looking into another section, which might have been a storage room; Martinez was drifting back to the beds. "Lenny? Do you copy? Dammit!"

"What? I don't understand." Halliwell was on her shoulder, squinting at the display.

"They're in a near-vacuum. If that were water, it would be evaporating."

"Okay. So what is it?"

"The way it glistened in the light? A gel. I'm guessing cold sleep gel."

"Cold sleep—?"

She keyed her mic again. "Lenny? Dammit! Answer me!"

Halliwell tilted his head. "How would cold sleep gel show up on that part of the floor?"

"Oh, no. No!" Benson pushed her seat out.

"What now?"

She pointed to the video feed as she got up. Martinez had squatted at the base of the wall just beyond the beds. His gloved finger ran through a small slick of gel on the floor.

Benson moved to the hatch. "Lenny! Lenny!"

"Faith, tell me—" Halliwell followed her.

"It's a cold sleep storage chamber. Probably like ours but smaller."

"Where?"

"Behind that wall!" She keyed the mic again. "Lenny! Can you—"

Her heart skipped a beat when she took a quick glance back at the display: the wall was opening.

Martinez looked up, tracking from a pair of gel-covered booties to some sort of insulated leggings, then up to a matching shirt wet with the same gel.

Then the camera locked on the gloved hands of the man just beyond the opening. He was big, bigger than Halliwell, wider in the shoulders but not with Halliwell's muscle definition. An oxygen mask covered the gel-slick face, but she had a sense of dark eyes smiling malevolently. And that was a bad thing for someone whose gloved hands held what looked like a laser rifle.

A brilliant light flashed on the display, then Martinez's camera feed died.

6

HALLIWELL'S BOOTED STEPS WERE LIKE THUNDER IN THE STAIRWELL, BUT HIS voice was louder. "What're you doing?"

Benson kept her eyes focused on the steps, trying not to notice the panicked heat coiling in her gut, trying to stay just ahead of the man she loved. She knew him well enough to guess his thinking—they had guns, they had armor, and they still had half the crew. He would want to speed across the umbilical and storm the other ship. He would do anything to save Grier, even Martinez.

But Martinez was already dead. Grier too, probably. They'd stumbled across a pirate ship, fallen for some elaborate trap, and they'd lost comrades.

And if Benson didn't do what any good captain would do, they would lose everyone.

Halliwell sped up once they were out of the stairwell and headed into the maze of cargo crates separating the forward part of the lower deck from the rear. "Faith, wait. Let me get the guns. I'll take everyone across. We—"

She bowed her head, fought back tears. "Take who, Clive? Dietrich? Parkinson?"

"You and me. We can handle a pirate."

"A pirate? We saw one man with a laser rifle. You think that's all there is?"

The cargo hold sped by, gray cargo crates strapped to mounts on the scuffed bulkheads by frayed, grimy straps. What could pirates want from what the *Pandora* carried? Medicine? Powdered food? Spare parts?

The secret cargo in the black crates secured in a fenced-off section at the forward end of the hold? How could they possibly know about that? Only Martinez had a clue what was in there, and he'd been stunned when they'd been forced to take the cargo aboard.

"We're taking it to Outpost-27." That had been all he'd said through a clenched jaw.

No, there was something more than sinister about stumbling across these pirates. Whoever they were, Benson was sure they hadn't been lying in wait inside the DMZ for a random ship to show up. That was absurd.

She pulled away when Halliwell tried to grab her upper arm as they approached the airlock.

His boots were silent now, his body rigid. "Faith, please."

"They're dead, Clive. And if the pirates haven't killed them, they've taken them prisoner. They'll use them as hostages or human shields. That's the same as being dead."

"We can free them. Let me do this. Parkinson's qualified—"

"He's an engineer. You've already seen how he reacts to one of his drones malfunctioning. You want someone like that protecting your back?"

"Dietrich can—"

"He's detoxing." She slapped the bulkhead above the airlock control panel. "Martinez took the best of our people. He screwed everything up. Again."

"I'm a Marine, Faith. This is my job."

How could he squeeze so much pain and vulnerability into such a deep and powerful voice? "I understand, but my job is to protect this ship and its crew."

His jaw quivered. "You sure you're not proving Martinez right, grabbing the first opportunity to have your own command?"

The words hit like a physical blow. She'd slept with this man, opened herself to him. How could he even think such a thing? How could he say it? She understood his connection with Grier and his sense of failure at her loss, but...the words were the sort that ended relationships. They could never be taken back, the pain of distrust never undone.

Could he actually feel that way?

Could he be right?

She swallowed and brought up the video feed from the umbilical camera. The other ship's airlock was still sealed. Retracting the umbilical required the slap of a button. It could collapse into its storage area in less than a minute.

They had time. "Ten minutes, Sergeant Halliwell."

He winced.

It's never pleasant when someone turns the pain back on you, is it?

Halliwell nodded, then stepped to the intercom and keyed it. "Chief Parkinson, Commander Dietrich, Lieutenant Clark, meet me at the armory."

"Bring my gear to me, please, Sergeant." Tears threatened, but she refused to look away from the display. She couldn't.

He reached for her. "Faith..." His voice cracked, but he knew better than to apologize.

His retreating steps nearly forced her to turn around. She had an obligation. The ship, the crew. At the first hint of someone coming through the other airlock, she knew what to do, and she wouldn't hesitate. Lives were at stake. Someone had to do better than Martinez.

And for several minutes, she kept her eyes glued to the display, knuckling away tears, fighting back against fraying nerves.

The shouting came from the direction of the armory. "I'm a goddamn engineer!" Parkinson.

"We're all military, Chief." Halliwell's voice was icy cold.

It wasn't just his loathing for Parkinson, either. The man's smugness had alienated so many of the crew over the years, even before his ego had killed Halliwell's Marines. But the Marine sergeant couldn't leave any doubt about who was in charge once they headed into the other ship. Hesitation, uncertainty—that's what got people killed.

They came out of the cargo maze, Halliwell looking sharp and dangerous, the others looking hapless. Armor not yet tightened, weapons dangling awkwardly from shoulders puffed out in environment suits. Dietrich looked sick—bleary eyes blinking rapidly, mouth open as he breathed unevenly.

Parkinson latched onto Benson once he saw her. "Commander Benson! This...you didn't approve it. Tell me you didn't approve it."

Benson held a hand out, taking the environment suit and armor Halliwell offered. "All we know right now, Chief, is that Commander Martinez was attacked." *And that you're a gutless, arrogant fool.*

"They're already dead. If there really are pirates over there, our people are dead."

Benson pulled her boots off while watching the display. "We'll find out for sure when we get over there."

"No! We need to go. You were right all along!" Parkinson cackled. "Who knew?"

"Chief, we've got crew at risk. Man up."

Dietrich leaned against the bulkhead. "How many..." He squeezed his eyes shut and shuddered. "How many did you see?"

"Just one. Before the camera went offline. The captain decided to slave all their comms through his system just before the attack, so we couldn't reach anyone else."

"Eve? Petty Officer Stiles?"

"They were okay." As far as Benson could tell, and that was all she was going to say.

She turned to let Lieutenant Clark check her environment suit; he patted the atmosphere pack. "All good, Commander."

"All right, Sergeant Halliwell is going to walk us through the—"

Her communicator buzzed. No name popped up on the display, but the buzz came again.

Someone was requesting an anonymous connection. And not using their standard comm gear but something more basic.

Did Grier avoid the pirates? She wasn't in the infirmary when the hidden door opened, was she?

"Hold on." Benson accepted the connection. "Who is this?"

"Commander Benson?" The voice was male, gravelly, older. Not one of her people.

Should she disconnect? The others were watching now. It was too late.

"This is Lieutenant Commander Benson."

"And this is Quentin Chung, Commander. You're the captain now."

Parkinson had stopped pouting. Dietrich's bloodshot eyes were on her.

"What do you want, Mr. Chung?"

"I want to talk about a business deal."

"We're not businesspeople, I'm afraid."

"I think we can change that with a little training."

"We don't have time for training."

"Make time. I've got something you want, and you have something I want. That forms the basis of any business relationship. That's the first step of training. See how easy it is? You'll have your own business in no time."

Her finger slipped toward the umbilical retrieval button. "What did you have in mind?"

"I have some people here who'd like to go home. You have repair equipment that can get my ship operational again."

"Let my people go, and we'll handle the repairs."

"That's a good offer. Really, it is. In a different situation, I'd consider it. But I have to counteroffer now."

"Is that part of the training?"

"You're a sharp one." He rasped a chuckle. "So here we go: Let us aboard, or the rest of your people die."

Benson punched the umbilical button. "No deal."

Halliwell reached past her. "What're you doing?"

"What I have to—"

The umbilical pulled back from the other ship's airlock, but stopped after a couple meters.

She slapped the button again.

Nothing.

Voices sputtered over Chung's connection. He shouted them down, then killed the connection. The airlock hatch opened. Two forms in basic environment suits rushed to the edge of the lock and jumped out, tether cables trailing behind them. They knew what they were doing, because both got a grip on the umbilical framework.

Had the pirates broken the umbilical somehow?

Benson glanced through the airlock viewport. There were more people in the other ship's airlock. The two who had made the jump threw back lines, which the others secured.

She took Halliwell's weapon and checked the load. "They've got at least four. Since I can't see our people, I'll assume six."

Halliwell's face twitched angrily. "You were going to abandon them."

"I was going to do whatever it took to save this ship and crew." She glared at the others. "Too late for that now."

Parkinson seemed frozen as he stared at the display. "They're coming? Here?"

"And they're going to use our friends as human shields." She shot an angry glare at Halliwell. "Which is why we should have bugged out the second they killed Martinez."

Dietrich groaned. "Those are our people. We…can't—"

"We can't save them. And if we'd left the area immediately, this ship would still be safe."

"But you're condemning—"

"I'm doing nothing, Dr. Dietrich. Commander Martinez condemned them to death when he decided to respond to the SOS."

Parkinson pointed at the display. "Eight. Eight of them!"

The pirates were moving along the ribbing of the umbilical with the speed and grace that only came from experience. Of course it made sense for pirates to be able to handle extra-vehicular activity easily. And they were tugging other people—her people—along on lifelines.

Benson was under no delusions how an assault would go. They would overcome the outer airlock hatch with the same tool used to open the hatches on their ship. Then they would open the inner hatch, releasing all the atmosphere in the cargo hold. Then it would come down to a desperate gunfight with her team outmanned, outgunned, and handicapped by trying not to shoot comrades.

With weapons designed for indiscriminate slaughter.

They were going to die. Unless she had it in her to kill her own people. Or to go into the airlock now and shoot everyone trying to make their way to the airlock.

Alone? Against at least one laser rifle?

Even with Halliwell, it would be a pointless martyring.

And that was finally sinking in for the others. Even Halliwell was looking down, shoulders slumped.

Then it hit her. "Breaching pack."

Halliwell's head came up. "What?"

"We mount a breaching pack in the airlock. Point the explosive charge at the outer hatch."

"That would blow the umbilical and kill them all."

"And if we let them in, they'll kill all of us."

Parkinson smiled. "I like that! I mean, it's terrible losing our friends—"

Benson rolled her eyes. "We're not losing anyone. It just gives us enough leverage to negotiate again."

The reality sank in for Halliwell. He sped back toward the armory.

"Okay. Suit up." Benson pulled her helmet on.

Parkinson stared at the helmet for a second, then put it on. He connected to her over the helmet comms. "What about just killing them all? Wouldn't that solve all our problems?"

Hearing it come from him, Benson realized just how cold-blooded such an act would be. The upside of Martinez dying was that he was going to take the fall for the idiotic decision to go deeper into the DMZ and enter a ship that looked like a pirate vessel. But killing the rest of the *Pandora*'s crew to save a handful? It wasn't a career-boosting act, and it wasn't something she was sure she could do.

If only Halliwell had backed her decision to separate and leave the area.

The big sergeant came running through the cargo container maze, breaching pack held over his head. She cycled the airlock. It would be close, with the front two pirates already nearing the hatch. But they were waiting for their comrades.

And their shields.

The hatch opened as Halliwell reached them. He didn't even bother with his helmet, instead jumping into the airlock and setting the pack over the aft section of the airlock, then adjusting the angle so that the bulk of the blast would be directed at the outer hatch. The backpack-sized demolition kit was meant as a way to handle quick access to damaged hatches or even to blow through bulkheads. The segmented plate on the outward-facing front would act as shrapnel, compensating for the lack of atmosphere to still deliver a major concussive payload.

It wasn't a selective weapon that could instantly turn things their way, but it gave her something.

Halliwell exited the airlock, and she closed the inner hatch. Instead of cycling atmosphere in again, she opened the outer hatch.

She transmitted to Chung's radio. "Mr. Chung, do I have your attention?"

He was apparently listening. "You really are a smart one. But do you have—"

"I'm not going to let you kill my entire crew, Mr. Chung."

"Of course not. Violence isn't necessarily the only outcome in these situations."

"So let's move to lesson three: my counteroffer to your counteroffer: You keep your hostages until we repair your ship, then we get our people back and we both go our separate ways."

"A fast learner."

"I'm being practical. We're a search-and-rescue vessel, not a merchant ship. We have nothing of value, unless you know of a market desperate for basic medicine and medical supplies."

"So your pretty little Brianna wasn't lying."

Had they tortured Stiles, or was she cooperating? "Commander Martinez hoped to save as many lives as he could. That's our job."

"A Kedraalian Republic ship out to save lives?" Chung laughed. "Maybe things change over time."

It was an odd thing to say, but she was growing used to odd things. "Take everyone back to your ship, and we'll begin ferrying repair equipment across."

"Oh. No. That won't work. The radiation would be lethal. For your people, too. I'm sure you've seen the hole near the back. The bomb that tore that hole also took out our life support and the reactor shielding."

She muted and turned to Parkinson. "Did you get Roddy back?"

"A-almost. Sam pulled him out, but—" He waved at the airlock. "—this happened before I could get Sam back."

"Can you outfit them to work in the radiation?"

"Yeah. I mean, I'll need to reprogram Roddy and get some shielding—"

"How long?"

"Two, three hours."

She unmuted. "Mr. Chung, we can get the shielding repaired. It'll take a couple hours. You can stay in your cargo bay. There wasn't a problem with radiation in there."

Chung made a clucking noise. "And now we go to lesson four, Commander Benson."

Two of the pirates entered the airlock, hands wrapped around the bound arms of her crew. Gaines and Stiles were right in front of the breaching charge; Kohn and Lopez were behind them.

It was entirely possible the explosion would only kill the six of them. Even the umbilical might survive.

Halliwell's finger froze, hovered over the remote detonator for the breaching pack.

"Do you know what lesson four is, Commander Benson?"

She could barely whisper her answer. "Calling the bluff."

"Exactly that." Chung chortled. "So, can you kill your comrades?"

Stiles's dark green eyes were huge. Gaines had her head down, but her lips were visible—moving.

"What do you want, Mr. Chung?"

"I want your ship." His laughter was dark and rich and malevolent.

Her leverage was gone, and he knew it.

7

COMPARING NOTHING BUT THE CARGO HOLDS, THE KEDRAALIAN SHIP HAD A different vibe about it. Dev Rai kept noticing the order and structure about everything—the way the cargo was secured, the way equipment was operational despite obvious age and hard use. Even the little details, like readable labels, were focused on. After days in cold sleep, he was pleasantly surprised to find the *Pandora* was warm. He wanted to strip out of his grungy environment suit and shower, maybe to stroll around a bit and just breathe in the comparatively fresh air.

Of course it wasn't fresh. No ship had fresh air. Scrubbers could only do so much, after all. But the Republic military apparently had a much higher standard when it came to minimally acceptable operations.

The jump in standards wasn't lost on Chung, either. The white stubble on his fat, wrinkled cheeks shifted around a broad, yellow-toothed smile. "Whatta you think of this?"

"Nice. I could get used to it."

"You will. It's ours now." Chung laughter. It was a dry, raspy sound that Rai hated for years.

The other privateers seemed more concerned with the Kedraalian crew than the ship. There were two lookers—the young nurse whose cooperation had probably saved her comrades' lives and this

Commander Benson. That was nice and everything; it probably helped with promotions, but it was a bad thing right now. Rai had never cared for the way some of his comrades could forget the tenets of a professional privateer. Executing an enemy combatant was one thing. Forcing yourself on them was another. And that seemed to be on the others' minds.

They were thuggish, violent brutes, the sort to rely on fear and strength.

Not like him. You grow up always a little smaller and spend all your time around tough people, you learn how not to be intimidated. That started with toughening up. Developing strengths.

Like speed.

Rai was quick. Really quick. And smart. His dark eyes were always on the move, sucking in information.

People always said, "Dev, you're a smart guy. I see it in your eyes."

Or they'd say, "You know, you're a good-looking guy, except for that nose. Can't you fix that nose?"

He liked his nose. Big, yeah. But dumb people fixated on that instead of his mind.

And that was what made him special.

He nodded toward the airlock. "Hey, we really want to keep this thing or get the *Rakshasa* running again?"

The old man glanced around the cargo hold. "Don't think we could get the transponder figured out?"

"Nah. I bet the systems are just like ours. But you want to relearn the quirks of a ship? What if we run into trouble before we can get out of here?"

That got the old man's attention. He looked around again through slitted eyes, rubbing stubby fingers through the spikes of white hair that remained on his scarred, dark gold head. "It'd take a bit to get a weapon system refit, I guess."

"What would you pull out to make room for one? It'd be a mess."

Chung's glee was beginning to fade. "Yeah."

"This thing looks like it's legit search and rescue. Probably not a thing on here we wouldn't have to modify."

"Yeah. Maybe repairing the *Rakshasa* would be better."

"I think so."

"Yeah."

Rai peeled off his environment suit. Gel clung to his clothes. His favorite black pants and shirt were wet and slimy with it. He hated that. "We really should get the guys off of the ladies."

Chung's eyes lazily swung over to the two pretty women, now surrounded by the brutish Vic Gabriel and Stef Nguyen, and by Chung's nephew Jimmy Wong. While Gabriel and Nguyen were thick, powerfully built bruisers who could always be counted on to set the bar low for behavior, Wong was a scrawny punk who always sought to curry favor with his uncle. The kid was probably a reminder of the young man Chung had been but certainly dumber.

Chung coughed wetly. "You sweet on them?"

"The ladies?" Rai shrugged. "I've seen prettier."

"You have? Hm. Then why get worked up about it?"

"We're professionals is all. We're not common rogues; we've got a charter."

"They're just looking to get some action."

"They can hire all the ladies they want when we get back to Minhath."

"Yeah, but they can have a good time for free with those two right now. It's harmless."

"Quentin, what you do in life matters."

The old man scratched his belly with cracked and yellowed nails. "You and your philosophy."

"It matters. It does."

"They're going out an airlock in a bit. Who cares about what happened to their bodies before that?"

"Anyone with a shred of decency."

The old man's dark eyes flitted back around to Rai. "I run this operation."

"You do."

"Remember that. My ship; my rules."

"Gabriel wouldn't be alive otherwise."

"Vic's a good kid."

"He's a psychopath."

The old man's gut shook from a quiet laugh. "You need people like him to keep everyone in line, especially after so long in space."

As far as Rai was concerned, keeping people in line started by getting rid of thugs like Gabriel, but Chung was right—the *Rakshasa* was his ship; the charter from the Azoren was in his name. Rai was just along for the ride.

"Hey, about being in space so long—how long did you think we were going to be in cold sleep? Because I thought we'd be out for years."

Chung's mouth twisted, not quite into a sneer but into something close. "People're looking for that cargo."

"In the DMZ?"

"Yeah, well…"

"But isn't it odd the way we wake up not even a week after going under?"

"I told you—people are looking."

"A search-and-rescue ship? A *Kedraalian* search-and-rescue ship?"

The old man scratched his scalp again. "Good fortune."

"Lots of it." Rai wasn't one to buy into luck, but he couldn't put his finger on why exactly he was feeling incredulous. Crazy things happened. That was how the universe worked.

Raised voices brought Rai around. The fat doctor who'd talked Gabriel down after he killed the first guy aboard the *Rakshasa* had inserted herself between the big oaf and the pretty nurse.

The others laughed.

Rai's skin crawled. "Hey, this ship, it's got to have a good infirmary, right? Doctors, nurses?"

Chung had turned to watch the drama, too. "Yeah." Distracted.

"So we can get folks patched up, huh? The cargo, too. She's worth more alive and in good shape, don't you think?"

Those dark eyes slithered over, squinting, serpent-like. "Yeah."

"So let me talk to this Benson lady. Get a look at her ship and crew. We can figure out how to get people taken care of."

The old man's stubby fingers scraped across the white beard stubble. "And it keeps your ladies unmolested."

"Conveniently. Unless you think it's necessary for Stef to get her hands down their pants?"

Chung studied the burly technician, who seemed to be even more aggressive going after the Benson woman than the men. "Hey! Bring the commander over here."

Gabriel groaned. Nguyen turned around, arms still wrapped around the Republic officer's chest. "She's mine, Quentin."

"Dev here wants to spend some time with her first."

"He can have grandma here!" Nguyen kicked the fat doctor in the ass, shoving her in their direction.

The wrinkles on Chung's face grew deeper as he frowned. "Wasn't asking, Stef."

The tattoos covering Nguyen's plain face twisted as she scowled. She shoved Benson ahead, muttering in one of the street languages Rai had never mastered.

He took the stunned woman from Nguyen and flashed a smile. "Could you talk to their engineer about how he planned to patch the reactor shielding? Maybe we could get the *Rakshasa* running again after all."

Nguyen's scowl deepened. "Fuck you."

Chung grabbed her forearm. "Do what he said."

She tore her arm free and stormed away.

Chung chuckled. "You don't make a lot of friends."

Rai ran his tongue over his teeth, which still felt like hardened rubber after the cold sleep. "Not my strong suit."

The shock seemed to be fading from the Benson woman's eyes, but her lips still quivered.

"Why don't you give me a tour of your ship, Commander?" Rai gave her a much warmer smile. It was something he was pretty good at. In fact, some women said he could be absolutely disarming and more than a little handsome.

Apparently, Benson didn't agree. She cringed. "I..."

"Just a tour. You'll find I'm not like them."

Her eyes darted back to the others, then she nodded. "O-okay."

He nodded down the aisle between the cargo crates, and she took a few hesitant steps. When he fell in behind her, she seemed to gain confidence, which grew once they were past the leering thugs. She didn't expend any energy on describing the cargo, instead stopping at a set of stairs and looking around.

Rai glanced aft first, then forward. "Nothing of interest down here?"

"Um." She still seemed dazed, but after closing her eyes and exhaling unsteadily it became less noticeable.

He put a hand on her elbow. "You work with me, I'll protect you. Hear me?"

Her eyes locked with his, and her brow wrinkled. Some people could really see into a person by looking into their eyes. Maybe she was like that.

She almost smiled. "All right."

That was the time to let go, so he did. "Good. Anything of value down here?"

"Cargo. Medical supplies and food, mostly. Engine room, the Fold drive, gravity system, the maintenance bay. Living quarters...for the non-officers."

"Ship like this, you must have a pretty good Fold drive."

"It's—" She licked her lips. "—the only good thing, really. *Was* the only good thing."

"Was?"

She smiled, but it was rueful, pained. "It's how we ended up in this mess. The system...we don't know what happened, but we ended up drifting about ten parsecs off course before dropping out of Fold space."

"That's a pretty significant drift."

"There's a lot of empty space in the galaxy, but you don't want to test the odds when you unfold."

The odds kept looking more and more unlikely. He looked up the stairs. "And up there?"

Her eyes dropped down to one of the Marines—the tough-looking big guy—then she took the steps. She kept a hand on the railing and never looked up. The whole time, Rai rolled around in his head the look the Marine and his commander had exchanged. It wasn't subordinate and boss—at least it didn't seem that way to the privateer. There was something personal between them.

More to store away.

The commander stopped in a passageway. There were hatches forward, aft, port, and starboard. "This is officer country." She winced at that. "The captain and I—"

No more captain; that was still settling in.

He studied the forward hatch she'd been pointing to. "Sorry about your boss getting whacked."

"No." She straightened her back. "If he'd listened to me, none of this would've happened."

"You knew the Fold drive was failing?"

"When we came out of Fold space, our inertia carried us into the DMZ. Rather than decelerate and reverse course, he wanted to figure out what caused the failure. And then your SOS reached us, and he insisted on going deeper into the DMZ."

"Against your advice."

"Yes."

"Sounds a little light on the search and rescue, Commander."

"An officer's duty is to the crew first and foremost."

"I thought you'd have an obligation to rescue people."

"We've got two Marines and a nurse in cold sleep with enough radiation in their bodies to kill them two times over, all because Commander Martinez took too many risks trying to rescue people from a ship even worse off than yours."

"Sounds like you two didn't get along."

"Lenny took too many risks."

"I guess so." Rai pointed to the starboard hatch. "What's in there?"

"A passageway that runs aft to the gym." She pointed to the port hatch. "That takes you to the break room, also aft."

He pointed to the aft hatch. "And this?"

"The rest of Officer Country—doctors and nurses. Chief Parkinson has a little cabin in there, too. The infirmary and cold sleep are beyond those."

"Parkinson. The weaselly guy?"

"Our engineer."

"Don't care for him, either."

"It was his arrogance that got those Marines and that nurse killed."

"I see." Rai nodded to the forward hatch. "You mind showing me the bridge?"

She went rigid. "What do you and Mr. Chung have in mind for me and my crew."

"Quentin usually runs a pretty tight operation. We hit ships with VIPs or critical cargo. Ship like this? We wouldn't go near it."

"You didn't answer the question."

She was regaining her strength and confidence.

"I can tell you what I'd do. I'd get you to fix the *Rakshasa*. I'd transfer any cargo you have that could be of use to us. Then I'd bug out, full speed."

"And Mr. Chung?"

Rai rubbed his nose. "You don't piss him off, maybe things go your way."

She seemed to get his meaning.

The passageway running forward passed two hatches on the starboard side and a third on the port. Another hatch was straight ahead.

The commander pointed at the first hatch—the one port side. "The head. My cabin's the next one up—the captain's is the one closest to the bridge."

"Show me your cabin."

She tensed but stiffly opened the hatch and led him in. It was a little nicer than his own accommodations and certainly better maintained. Her scent was in the air—a sweet perfume combined with a personal aroma. There were a few knickknacks on the shelves. His eyes were drawn to what looked like a glass globe, maybe some recognition trinket like he'd seen on a couple ships the *Rakshasa* had raided.

He pointed to it. "Can I?"

She nodded but clearly wished they weren't in such tight quarters.

The thing came away from the shelf with little effort, once he figured out the right angle to overcome the smart adhesive. Almost immediately, he realized there was more to it than the simple trinket he'd imagined.

Holographs flashed in the heart of it when he rotated his wrist—some sort of insignia, what might be a medal, a starship.

They were revealed only with care and study.

"What's all this?"

She seemed to relax a little. "Silly things."

"Like…?"

She shrugged. "Nothing."

"Your dreams? Goals?"

"Y-yes."

"What's this rank?"

"Captain."

"And the… Is that a medal?"

"The Republic Ivory Order of Meritorious Service." She blushed. "There've only been three given out."

"Is that big ship important?"

"The *Valor*. It's slated to be the fourth fleet flagship, if they ever finish it."

"One problem everyone seems to have in common—pushing a big ship out."

"The technology keeps changing before—"

Rai caught an image of a man he'd missed before and nearly dropped the trinket. "Who's this?"

She blushed harder than before. "No one."

"You wouldn't put no one in this thing, now would you? Brother? Boyfriend?"

"My father."

"This is your father?"

"What?"

"Nothing." He snorted. "It's just that the universe seems to have a strange sense of humor is all."

"What do you mean?"

"He's young. Handsome. Left you as a kid?"

"I was eight."

"Crazy." He put the globe back on the shelf a little unsteadily. The odds seemed to be spinning out of any reasonable semblance of control. "Let's check out the—"

His radio squealed.

Chung shouted. "Better get your ass down here."

"What's up?"

"Just put your dick away and get down here."

Rai jerked his head toward the hatch, and the commander led him back to the stairs and down. She seemed just as curious as he felt. That didn't mean much, though. Marines could be trouble. It was possible they'd tried something.

And it looked like they might have. Gabriel had the big Marine pressed up against the bulkhead with a pistol pressed against the base of his skull. Nguyen had the muscular, hard-looking female Marine similarly ready for execution, and Wong had the skinny Marine kid face down on the deck while the fresh-faced kid Penn covered them all with the laser rifle. Bug-eyed, with a little sliver of a mouth—he wasn't really someone Rai would have pictured running around with hardcore privateers, but Penn had shown he could handle himself.

Benson stopped.

Rai put a hand into the small of her back and pushed her forward. It was a nice back. "What the hell's going on?"

Chung kicked something on the deck, and a groan floated up. There were cargo crates blocking Rai's sight, but when they came out of the maze, he saw the weaselly engineer sprawled on the deck, now with a bloody face.

"Stef—" Chung kicked the engineer again. "—tell him."

The tattoo-faced woman quit glad-handing the female Marine long enough to turn to Rai. "Shithead there was showing me the engineering section when I noticed something flash on the console."

The commander's muscles tensed against Rai's fingers. "Like what, a bomb?"

"An SOS. He tried to cover it up, but I was able to bring it back onscreen."

Gabriel howled. "Fuck! I told you! Oh-ho! I *told* you! Waste 'em!"

Benson twisted around, eyes imploring. "You triggered something. That's all it was, some sort of automated SOS."

It didn't seem all that unlikely to Rai. He'd seen a lot crazier.

The engineer groaned. "I didn't do it. I swear."

Chung kicked the guy again. "See? Trouble. Lying troublemakers."

Gabriel pushed the big Marine toward the airlock hatch. "Space 'em!"

Tears formed in the commander's eyes. "Please. I-If it's an SOS, it's not going to do anything. Your SOS fired off first, and there's no one out here."

"Shit." Rai sighed. "She's right. Anyone listening for an SOS already heard ours, Quentin. Whoever did it, they were just being stupid."

Gabriel shook his head. "Nah. Uh-uh. Let me space 'em. Ho-ho-ho! Space!"

Muscles bulged on the big Marine's neck. He seemed ready to turn things into a pointless massacre. All Gabriel and his little crew were looking for was an excuse to splatter brains all over the bulkheads.

Rai pushed Benson over to the rest of her crew, who were looking on in terror. "Let it go, Vic. Quentin, this is pointless."

Gabriel's teeth pinched his bottom lip. "Uh-uh. No. No-no-no!"

Rai slid his hand to the holster on his hip. "Quentin, you tell this fucking ape to back off now, or the bulkhead gets a new coating of brain paint."

Quentin grunted. He kicked the engineer again.

Gabriel growled as he wrestled the big Marine closer to the airlock hatch.

Rai pulled his pistol. "I'm not kidding, Quentin."

The old man squinted. His eyes drifted to the commander. "She got something you never had before, Dev? Some magical Kedraalian pu—?"

"We're being stupid is all. We need these people for repairs."

That seemed to get to Chung. "Yeah. Repairs."

Gabriel's head shook. "I wanna space one. Let me space one. Just one."

Rai kept the pistol low, but he could snap off two shots, killing Gabriel and Chung's idiot nephew before anyone could do a thing about it, and they all knew it.

Chung sighed. "Let 'em go. For now."

As the goons pushed the Marines back in with the others, Chung stomped over to Rai, not even looking down at the pistol. "You draw that gun on my crew again, Dev, it'll be the last time."

Rai put the weapon away. It was a strange feeling, risking his years of reputation on a few Marines.

Or a pretty Kedraalian officer.

"Sure, Quentin. I hear you." Rai smiled. "Maybe we should get our wounded tended to?"

Chung's little eyes held an unfamiliar fury. The message was clear: The damage that had been done to their trust was permanent.

8

BENSON'S HEARTBEAT FINALLY RETURNED TO NORMAL. FOR THE MOMENT, the cargo bay felt like it might on any other day during any other mission —a little cooler, a little darker, a little more dangerous. But almost normal.

Partly, that was the work she and her crew had returned to. Having her team suit up to cross back over to the *Rakshasa* presented an imme- diate risk that drew her mind back to the safety of those in her care.

There was decontamination to do, pulling out heavier suits to deal with the radiation, a more robust radiation detection system.

The privateers seemed to have no concept of something so essential. They made strange faces at the pungent detergent sprayed onto the cont- aminated suits. They challenged the need for the injections, even after Dietrich administered them to the *Pandora* crew.

It was like dealing with savages.

Seeing the monsters from the privateer crew leave the *Pandora* also helped add normalcy, even if they would only be gone for the short time it would take to retrieve the seriously injured from the privateer ship's cold sleep chamber.

Of course, the threat was still present. As civil as he seemed, the priva- teer named Dev Rai watched over her, and three of the others watched over the rest of her crew. She'd seen Rai draw his pistol and recognized the threat someone so quick represented. And he had a charming smile that he could probably flash while shooting someone right between the eyes.

But he was the only one of the privateers who seemed remotely human.

Well, him and one of the three standing guard over the rest of her crew.

Penn. Eli Penn. He was younger, clean cut, without any of the tattoos and piercings of the thuggish brutes now back aboard the *Rakshasa*.

But there was no mistaking him for a harmless young man. He was hard-eyed. Cold.

And she couldn't tell where he fit in the strange little tribes that made up the privateer crew. It was easy making out who ran the show: the chunky, white-haired man with scars on his face. Quentin Chung. Everyone seemed to respect him or at least to defer to him.

They also seemed to see Rai the same way. He was the clear second, but he also seemed to stand alone. Did that add to his influence?

But the big brute who'd nearly shot Halliwell. Gabriel? The younger privateers seemed to marvel at the man's beastly power and savage behavior. Maybe he would be valuable in a fight, but he seemed just as likely to kill an ally as an enemy.

Rai's dark eyes lingered on the stairs leading to the top deck. "They'll be a few minutes. Think I could clean up in your bathroom?"

Bathroom. He had to be a civilian. She caught Halliwell's attention just to keep him aware of what was going on, then headed to the stairs with Rai in tow.

When they reached the passageway outside the head, she crossed her arms. "How do you plan to work this?"

"I just need a shower. Can I trust you not to do something stupid? You've seen what Gabriel's like."

"And I've felt what that woman's like, thanks."

"Stef? She's got her own problems, yeah. You come up the way we did, problems are a given."

Benson opened the hatch to the Officer Country head. "Two showers, two stalls, two sinks. Towels are in the cabinet, soap dispenser in the showers."

"Underwear? All I've got is the insulation suit underneath."

She pointed to a clothing printer. "Punch in your size and what you wear."

He chuckled as the printer spat out a pair of briefs. "Not too hard a life."

"Right. Except for the three dead we have in cold sleep and my crew being prisoners, I guess it's pretty easy."

"I was talking about the printer. I can't help the rest."

"It's practical. We recycle almost everything."

After digging around in the cabinet, he took a towel out, then undid his holster and set it on a sink counter. When he peeled off his shirt, he revealed the dull white insulation suit beneath. It was slick from the cold sleep gel and was saturated with the sharp mineral smell of it. The material was like a transparent second skin, revealing his dark gold flesh. Compact muscles bunched as he stripped the insulation suit top off. There were scars on that flesh, the sort of wounds a veteran might carry. "Gets a little crowded, I'd imagine."

She turned away. "During shift turnover, it can. We try to give everyone space."

"Sorry you had to see that display earlier. That big Marine mean something to you?"

How could he have figured that out? Or was he just guessing? "Sergeant Halliwell's been dealing with a lot of issues. He didn't take losing half his team very well."

The shower stall door closed, and water turned on. Rai had left his clothes in a pile on the floor and the holster sitting beside the sink.

The pistol grip was pointed toward her.

She could get to the gun before he could stop her, but could she pull it from the holster in time? Was it keyed to his biometrics like privately owned Republic weapons were? Even if she could pull it out and it wasn't keyed to his biometrics, was it even charged?

It could all be a trap, an excuse for him to attack her.

She shivered. Her first concern was for her crew. She couldn't risk putting them in danger again, not after what Martinez had done to them.

Ventilation fans spun up as steam heated the small compartment. The soapy aroma was a welcome replacement for the sharp, mineral smell of the gel.

And then the shower was done, and she turned away again.

If he'd set her up with a test, had she passed?

The towel rasped against his skin. "How long have you been on the *Pandora*?"

"Nearly four years. How long have you been…a privateer?"

He stopped toweling himself, as if considering his answer or maybe trying to figure out the truth of it. "I joined Chung's little gang about three years ago, after he got his charter from the Azoren. I ran with another of his gangs a few years before that for a little while."

"I hope it doesn't offend you if I admit I had no idea you were Azoren."

He snorted. "We're not. Most of the privateers working for them are from the Gulmar."

"Union? So you're traitors?"

The stall door clicked. "Hard to be a traitor when you aren't accepted from birth. The Azoren might be monsters, but they're merit-based monsters, and they pay. In the Union, if you're born poor, you'll always be poor. You don't get access to education and opportunity, so you either drift into dead-end jobs where you're constantly exploited, or you waste away. Some of us aren't okay with that."

"So you take money from the enemy and raid ships of your own people—"

"Hey, look, if you don't know what it's like, maybe you should lighten up on judging, okay? This gig pays. We have a decent life."

She bowed her head. "I'm sorry. I was trying to understand what you do."

"Kill and steal, that's what I do. It makes money I could never have made otherwise. Sort of like being in the military but without all the hardware and training."

Had he meant that to sting? "I certainly never intended to kill and steal for a living when I went to the Academy."

"Yeah, they probably use different words, don't they?"

She wrapped her arms around her. "I guess."

"Look, you go your whole life never being given, seeing others born to ease, you learn to take."

"I'm not judging you."

"That globe of yours, the medal and all that, it's a nice thing. Your goals?"

"Yes." Her gut flipped at the realization he was the only person to have ever recognized all the holographs.

"Realistic ones?"

"I was a distinguished graduate."

"That's impressive, right?"

"I guess. It... It won't matter now. Even if I survive, my career is over."

"Why?"

"Aiding and abetting privateers, entering the DMZ... The military has a way of piling up charges when they prosecute you. Who knows what a Kedraalian ship entering the DMZ will mean in the end."

The whisper of his clothes preceded the scrape of his holster sliding on. "You thinking war?"

"It seems likely. The Azoren said they would take back everything one day."

"Did they?"

She turned on him, eyebrow cocked. "You think they're peaceful? They're paying you to raid Gulmar ships."

"I mean I wasn't around when the war happened."

"But you think they're peaceful?"

Rai snickered and waved for her to precede him out of the head. "I'll tell you something about the Azoren. They're the last people you want to be on the wrong side of, okay? They're cold-blooded and ruthless."

His head was downcast, but she noticed a strange look in his eyes as they headed back for the stairs.

Were things worse than she'd feared?

Penn was at the airlock hatch when they reached the others, eyes locked on the viewing portal. "They're almost here!"

Rai nodded, but he still seemed distracted. "Let the doctor and nurse help."

Dietrich and Clark showed their hands to the two privateers watching them, then edged toward the hatch. Once it was clear no one was going to trouble them, the two prepared the decontamination gear.

Rai smirked. "You going to be able to recycle those environment suits?"

The slender nurse shook his head. "Not recycle, no. We run them through a process to get out any radiation. The decontamination is more to seal any particles clinging to the material."

"Some things you can never get out, though." The senior surgeon sneered.

That drew a curious look from the slender privateer. "I guess."

The inner hatch opened, and the privateers and her crew came through. The big privateer once again didn't seem interested in being decontaminated; Dietrich and Clark didn't argue but kept their distance.

Once Gaines was out of her environment suit, she turned to the two body bags that had been brought across. "All right. Who can tell me what happened here?"

Chung was still pulling his suit off. "They died. What more do you need?"

Dietrich's head popped up from where he was examining the first body bag. "You want us to give optimal treatment to your people, we need to know what happened to them. And their medical records would be helpful. We're not witch doctors, dammit."

"Who the hell're you?" Chung twisted around. "Who's this fucking drunk?"

Gaines clasped her hands in front of her. "He's Dr. Ernest Dietrich, one of the best surgeons you're ever likely to meet, Mr. Chung."

"Best surgeon, huh?" Chung shuffled up to Dietrich. "You know your shit?"

Dietrich sneered. "I'm an expert in my—"

Chung pulled his pistol from its shoulder holster and pressed the end of the barrel against Dietrich's forehead. "So why don't you tell me what kind of surgery would be needed to stick your big brain back in your head if I blow it open. You got any idea?"

Gaines's eyes bugged out. "Mr. Chung, please! Dr. Dietrich didn't mean anything. He was upset because he wants to save lives."

"Like his own?"

Dietrich blinked slowly. "I'm sorry if I came off as insensitive."

"Yeah." Chung put his pistol away. "Well, that's my son, and he took a bullet to the face."

Dietrich opened the bag again and went pale. "His skull has been—"

"I know what happened to him. Can you fix him or not?"

"Well, with a resuscitation system, even a small amount of brain—"

"He wasn't wearing one." Chung sniffled—soft but audible.

"Then..." Dietrich looked to Benson.

She cleared her throat. "Mr. Chung, we could keep your son in cold sleep until we get to a regenerative center in Kedraalian space. If he's been in cold sleep the whole time, there's always a chance they could save him. They have remarkable capabilities. We have people of our own we'll be sending in for lethal radiation rehabilitation when we get back." *If we get back.*

Chung shrugged, but there was no hiding the pain in his eyes. "The other one is what matters. Took a round to the chest. Her own people."

Rai grunted and leaned a little closer in to Benson. "Asset denial. Worth a small fortune to us. Apparently worth more to them."

Dietrich probed inside the bag. "Female. Significant surgical enhancements make it hard to assess age. Let's assume mid-forties to mid-fifties."

Chung guffawed. "Eighty-nine. Money buys so much."

Dietrich glanced at Gaines. "Looks to be in good shape. She died before going into cold storage?"

"Heart stopped a couple times. Our 'medic' is more of a butcher." Chung glared at a third privateer who'd been left behind to guard Benson's crew—a skinny, big-eyed man with a wide nose bridge and sunken cheeks; the guy's shoulders slumped.

"I think we've got a chance to save her." Dietrich stood unsteadily.

"Someone like this usually has a resuscitation implant. We'll need to see the exact damage done, obviously, but her initial—"

"Doc, just fucking do it."

Dietrich bowed his head. "Petty Officer Stiles, Lieutenant Clark, if you could, please."

The two nurses hefted the bag and followed after Dietrich, with Penn and the privateer medic bracketing Gaines, who was close behind.

Chung nodded at Rai. "Stay with her. Looks like I'm with the babysitters."

9

BENSON LED THE MYSTERIOUS PRIVATEER UP THE STAIRS AGAIN WHILE THE
others took the forward lift. It seemed strangely silent the entire way,
with even their steps like whispers. They reached the infirmary first. As
the lights climbed to full brightness, she led Rai aft, past the treatment
bays toward the surgery chamber. It was an enclosed, clear cube that
took up the back half of the infirmary. The only way in was an airlock
that rested midway along the forward wall. To the left of the airlock was
a narrow room, barely wide enough to walk into comfortably.

She pointed him through the door to the small room and closed it
behind them. The room took up half the surgery chamber wall running
to starboard. "This is the observation room."

Rai looked around. "Seems a little snug."

"It wasn't built for comfort."

"More like a meat locker."

"They keep the surgery area cold. Cold sleep is just beyond there." She
pointed to the back wall, where a hatch granted access to the place they
called the sleep room or chiller, depending on who was going in. "People
don't usually stay in here too long."

"Can't imagine why."

The outer hatch opened, and Clark and Stiles came through, the body bag between them. Penn followed a second later, weapon still at the ready. Like Rai, the young man had a professional bearing and a level of discipline that seemed almost reassuring, a sharp contrast to the other privateers.

The sunken-cheeked medic led Dietrich and Gaines in but stopped in the outpatient area and took a seat at one of the treatment stations. Once the medical personnel were all within the surgical area, he returned his gun to its shoulder holster.

Penn paid the other man no mind, instead watching the surgical area through the forward wall.

Benson nodded toward Penn. "He seems to really care about this woman."

Rai chortled. "We all care about her. She's like a mother to us."

"What's that mean? She's a relative?"

"No." He shrugged. "Like I said, she's valuable."

The nurses removed the body from the bag and set the woman out on the closest of the two surgical tables. Benson's eyes went to the woman's clothing, which looked stylish and expensive: a deep blue jacket and pants, a bright gold top where blood hadn't darkened it.

"That blouse probably cost more than I make in a year."

Rai squinted. "People like her, they hire top designers to produce one-offs. It's a show of power."

All that money—wasted. The nurses cut the clothing away and tossed it into a pile.

Benson had seen some gruesome surgeries, so she wasn't really affected by the bloody wound. It looked like it was almost dead-center of the sternum; the shot had come close to the heart.

Rai gnawed on a knuckle but seemed undisturbed by all the blood and ruptured skin.

Benson couldn't help feeling a little envious at the sight of the woman's flesh away from the wound. On the arms and legs, the woman's skin was smooth and seemed to have the elasticity and fullness of youth. The bronze coloring spoke of time under a warm sun. Eighty-nine seemed unlikely.

"She's pretty."

Rai screwed up his face. "You can't really know that."

"Just look at her. Thick black hair, full lips, a really nice nose."

"All after-market. It's not the real person."

Benson felt insecure in the presence of such harsh analysis. "Who is?"

"Nah, I mean you shouldn't defy age like that. It's not right."

"If she's young in every way, does her real age matter?"

"It's the mind, the experiences. After a while, you see too much."

"Would you feel that way if you could be that old and look that good?"

Rai glared at Benson, then smiled. "Fair question."

Benson fought back a smile of her own. "You called her people killing her asset denial. Why would they do that?"

"That's the way things are. This isn't a struggle with starships and armies blasting each other apart. Not yet. For now, everything happens in the shadows, out of sight or hard to make out the details."

"Espionage."

"Yeah. Everyone wants to be in the best position when the missiles fly."

Dietrich glared at Benson as the nurses helped him into his gown. He wasn't used to having guns waved around at him, and in his detoxing state it was probably worse than it would have been if he'd been sober.

Suck it up, Doctor. She broke eye contact. "We were always told the Azoren were the worst and would be the ones we had to fight again one day. Don't they have all the advantages?"

Rai's smug amusement was irritating. "You don't know much about the Azoren."

"We've been hoping to avoid war with them for decades."

"Uh-huh."

She blushed. His smirking really was getting to her. "You don't think it's a good idea to hope for peace?"

"Sure. Is that what your people do—hope for peace?"

"And train for war."

He bit his lip. "Well, that's one way to do things."

"You didn't answer my question. Don't the Azoren have all the advantages?"

"For war? Not yet. That whole superior race thing hasn't really panned out like they thought, I guess."

That was a relief. "But they're preying on the Gulmar Union."

"It goes both ways. The Union has a lot of money. You'd be surprised how many 'superior' people can be bought, how many secrets they'd be willing to sell themselves out to keep." He looked at her, but his meaning wasn't apparent.

"If you don't like the Azoren, why work for them?"

"You've seen the way Chung's people fight amongst themselves."

Chung's people. Rai didn't see himself as part of their crew. "Yes."

"They hate each other, most of them. But fear keeps them together. And hatred, too. We all hate the Union." He looked down at his boots. "Although we aren't all that different."

"How could you be? You were raised there. They're your kin."

"Not really. But we really like money more than anything, so…"

The overhead lights came on, brightening the surgery area. It drained color from the woman's body and gave the illusion of age.

Or maybe it revealed more of the truth of her age.

Stiles covered the body with paper sheets until only the wounded area was left exposed.

Benson turned Rai's words around in her head. The privateers hated each other. They feared each other. They were held together by their hatred of the Gulmar. Did that leave the pirates vulnerable? Was there enough friction between them that it could be exploited?

She pressed her forehead against the glass. "What was the plan, then?"

"The plan?"

"For this woman you kidnapped. Sell her to the highest bidder among the Azoren?"

"They don't work that way. Chung's charter is simple: They pay; we do what they say."

"Like soldiers."

He looked her up and down. "Without the uniforms and ranks, yeah."

"And they told you to grab her?"

"Well, we sort of stumbled onto her ourselves. That's how we picked up Penn." Rai nodded toward the young man, who stood still in front of the surgery area, eyes locked on the ring of medical personnel.

"He wasn't part of your...what are you, a gang?"

"Sure, gang is fine. He joined us about six months ago. He came to Chung, said he knew someone who knew someone, but he couldn't get his own gang together. So he told us about this mark for a cut of the payout. Chung made him a deal to let him come along."

"What's that face mean?"

"What face?"

Benson imitated the face Rai had made. "Like you smelled something horrible."

Rai laughed. "I didn't make that face."

"You did."

"Okay, so I did. So what."

"You don't like this Penn?" They *all* seemed to hate each other.

"I don't like unknowns. You let unknowns get into the mix, the odds go against you. But the kid proved good. Better than Chung's son and nephew." Rai shook his head.

"Did they screw things up?"

"Nearly got Penn and me killed. Them and Gabriel."

"The crazy one?"

"Yeah. Another unknown. Hurley over there took a hit but happened to be wearing a vest. He would've been dead for sure."

Benson turned around to check on the man with the sunken cheeks. He was slumped in his chair, greasy hair hanging down over his big eyes. "Real lucky he made it."

"Hey, he knows what he's doing. He saved my life before."

One of the scars she'd seen on Rai's chest? "Do you trust them?"

"My gang? Not all of them, no."

"The psycho."

"Yeah. Not him. Not Stef. Not Wong. I trust Chung. Hurley. This Penn guy seems good."

"Brought a lot of money to you, if you can pull this off."

"A lot."

The trust didn't seem to go far or deep. And if Rai felt that way about the others, they probably felt that way about each other. She'd already seen friction among them. Could she find the right situation that would lead to a breaking point? Rai had been ready to shoot earlier, in the cargo hold. Chung had made it clear he wouldn't put up with something like that again.

Maybe the particulars of the divisions would make themselves known. Or maybe she'd have to figure them out. She would need time for that.

How long before she and her crew were no longer needed?

Someone rapped on the door to the observation room: the guy with the sunken cheeks. Hurley. He pushed the door in. "Hey, Dev, the Old Man's sending some people across to start repairs. I gotta go play guard."

Rai shrugged. "Nothing's gonna happen here."

"Yeah, I know. I was hoping to catch some shuteye."

"You were asleep for a couple weeks."

"Not the same, man." The gangly guy shrugged. "Every time I come out of cold sleep, I feel like shit."

"Yeah, well, you take too long getting back down there, you're gonna feel worse."

Hurley let the door close and jogged out of the infirmary. He seemed dangerous enough, like Rai had implied, but not motivated and disciplined like him and Penn. That was another exploitable difference.

Benson turned back to the surgery. Dietrich was digging around inside the dead woman's chest, watching a display that showed imagery of her insides—arteries, veins, muscles, bones.

The little room suddenly felt hot to Benson. She looked away. "So, who was this woman who's going to make you rich?"

He chuckled. "You sound jealous."

"We'd all like the kind of money you're talking about."

"Amanda Carone. A pretty important executive with Haidakura. They run a lot of the Union defense systems. She was on her way back from a research center, delivering important data on the big upgrades underway."

"Physically delivering? Isn't that a little backwards?"

"Not really. It's the kind of data you don't transmit in the open."

"How is carrying data physically safer than transmitting it?"

"You should've seen her security."

"But you captured her."

"We did, with a lot of work. Hackers could get transmitted data easily."

"Encrypted?"

"Nothing can't be hacked. It was the right call."

Had there been anything on the other ship that could have held the data? An attaché case? A data device? She hadn't seen anything. "Did you get the data?"

Rai nodded at the woman on the table. "She's the data. It's in her head."

"Memorized?"

"Sure. But through a cybernetic implant."

"Can you get it out of her?"

"If we have too. It's better to have her alive, but there's always a chance the implant could be extracted and salvaged."

"You think the Azoren could do that?"

"Maybe."

"You don't sound keen on that. Why not?"

"Well, there's better money to be had."

Mercenaries. They would sell out the Azoren? To whom? "Who would pay more?"

"The Haidakura."

"The same people who tried to kill her?"

"Yeah. Penn says the same people who sold her out could guarantee twice what anyone else would offer. They could take the credit for the rescue. It's a big win all the way around." He smiled.

"You like that?"

"Turning her over to the Azoren would've been bad for business."

"How's that?"

"Compromise the defense network or force the Union to back out of the planned upgrade? It would've given the Azoren the last advantage they needed to start the war. We would've either been out of a job or pressed into military action. Or executed."

His calm assessment was unnerving. Didn't he fear death at all? "What about the others? The Khanate and the Moskav Alliance?"

"No one knows if the Khanate is even around anymore. Most people don't think it is."

"What about the Moskav?"

"Not a serious threat, not to the Azoren. No, the real money to be had is working against the Union. You'll never find a society more likely to sell itself out than one where money means more than the people."

Wasn't that everyone? Didn't every society have something they valued more than their people? Why else would the *Pandora* ever have been at risk?

It hit her then that the privateers were actually in even greater danger than she'd realized. If word got back to the Azoren one of their chartered privateers had kidnapped such an important Gulmar executive, then sold her back to her own people, Rai's worries about execution would almost certainly prove true.

It was yet another reason for Chung's crew to kill the *Pandora* crew. And unless Benson could figure out some way to turn things around, that execution seemed like it would be coming sooner rather than later.

10

ALTHOUGH THE NARROW CHAMBER WAS TOO CHILLY AFTER DAYS IN COLD sleep, Rai was enjoying the warmth. Whether that was coming off the pretty Kedraalian commander or was in his imagination, he wasn't sure. And he didn't care. It wasn't lost on him that she'd chosen to stay in the bathroom while he cleaned up, and he was still impressed she hadn't gone for his weapon.

She wasn't some gullible rookie who didn't know where her head was. No doubt, she was scheming already, just as he would in her situation. That was dangerous, but he liked a little danger in his life. In fact, he'd never known anything *but* danger. You don't grow up on the mean streets of Hyberanon and not know danger.

He sucked in a breath, caught the now-familiar perfume coming off Benson. It was almost hidden in with the antiseptic tang and the remnants of the gel that had soaked into his clothes.

His priorities bounced around, shifting too quickly to keep up with.

They needed to get the *Rakshasa* running. They needed to get the old Carone bitty on her feet again or at least breathing before stuffing her back into cold sleep.

They needed to *go*.

But he could make some time for the Kedraalian commander, if she wanted.

She turned to him the way people do when they realize someone's been staring at them. "Does it really matter if they save this Amanda Carone?"

"Matter? It could save us thousands we'd have to spend otherwise."

Benson smiled. He'd misunderstood her meaning. "Will it keep her alive?"

"Oh." She was in his head. Normally, he was a master at reading body language, picking up on contextual clues, and inferring. It was what his old man Masran had taught from an early age, even before his mother and siblings had died. Rai's stomach twisted at that little lie. What was one convenient lie in a lifetime built on a framework of them? "That's gonna depend on the Haidakura."

She glanced back into the surgery area, then bowed her head. "It's a lot of effort. I'd hate to see it wasted."

"That's how life is in the Union. A human life's not worth much."

Penn turned from the place he'd been glued to since they'd taken Carone into the glass cube. He headed to the entry, searched for a second, then reached a hand out.

The intercom. Someone must've called, and the noise wouldn't reach them in their own sealed-off glass room.

The way Penn looked at Rai, he realized the call was for him. "Gotta take a call."

Penn jerked a thumb back at the intercom on the way back to his guard post outside the surgical chamber. "Chung."

Rai hit the intercom button. "Yeah?"

"Need you down here in the cargo bay."

"Something wrong?"

"Just get your ass down here."

Benson was watching from the intimate glass room. Rai waved, then strolled out. There was no reason to hurry, not with her watching. Chung could be a grumpy old fuck, but losing his stupid kid had made it worse. All the years working for the old bastard, it was sometimes hard to reconcile. He'd always allowed a more flexible work relationship with

Rai, something that was absolutely essential in his line of work. Most of the time, someone like Chung required loyalty. You couldn't disappear for weeks or months at a time and show back up and slip back into place as if you'd never left.

It was Masran's history. Rai's father had probably been the most respected bookie on Karkos, and he'd made good money for Chung's old man Wan.

Legacies mattered.

About halfway down the final flight of steps, Rai slowed. Chung's people had the Kedraalian crew herded closer together. Stef and Rainier Volker—her balding, tattooed assistant—were whispering, and Rai was pretty sure they weren't talking about the repairs. Even though Volker had been sluggish coming out of cold sleep, he was fully awake now and eyeing the captives like meat while the repair crew piled their gear into the airlock.

Chung stepped away from the others and headed toward the stairs. He met Rai in the cargo maze. "You get your piece of Kedraalian ass yet?"

"What the fuck's going on?"

"Our little roundup?"

"Yeah. You think they're animals or something?" Rai's voice seemed to roll up to the ceiling high overhead. With all the clutter, the look in Stef's eyes, the way the lights seemed to be swallowed by the darkness in the big cargo space, it felt like a slaughter waiting to happen. He swallowed and lowered his voice. "No reason to treat them like that."

Chung patted Rai's cheek softly. "Hey, look. You with me? Need you with me, Dev."

"I'm with you."

"You can get better than that commander."

"Lay off that, okay?"

"Sure, sure. But I want your head in this."

"My head *is* in it. What's up?" Rai glared at the other privateers, who were laughing among themselves now.

"We gotta plan for the next move. They got the Carone lady on her feet?"

"Fuck no. She's still half-frozen. They're digging around in her guts to see what happened."

Chung ran stubby fingers over his whiskers. "Can they save her?"

"This drunk guy's supposedly the best around."

"She had a hole as big as two fingers in her chest."

"Sure. Because Jimmy fucked up."

"Let it go, huh. He's a kid."

"I was younger than him when I started working for you. Was I ever that stupid?"

"So he's a stupid kid. Let it go. I want you thinking about what comes next. Okay?"

"Sure."

"Say they get her stabilized, what do we do?"

"We take anything worth a damn from this ship and get the hell out of here. Head for Radetta at full acceleration."

"I thought you wanted to shoot for Minhath."

"We've got to get rid of Carone as soon as possible."

"Sure, but what about this ship? I thought you were gonna think about it."

"What? No. It's no good. No gun to speak of. It's built for speed and rescue."

Chung flashed his yellow teeth with a wolfish grin. "Perfect cover. Get another big gun on the belly. People let you in close when you're a rescue ship."

"Only if they're expecting rescue, and if they are, we don't need guns."

"But the Fold Drive's good."

"Nah. Not worth it. She said it malfunctioned, and they can't figure out why. That's how they got here in the first place. They were supposed to be parsecs away from this place."

"You gonna look fate in the eye and let this walk away?"

"I'm telling you, it's not worth it." Rai smoothed his shirt. "We don't need any more distractions than we already have."

"What's that mean?"

"Gabriel. He's a fucking animal." Rai nodded toward the big thug, who was harassing the skinny Marine as he pulled on his environment suit.

Wong was pitching in, jabbing the scrawny guy with the business end of the laser rifle.

"Yeah, an animal."

"We need brains now. We're in Azoren space. What good is it to have a hostage and a working ship if your little psychos fuck everything up again?"

"What'd I tell you? Let it go."

"Sure. But if you don't get that meathead away from the others, we're going to have trouble."

"Vic's a good kid. I got him under control."

"Yeah? Like when he used Carone as a meat shield?"

"Everyone was in a panic."

"When the blaster bolts fly, that's when you have to be your coolest."

"Sure, but not everyone can be you." Chung patted Rai on the cheek again. "So, this weaselly engineer says he can get us running in a bit; you say load up and bail. You're not worried about this SOS?"

"No. I told you, we're in the middle of nowhere. Anyone hears an SOS, they'll hear ours first."

"But this fuck sends an SOS, maybe we can't trust him."

"Who cares. Leave it. We'll be long gone before it matters." Rai edged closer toward Gabriel. The gorilla had the skinny kid pinned to the bulkhead. The big Marine was at the edge of the herded group. He looked ready to charge through Stef. That would set everything off. There'd be a bloodbath. They didn't need that. Not right now. "Look, Quentin, this engineer's a coward. He's not gonna do shit to endanger himself."

"Yeah. But *someone* triggered the SOS."

"Fine. Keep an eye on him."

"I'll have Jimmy watch him."

Wong had the laser rifle barrel pressed against the struggling little Marine's forehead.

The big Marine's hands balled up into fists.

Rai reached for his pistol, thought better of it, and took a step toward the fracas. "We need to ratchet this shit down, Quentin, or the Marines—"

"Fuck the Marines."

"No, no. They're good for the dangerous work. Better them getting radiation than us. Better they move shit around so we can keep our weapons handy."

"Yeah, sure."

"So tell that gorilla to lay off."

Chung shrugged. "We're good."

"No. We're not. And tell Stef she's gonna push the Marine gal too far, getting all handsy like she is."

"Yeah, sure."

"You're talking but not doing anything." Rai took another step out of the maze.

Chung didn't move. "Hey, you falling for that piece of ass? That what this is all about?"

"No. Doesn't mean we have to act like animals, right?" Rai took a step, then turned back on Chung when he didn't follow. "What matters is the ransom. Right? Why bother killing these people off? They didn't do shit. Let 'em go. The Kedraalians aren't going to sell us out. They got fuck-all to do with the Azoren."

"Maybe."

The old guy wasn't going to rein his thugs in.

Rai stomped over to the scuffle. "What's going on, guys?"

Gabriel twisted around. "Just having a little fun."

"Fun time comes later. This is business time."

Chung scraped to a stop behind Rai. "We got repairs to make. Where's the weaselly guy? Jimmy, you're supposed to be watching him."

The sadistic smile disappeared from Wong's face. "H-he's back in the engineering area."

Rai sensed the sudden tension in Chung and intervened. "Go check on him, Jimmy. Never take your eyes off of him."

"S-sure." The stupid kid jogged back toward the open engineering hatch.

There was a popping noise coming out of the space, probably some sort of maintenance to get the robotic drones ready for all the radiation. That's what the chickenshit engineer had stammered when he'd promised he could get everything running soon. But it was better to have Wong away from Gabriel.

The musclebound oaf was smirking at the big Marine, daring him to do something.

Gabriel was too stupid to realize that it was only guns keeping him from spitting teeth right then. The Marine looked dangerous and not the least bit afraid of the big oaf.

Chung tugged on Rai's shoulder and led him back toward the maze. "This deal with the Haidakura, you think it's a good idea?"

Rai held his breath until the big Marine seemed to calm down. "What? Selling Carone back to them?"

"They're nothing but a bunch of scumbag double-crossing fucks."

"Sure. But they have all the money."

"But they won't *pay* us. They'll just kill us all—her and us."

The dark seemed to swallow the lights even more. There were no good sides to play in this job. That was what his father had taught him from day one. You trust yourself. You have loyalty to yourself and to the one thing you believe in, but you never could tell anyone who you believed in, who you *were*.

And he sure as hell wasn't Azoren or some wealthy merchant.

"All right." Rai ran the back of his hand over his brow. Dry. He only thought he was sweating. "So what about selling her to someone else?"

"Yeah. That was my thinking." Chung glanced at the stairs. "But who else has money?"

"You're thinking the Kedraalians?"

"Sure as hell can't be the Moskav, right?"

If there was someone more money-strapped than the Azoren, it was the Moskav. "What would the Kedraalians do with her data? They're not looking for war."

"They got a military, right?"

What had Benson said about the big ship? It would never be finished because the technology kept changing before they could launch it. "I don't think they've got the sort of military the Azoren do. They sound afraid of them."

Chung's whiskers sounded like sandpaper under his fingernails. "I'll think about it. Maybe it could work."

"The Haidakura are offering a lot of fucking money for her."

"Yeah." Chung quit scratching. "And we fuck them over, we'll have contracts on our heads from the Azoren *and* the Union."

"So we take the chance. We arrange the transfer. We scout and plan like we did for the kidnapping."

"We lost people doing that."

"Because of Gabriel. Get rid of him. Leave your nephew on the ship. We can hire some muscle we can count on."

"I ain't giving up any of this fucking money."

"Gotta spend money to make it, Quentin."

The old man hissed. "Why the hell couldn't we have gotten the charter when the Azoren were wiping out the Moskav?"

"Or the Khanate."

That drew a laugh. "You ever hear about their ships? Little shells they'd send into battle by the thousands. Death traps."

"The metal horde. Keep sending people at the enemy until they run out of ammo."

Chung sniffled. "That's how we all win. The survivor comes out on top. Everyone's expendable."

"Doesn't have to be that way. Not everyone has to be like that, y'know."

"Maybe." Chung looked around the cargo bay. "You sure we couldn't do well with a second ship?"

"Too much trouble."

"Yeah. I guess." He kicked at the deck plates. "The crew quarters look nice."

"Pretty nice, sure."

Chung's brow arched. "You know we gotta kill them."

Rai's heart sank. "I know."

11

DIETRICH STRAIGHTENED AND ARCHED HIS BACK. BENSON HAD SEEN HIM DO that enough times to know he was done. Gaines would take over with the nurses' help, and then—

Something was different this time. Dietrich waved for Benson to come into the surgical area.

Had they run into a problem?

She pulled the door open; the young privateer—Penn—turned. Not alarmed or panicked but curious.

"I think there's been a complication." Benson smiled hopefully.

Penn stepped back. "It was a pretty ugly wound."

"It looked bad, didn't it?"

She passed through the airlock, which cycled with a mechanical hiss, then into the chiller freeze of the surgical chamber where it seemed that all sound had died. The body lay on the surgical table, surprisingly not that gory. There was blood, but it was thick, in dark globs—thawed. Dietrich's pale eyes almost glowed in the blinding surgical light.

Stiles was there with a surgical gown and mask, dark green eyes going from Benson to the privateer guarding them, then back. "Just that one, Commander?"

"Just him."

Benson stretched her arms out to get the apron over her flight suit. The material was coarse against her neck, and it smelled like it'd been dipped in alcohol. The mask was even worse. They were sterilized, certainly, but she would've preferred something less…medicine-like.

Was this what it was like to be interrogated? Something the Azoren might do? Or would they prefer to sweat the strength out of their victim?

Clark nodded to the space beside Dietrich, which Stiles had abandoned. The young woman seemed close to panic, even in the relative peace they'd been afforded to save this poor Gulmar woman's life.

Eighty-nine, but she could have been in her thirties.

Then again, given the way Rai had talked about the Gulmar, maybe it wasn't so right to feel pity for the woman.

Was it really that bad to live in Union space? Before the War of Separation that had torn apart the once-promising human hegemony, the factions had certainly all been dramatically different. Millions—billions—caught up in the belief that their philosophy was tied to the species' destiny. War seemed inevitable in hindsight, at least based on her reading about the events leading up to the conflict. But the Gulmar had seemed the least crazy of the four splintering groups. Was it really so wrong to believe that an individual should determine his or her own success? How could that compare to the Azoren philosophy of racial purity or the Moskav belief in a single collective that elevated the power of a small group of elite? And what about the bloodthirsty Khanate, willing to put to the sword anyone who wouldn't bend a knee to their strange god?

Dietrich cleared his throat. "Commander?"

"Oh. I'm sorry. I was just…"

"The wound looks bad, I imagine."

"Yes."

"Well, it was, actually. Almost instantly lethal." He plucked a metal rod from the surgical instrument tray that stood between them. It gleamed in the overhead light. "I'm going to walk you through our findings and what we've done."

She swallowed. No matter the number of corpses she saw, she would never grow comfortable with the gore. Not up close like she was now. "All right."

Clark turned on a machine that gave off a deep, bass hum.

Dietrich dropped his voice to a whisper. "I'm also going to talk to you about something much more pressing: How do you plan to get us out of this mess?"

Benson realized then that with the surgical masks on and the machine generating a hum, there would be no lip reading or recording what was being said, not if they kept their voices low enough.

She leaned over the body to stare uneasily at the open wound. "They're at each others' throats."

Dietrich raised his voice. "The round entered here, punching through the sternum easily. She must have been wearing a little armor, though. We removed fragments." He tapped the cavity with the probe and his voice dropped again. "It's possible they could kill each other, Commander. We would all welcome that gleefully. But I must point out that their bodies would still be warm long after ours would be cold. They mean us ill, there can be no misconstruing that."

She nodded. "I figured that out."

"Yes, well, I don't intend to die, Commander."

"It makes sense the wound would have been worse without armor."

"Do you have a plan, then?" His voice rose slightly.

"I think we could take advantage of the friction. If we could just get weapons to Clive and—" She'd called Halliwell by his first name.

Only Dietrich seemed surprised, but he went back to probing the wound. "We've patched up some damaged blood vessels and a little nick in the heart. There was also a collapsed lung, now re-inflated. Rather, if she ever breathes again, the lung will be functional. Also, that little slice in the heart—there's a matching nick on her vertebra. It shouldn't endanger her beyond discomfort while it heals the rest of the way. I've put bone glue in there to stabilize it."

"That sounds promising."

He was back to whispers. "Promising, Commander, would have been finding a blaster pistol with a full power pack inside of her."

"Well, you didn't. We'll need something else."

"And since you haven't produced such a thing yourself, I have an idea."

She blinked away threatening tears. Was the alcohol leaking from his pores? "I'm listening."

"Sedative gas."

Penn knocked on the airlock door and pointed at Benson, then waved for her to come to him.

Could he have heard somehow? Maybe they'd slipped a listening device into the dead woman's clothes, or when the big female privateer had her hands inside the flight suit...?

Benson fought against the shaking in her knees. A few steps from the surgical table, she lowered the mask. There was an infirmary-only intercom near the airlock. She pressed the button. "What is it?"

"How much longer do you think you're going to be?"

"A few more minutes. The injuries were surprisingly extensive."

Penn bowed his head. "We almost had her out of the line of fire. It was Gabriel's fault. Him and Chung's stupid kid."

"If it matters, I wish you'd managed to escape and we'd never met." She smiled and hoped it appeared warm.

"I understand. So, is she going to make it?"

"I'll let you know in a few minutes."

"Thanks."

He stepped back and returned to his almost military stance.

Benson sucked in a breath and pulled the mask back up. Her legs were jelly, and her heart... How could Penn not hear it?

Dietrich wiped a black blob of blood from the end of the probe. "We can resume."

"Yes." She barely managed that. "Sedative gas?"

"We have enough to fill this chamber."

"You plan to knock yourselves out?"

He glared. "I plan to lure a few of them in. We could have them help move the woman. She'll need to go into a treatment station. Blood transfusion, anti-inflammatories, boosters to fight infection. All very real."

"And what about us?"

Dietrich tapped a gas mask attached to the table. "Two of us will be alert. I'll administer stimulants to counter the gas. We'll acquire their weapons, then it's down to exterminating them."

The plan didn't sound very much like something a doctor would concoct, but she wasn't really in need of something soft and forgiving at the moment.

"All right." She cleared her throat. "I think we'll want Sergeant Halliwell up here."

"Yes. All of the Marines would be ideal."

"They've got Corporal Grier and Private Lopez on the repair team."

"Then Halliwell will do."

Gaines leaned in. "The risk seems too high, Commander."

Benson wanted to pat the older woman's bloody glove. How many times had Gaines called the crew her kids? There was no way to tell someone who had lost her entire family in one form of service or another to just suck it up. Die fighting for freedom or die being shoved out into space, you were dead either way.

But Benson had to say something. "We need to take a risk now, or it's pointless later."

The big woman's eyes watered. Was there fear in them because the man who'd come up with the idea was still detoxing? Could there still be a suicidal instability to Dietrich, something so dark he would put the whole crew at risk?

Gaines finally lowered her eyes. "I understand."

Clark hugged her.

Would that make the privateer suspicious? Who could question that? After all they'd been through, would even a murderous privateer wonder why hostages would comfort each other?

Benson returned to the intercom and pulled her mask down. She wasn't sure she could maintain her wavering calm, but she would have to do better than Stiles, whose eyes were absolutely huge. The young woman seemed ready to collapse.

How could someone who went through military training be so anxious? Stiles was smart. She had high marks. But anything other than partying and flirting—

Benson sighed and pressed the button. "Mr. Penn, was it?"

"Yes."

"We're going to need some help up here. Could you ask some of your people if they could assist us?"

Penn squinted. "Assist you with what?" He sounded as if he suspected something.

Calm. She had to sell him on this. "Well, we believe there's a good chance we've got Ms. Carone in a situation where she could be stable."

The squint softened. "That's great!"

That was the hook she'd needed. But how could she convince him of the—

What was it Dietrich had said? The vertebra was damaged. They needed more people to ensure the spine was kept stable!

Benson relaxed a little more. "It is great. Unfortunately, she suffered some spinal damage from the projectile. Doctor Dietrich did what he could to stabilize her, but we don't want to risk things worsening when we move her to a treatment station." She pointed toward one of the beds against the bulkhead. "We need to do a transfusion, get her heart going again, and get some medicine into her."

"Oh." Penn looked worried now. He was sold.

"If we could get some of the stronger people up here? Maybe Sergeant Halliwell could help?"

"Sure."

The young man held up a finger to signal he'd be right back, then ran back to the intercom near the entry hatch. He kept her in his peripheral vision the whole time. Smart. Efficient. She could see why someone like Rai felt compelled to trust the young man. If he were on her crew, she imagined he could be left to run things on his own.

Too bad he's a cold-blooded pirate.

Seconds ticked by. It didn't look like Penn was talking on the intercom anymore but was watching her. Waiting, maybe?

And then she had her answer: The outer hatch opened.

Halliwell stepped through, followed by the gaunt-faced guy—Hurley —and the youngster who seemed perhaps a little too stupid to last long in his line of work. Wong? Hadn't Rai said Chung had his son and nephew on the operation? Was this the nephew?

Penn waved them forward. They listened as he chatted and smiled just before he opened the airlock to the surgical area.

He must have told them about Carone possibly surviving.

All because they saw her as money. Or maybe there was something darker if she recovered.

Benson shivered. Rai wasn't like that, was he? He seemed...noble.

Halliwell's eyes locked on hers as he stepped through: *What's going on?*

She wished she could tell him. "We're going to want to be extremely careful moving Ms. Carone. The spinal damage was fairly significant."

The Wong boy snorted. "Don't care none if she's crippled. Not for what I need."

Penn rolled his eyes. "Use your own hands, you idiot. This lady's worth a mint." When he looked at Benson, was it embarrassment she saw?

Halliwell and the three privateers moved to the corners of the surgical bed.

Dietrich glanced at the corner across the table from where he stood: the other mask. He wanted Benson on it, awake.

She shuffled over.

"All right." Dietrich lowered his surgical mask. "I've unlocked the mattress surface. You'll all need to lift the handles at the same moment and move with caution."

There was a strange scent to the air—almost sweet. Heavy.

The gas!

She held her breath.

Penn looked around, confused, then began to wobble.

Benson grabbed the mask and put it to her face, almost missing her mouth. She sucked in the oxygen.

The Wong boy went limp, then collapsed.

Halliwell seemed to figure out what was going on, shaking his head and covering his face with a bicep.

"Hey!" Hurley's big eyes lit up. His sunken cheeks reddened. He pulled his pistol.

How? He should have been as wobbly as Gaines and Clark, who collapsed against the surgical bed, then fell.

Halliwell didn't wait to see if the pirate would be affected. Years of training seemed to take over, and the Marine's anger from so many setbacks apparently went into a brutal chop that caught Hurley just below the throat.

At the same time the gun fired.

Gangly arms flew up, the pistol clattered to the floor, and the privateer followed.

Then Halliwell hacked once and did the same.

Benson rushed to his side. "Clive! Dr. Dietrich!"

Fans kicked on, whirring loudly.

Dietrich placed his mask over Halliwell's face, then pulled a hypodermic tool from the surgical instrument tray and pressed it against the Marine's shoulder. Compressed air fired.

"Their guns!" Dietrich coughed. "Petty Officer Stiles?"

But Stiles staggered back to the wall near the airlock and slid down.

It was just Benson and Dietrich.

Gas plumed down from a section of the ceiling. Red lights flashed. An alarm boomed.

The gun! Hurley had hit something with his wild shot!

Dietrich hissed, then hurried over to a console and tapped through an interface. The gas shut off, but the alarms continued.

Benson felt woozy. She slapped Halliwell's cheeks. "Clive!"

Where had the pistol gone?

Everything had a haze to it. Hurley lay a meter away, spread-eagle. There had been others, right?

Yes. The Wong boy. Right there within reach. No. So far away. But her arms were long, too.

She pulled the gun out.

The holster wouldn't let go.

She slapped it. "Let! Go!"

Dietrich was there, fumbling with the thing until the gun came free. "Get him up, Commander!"

Then the doctor was off at a clumsy jaunt with the hypo-gun, squatting beside the pretty, pretty young nurse who just didn't seem capable of contributing anything more than her pretty, pretty smile and a shake of her pretty, pretty—

Halliwell's hand was on Benson's, pulling the gun free. She'd been pointing it at him without meaning to. Unless he'd looked at Stiles.

Was that what had happened?

Something had made Benson so woozy.

The sedative?

But it was too loud to go to sleep. How did it get so loud?

Dietrich stumbled past. He'd found another gun and now he pressed it into her hand before pinching her upper arm.

"Hey!"

The doctor seemed to be having trouble focusing his eyes. "Of all the things he could shoot, he hit the sedative line!"

And of course the detoxing was keeping Dietrich up. Sort of.

Benson's toes and fingers tingled. There was a weight in her hands. Something hard. "Clive?"

He slapped her cheek. "Was this the plan?" He seemed a little more alert than her. Was that why he was slapping her? Because of their fight?

"No." Wait. That wasn't true. "Yes. Kill them. All." She pointed the gun at the airlock.

His hands were around her then. Oh, how she loved his hands, but it was always better when they were on her flesh.

Let me get out of my flight suit, okay?

And then they were through the airlock and he dropped her on her butt. "Don't you like my—"

"Faith!" He grabbed her chin and pointed her eyes toward the hatch. "If one of the privateers comes through—" He raised her arms and pointed the gun at the door. "—shoot them!"

"Okay."

But her head was pounding. Something was behind her eyes, pushing them out of their sockets. How could she shoot like this?

The surgical chamber airlock hissed, and a moment later, Halliwell plopped Stiles on the floor so that she was leaning against Benson.

"Oh, don't you wish." But Benson realized she hadn't actually said it.

The petty officer stared down at her hands. Halliwell had put something there. A gun.

Benson set her own gun down and tried to help the nurse wrap her delicate hands around the gun.

"Shoot. Pirates." It sounded right to Benson, like what a captain would tell her crew.

But Stiles dropped the gun like it was a snake.

How incompetent could she be?

And then the hatch cycled open, and two people were there: the burly woman with tattoos and the guy Benson had never heard anyone call by name. They seemed surprised, even though their weapons were right there—*right there*!

Gunfire. High-pitched, like the biggest sheet of linen in the universe being torn in half combined with the growl of electricity.

Blasters. The stupid pirates had blasters! In a ship! *Her* ship!

But it wasn't them firing. It was her. And Halliwell.

And boy were they firing!

Bright blue light that appeared just long enough to register, then—

Holes in the bulkhead. Black holes. They wouldn't go all the way through, right?

The handsy pirate woman squatted and returned fire, and the surgery area glass crinkled and popped somewhere close to Benson.

Really close.

The nameless guy fired, and Halliwell groaned.

Clive!

Benson kept squeezing off shots. *No holding your breath and aiming at this point—you're high as a satellite!*

Handsy pirate's head snapped back, and she dropped.

Ka-thump!

And her pistol dropped. Another pistol!

Gone. Dead. Just like that. Life was so fragile.

And then no-name took a shot to the gut, and a whole bunch of dark stuff sprayed out of his back and onto the once-immaculate bulkhead.

Stiles was going to have to clean that up. She was the junior nurse.

Just a med-tech, really.

And she! Wasn't! Helping! At! All!

Halliwell staggered over. "You okay?"

Benson licked her lips, expecting them to be chapped and bloody. They weren't. "Thirsty. And I've got a headache—"

The airlock cycled, and Clark staggered out. "Anyone hurt?"

He had a scalpel in his hand.

Good on you, Lieutenant! Benson wiped blood from Halliwell's flight suit. "He's bleeding."

Halliwell gasped. "I'm okay. We need to get her to her feet. Can you grab those guns?"

Clark set his scalpel down, then helped haul Benson up. He grabbed the scalpel again and rushed to the fallen female privateer. "Oh. Wow."

Benson leaned against the glass. It was just now dawning on her how close she'd come to being killed. Her head was clearing but wasn't all the way out of trouble yet. She touched Halliwell's chest near the burn mark. "Another few centimeters—"

"I'll be okay."

The hatch opened again. It was the giant. Gabriel.

For being so stupid, he put things together almost immediately.

Clark stood and was immediately grabbed by the big brute, who then spun the nurse in front. Bone snapped, and all color drained from Clark's face.

Then Gabriel rushed forward, keeping the smaller man between him and Halliwell until the giant simply squished the Marine against the glass cube.

It was an ugly, meaty sound.

Benson lost her balance and nearly fell on top of Stiles, who was crawling away.

The commander's gun slipped from her hand as she dropped, then skipped across the room, disappearing beneath a bed. Her head smacked against the floor, and stars danced in front of her eyes.

But she had just enough awareness to see that the pretty nurse knew exactly what was going on yet had abandoned her gun.

"Dammit, Petty Officer! Help!" Benson's words came out all mixed up.

Her gun had gone somewhere...

A scream brought her attention back to the giant. Clark's scalpel was in a big, meaty hand. The nurse's arm hung limp and twisted.

Gabriel snorted as he slashed the smaller man's throat open, then threw him against the glass wall. Arterial spray painted the surgical chamber airlock.

Clark slid down, clutching at his throat with his good hand. Air wheezed from the wound. There was a horrifying desperation in his eyes as he slumped to the blood-slick floor.

And then shadow slipped over Benson's eyes.

12

"WHAT THE FUCK, DEV?" CHUNG'S CHEEKS WERE RED BENEATH THE WHITE whiskers that shook on trembling jowls. His damp eyes scanned the cargo bay floor, where the *Pandora* crew were on their knees, hands locked behind heads.

Except for the commander. As far as Rai could tell, she was okay. There was a small knot on her forehead and she was covered with blood spatters from the nurse Gabriel had slaughtered.

It could've been a lot worse if Chung and Rai hadn't gotten there when they did.

Rai forced his hands to open fully. He'd come close to putting a hole in Gabriel's head at the sight of Benson sprawled on the floor, bloody. And the way the ogre had been looking at her...

Her eyes opened, closed, then opened again. She groaned softly and pushed up from the deck.

That's when it appeared to fully register for her: metal deck, warmer air, darker.

Rai felt it himself. There was just a sense in the air, the way the cargo maze seemed draped in shadow that sucked in the crew's anxious breathing—things were about to get primitive.

Chung's boots thudded against the deck as he circled the prisoners, gun hand swinging at his side. "I mean what the fuck?"

Gabriel snorted. "Ho-ho-ho! Look who's awake."

Rai kept his hands frozen at his side as the big oaf grabbed the commander by her long hair and hauled her up from the deck. She gasped and clutched her hair below where he'd grabbed it but didn't otherwise give the bastard the pleasure of a reaction.

When Gabriel released her, she got her knees beneath her. He leaned in. "Now look at this. Just in time to take a walk out the airlock." He made a popping noise, then laughed.

It was a good thing the big Marine was still down. The guy's flight suit was dark from a fairly nasty wound, but his face was puffy and bloody from the beating Gabriel had delivered. Once again, Rai had to wonder how it would've played out if the Marine hadn't been at a disadvantage. Gabriel was a brainless bundle of muscle, a brute who was too stupid to imagine someone else might be a threat. Someone close to his size and trained? Yeah, Rai would've paid to watch that.

Chung stopped at the Marine sergeant's side, pistol shaking. "Get this fucker up, too."

Rai wished he could tell how much of Chung's anger was from losing Nguyen and Volker, and how much was from nearly losing Wong again. A leader's respect came from exhibiting strength and competence. Losing crew…that wasn't so good.

Penn and Hurley got the Marine onto his knees, but his head was slumped forward. Hurley slapped the wounded man's face, which made him rock back.

The Marine came around quickly; his head whipped from one side to the next.

Comprehension was right there in the guy's dark eyes.

Yeah, you're fucked.

Rai didn't like the look of it, the way it smelled like a mass execution was just a couple shouts away, but it was Chung's show. The old guy had to show his crew he was still capable. It had been his call ultimately to keep the Carone woman rather than turn her over to the Azoren. If things went sideways, their days as privateers would be over.

Definitely his show.

The commander's eyes came up as she locked her fingers behind her head. She got a good look at the cargo bay and where Chung's people were—she was counting, figuring out how her plan had gone. Good job.

But when her eyes met Rai's, she bowed her head.

It was kind of a nice signal. She'd been planning to kill as many as she could, maybe even him. And she felt a little ashamed.

What the hell, though. Anyone would do whatever they could to survive.

Gabriel shook his hips, dancing to music only he could hear. "Go-ing out the air-lock."

Chung waved his pistol in the air, irritated. "Shut the fuck up."

Gabriel rolled his neck. "Hey! They tried to kill us."

"Yeah. Where's the fucking—" Chung spotted the drunk doctor and plowed through the others, stopping at the man's side. The old man squatted until his eyes were level with the doctor's. "Hey. Hey! You save that bitch or not? Huh?"

The doctor nodded.

"She alive?"

"She'll live. She needs treatment, but she should live."

"Should live or alive?"

"Should live." The doctor's voice dropped to a whisper.

"Not a lie?"

"No."

The guy's smart mouth had abandoned him. Maybe he was sobering up. Looking death in the eye could do that.

Chung turned around, slitted eyes burrowing into Rai's. "What're we gonna do about this? Who the fuck is gonna die?"

One of the women whimpered—the fat doctor. "Please. No."

Gabriel drove a knee into the big Marine's wound. "Space them. All of them."

"Yeah, yeah." Chung sighed.

"I—" Another woman sobbed. No. It was the engineer. Tears ran down his cheeks. "I didn't do anything. I...just wanted to fix your ship."

That got the little man a couple glares. The Marines, then the commander.

Then the others, even the fat doctor.

Not the best way to make friends on a team.

Except the pretty, young gal didn't glare. She just stared into space, odd like. Almost vacant. It wasn't quite terrified, but it came close. Rai had seen people completely lose their minds in deep shit. And this was definitely deep shit, no doubt. But...nah. She was still hanging around. She'd just sort of hung up. No one home.

Weird.

Gabriel left the Marine alone long enough to get behind the weaselly man. "Heh-heh. Maybe we should start with you. Would you like that? Suck in a little vacuum?"

The engineer shook his head. "I'm just an engineer. I make things. I fix them."

Rai crossed his arms. "That's enough."

"Ho-ho!" Gabriel straightened. He was a sight, his coveralls stained with blood from the fight. "You making decisions now, Dev? Took command?"

"Quentin's call, but the shitbag's right. We need our ship fixed."

"Okay." Gabriel ran bloodstained fingers through the engineer's curls. "Fine. So we kill everyone who don't do the maintenance." He turned around quickly, grabbing the commander by her throat. "Like you, you piece of shit."

She gasped weakly, then no sound came out of her as she looked around, desperate.

Rai's body went rigid. "Let her go."

Gabriel's crazy eyes came around, but he kept choking the woman. "Don't like me fucking with your sweetie?"

"She keeps these people in line. You kill her, things fall apart."

"Nah. You just want a piece of ass."

"I could get that off you, Vic."

That got through to Gabriel. He let her go and stormed toward Rai. "You want—"

A gunshot brought Gabriel and Rai both around. One of the cargo crates at the maze entry had a sizzling hole in it.

Chung lowered his pistol. "You two put that shit aside."

Gabriel jabbed a thumb at the woman. "It's the bitch's fault. It was her plan. Makes sense to kill her."

The big Marine snorted. "Fuck you, moron. This was my plan."

Chung held his pistol up when Gabriel took a step toward the Marine. The brute froze, and Chung shambled over to the Marine's side. "Your plan?"

"Yeah." Not a hint of fear in the guy's eye. Just anger. Lots of anger.

"You talked to them while they figured out how to lure my people up there and kill them?"

The Marine just glared. He was good at that. He had some sort of history.

"How'd you do that, huh? How'd you connect to them?"

Nothing but glare. Bottled fury. A hard life would do that. A terrible event.

Chung chuckled. "Yeah, I didn't think so."

He turned back to Gabriel. "This is my operation, remember?"

Gabriel shrugged. "Sure."

"All right. Then shut the fuck up about the airlock."

Chung's eyes caught Rai's, then drifted aft, toward the engineering section.

Rai followed the old man back that way while the rest of the privateers stared. It didn't have the feel of a chewing out, but Rai knew he was cutting it close with Benson. He was usually good about hiding things like that, but something about her got to him. Maybe it was what had been in that globe of hers.

Once they were inside the engineering bay, Chung holstered his pistol. "Hey, you listening?"

"Sure. Listening to everything."

"Okay. Well, listen to this. We've got to kill one of them. Make a point."

"Who?"

"Like the fucking moron said: whoever figured this scheme out."

Rai tensed. He'd been expecting something like that, but it sounded like Chung had something figured out already. "You got an idea?"

"Sounds like something that commander would do, don't it?" It wasn't a test but a sincere question.

"Sure, might be. Would you? You're in charge."

Chung smirked. "Yeah. Maybe I would've."

"Hey, the big Marine wants to be the one to take the fall. Whack him. Makes it easier on everyone. Give Vic something to fix his hard-on."

"Nah. The guy's protecting someone."

"Sure. His Marines. He lost a bunch during a rescue gone bad."

"Did he?"

"The commander said that. That's why he doesn't get along with the engineer."

"None of them seem to."

"He's a jerk."

"Yeah. Look, there's something else." The old man's voice dropped noticeably.

"To do with this execution?"

"Nah. Before they went up there, Stef told me something. About that engineer, sort of. When she was looking over this area in here earlier with him, she noticed something odd."

"Odd?"

"Yeah, that's what she said. Odd."

"What the fuck's that—'odd'?"

"Some sort of antenna array on the belly."

Rai chuckled. "Ship's gonna have an antenna array."

"Not something like this. She said it was really advanced. Like, something you'd see on a signals ship."

"No shit?"

"She was gonna show me when the alarm went off."

"I saw you two talking. I just thought she was asking about getting some bunk time with the pretty nurse."

"That too."

"So, you want me to beat it out of this engineer?"

"He might delete whatever she found if he knows you're looking."

"Okay." Rai rubbed his chin and gave the bay a good once-over. "I've got an idea."

"I knew you would. If Mr. Pants-Shitter's trying to hide something from us, I want to know."

Rai strolled back to the prisoners just ahead of Chung and curled a finger at the engineer. "You. What's your name again?"

The little guy unhooked his fingers and pointed at himself. "Me?"

"I'm not pointing at anyone else, am I?"

"I—" The engineer looked around for approvals, then got to his feet. "I'm Chief Warrant Officer Will Parkinson. I'm the ship's engineer."

"Come with me." Rai spun on his heel and headed back to engineering.

Parkinson rushed to stay close behind. "L-look. I know I'm in uniform, but I'm like the medical team: a noncombatant."

"Your medical team was involved in getting two of my team killed. Not very non-combatant. Chief."

"Oh."

"You and Stef were back here earlier."

"She wanted to see our systems. I showed her everything. No hidden weapons or anything. That's what she wanted to see. Search and rescue, just like we said."

"Show me what you two were looking at before."

"Um." The engineer squeezed his eyes shut. "Well. Everything, I guess."

"Relax, okay? It would've been something she was excited about. She loved tech, too. If she'd had the money, maybe she would've been an engineer like you."

A sneer twisted the little man's face. "Not likely. I really am about as good as there is."

"Hey, Chief? When I told you to relax? I didn't mean that much. I could still blow your brains all over your consoles, okay?"

Color drained from Parkinson's face. "Oh."

"Show me what you two were looking at."

Parkinson twisted around. "Well, while I was testing the robot drones, yeah. She got excited."

"Show me what she saw."

Parkinson settled at a chair. His hands sped across buttons so fast that Rai couldn't keep up. A video popped up on one of the big displays.

"Those your drones?"

"Their cameras, yeah." Parkinson beamed. "They're really agile when I pilot them. I'm probably better at remote piloting than engineering, and I'm phenomenal at engineering. Really. Top of the line."

"Modest, too."

"I am! I could've been much higher rank by now if not for politics."

Rai let the little guy blather on and focused on the video. It was the *Pandora*'s hull, all right. There were things that were telltale: the way the top deck was broken into three pieces—the bridge, the aft compartments, and the passageways connecting them. And the way the bottom deck swooped down into almost a third deck starting about halfway back from midships. That was probably the big Fold Space drive that let them move around so fast.

But...

Rai squeezed the little guy's shoulder. "Hey. Freeze the image."

Parkinson shut up and reversed the video. "That's the underside. We recently had some systems—"

"Let me have your seat. Stay logged in."

The engineer backed up, pouting. "Be careful. I do everything at super-user level. Because I'm good enough not to make mistakes."

"I get it."

Rai fiddled with the video controls until he had the image back to where he'd seen something. He drilled down.

Foul, hot breath. Parkinson was leaning in. "That's, um, that's the upgrade—"

Rai backhanded the other man on the forehead, then went back to the console. "Did Stef look at any of this?"

"Oh. Yeah. She was looking at all the stuff I maintain. She was really impressed."

"I'm sure she was."

"I, um, I had to tell her I'm involved. With Brianna."

Rai covered his mouth. "Which one's that?"

"Oh. Petty Officer Stiles. She's the really pretty nurse. Med-tech, officially. But she has the scores to be a nurse. A doctor if she wants."

"Ah. Broke Stef's heart hearing that."

"Y'know, I thought she seemed a little hurt. Yeah."

The guy had no idea. Not about anything. Rai scrolled through what he guessed Nguyen had been looking at. The engineer was going on about upgrades. Could that be—?

There! The ship had modifications done to it at its last port of call.

Rai poked through some more interfaces until he found what he was looking for: maintenance logs before and during the upgrade and operational logs since.

Parkinson made a hissing sound. "Um, you're really going through a lot of sensitive stuff there pretty fast."

"Don't worry, you're logged in. You know what you're doing."

"Um."

There were logs for the maintenance work, just like the weasel claimed, but nothing seemed to map to what he'd seen.

And he was pretty sure of what he'd seen.

"This all the operational logs?" Rai pointed to the display.

"All of them."

That meant someone had put the system into place and it had been running on its own with nothing showing for all it was doing. Data was being dumped somewhere that even Parkinson the big-time engineer didn't know about.

Rai pulled the chief's credentials card and handed them back to him. "Let's go."

The little guy fell in reluctantly. "I-I helped you, right?"

"Sure."

"S-so maybe you could lock me in there until this whole recriminations thing is resolved."

"We may go with a lottery."

"Lottery? But I *helped* you! I—" The engineer swallowed as they approached his comrades.

Something was going on. Chung had his pistol out again. He was circling the search-and-rescue crew again. There was terror in their eyes, except for the big Marine. But the other Marines were afraid; the skinny kid looked ready to cry. Chung had said something to them, maybe done something to them.

After sending me off on a wild goose chase!

Chung glanced at Rai and Parkinson. "Eye for an eye. You make it easy on yourselves. You killed two of my people, we killed one of yours. Now I need a second name."

The big Marine shook his head. "You need blood to make you feel better? Take mine."

"Shut up!" That was the athletic Marine woman and her commander yelling at the big Marine at the same time.

The big Marine glared at the two of them. What was going on? He had two?

"No one needs to die." Benson lowered her eyes to the deck; Rai had caught a look of dread. "I-it was my plan."

The big Marine tried to get to his feet, but dropped when Gabriel punched the bloody wound.

Chung pointed his pistol at Benson. "Your plan?"

Rai's hand drifted slowly to his holster.

"Yes. And—" She closed her eyes. "I dare you to tell me you would've done any different."

Chung's tongue ran over his lips.

She brought her eyes up to look at him. "Tell me that you weren't planning to kill us all."

A raspy laugh shook the old man's chest. "Sure! Later. But—"

He spun around and put the barrel against the skinny Marine's forehead.

The gun screeched, and the young man's head snapped back. The doctors screamed as the gore spattered onto their faces, then the corpse slumped to the deck with a thick thud.

Chung holstered his pistol. "See what happens when you plot against me?"

Gabriel guffawed. "Oh! Oh! That was great!" He rushed over and kicked the corpse. "Can I put him in the airlock?"

Chung sniffled and caught that Rai was staring.

The old man's eyes dropped to where Rai's hand rested on his pistol grip. There was a silent chuckle in acknowledgement, then the old guy said, "Sure. Toss all the bodies in the airlock. We don't need the dead. They only drag us down."

13

TERROR. HORROR. SADNESS. RELIEF. *SHAME.*

So many emotions hit Benson at the same time, she couldn't be sure what was real and what wasn't.

They were all real, she realized with a shiver.

Lopez had nothing to do with the plan. Why him? Why?

The private's corpse had barely hit the deck when her stomach twisted. She held the vomit in but only just. The stench of the kid's gore and fluids were drowned out by the acrid smell of the blaster discharge. It was like a power overload: metallic, burned, ionized air.

And then the big brute was dragging Lopez by the boot.

Lopez's flight suit rasped across the plating, a blackish-red smear marking his passing. His head wobbled, but when she finally forced herself to look at him and see what happened because she didn't act decisively, his face turned toward her. Dead eyes condemned her.

I failed you. I failed all of you.

Whimpering from the doctors. Groaning from Halliwell. Her own ragged breathing.

Failed.

What was a commander supposed to do? Certainly not blame the situation on the previous commander. When Martinez died, the responsibility of command fell to her. She owed these people a solution to the problem. She owed them her life if it meant saving theirs.

How could she have felt relief over a kid dying instead of her? Instead of Dietrich? Halliwell?

She didn't deserve to be in command, not even of the *Pandora*.

Could she blame Dietrich? No. It was a good plan—the right plan. She could've used more time, that's all. Refined it a little.

No. You don't question someone showing initiative, not even a drunk.

They hadn't done anything wrong. Two pirates were dead. How close had they come to killing four? Five? The broken gas line spoiled the plan.

The airlock door hissed, and the big brute cackled. He took the body in.

Could she run to the airlock door fast enough to cause an override and send the monster into the vacuum he seemed to love so much? Could she outrun blaster bolts?

That was exactly the sort of selfish thinking she had to set aside.

Solutions were called for, not revenge. She had to focus only on solutions.

Rai had come back with Parkinson at some point. The dusky-skinned man had his hand on the grip of his pistol and his eyes locked on the old man's. Chung.

Friction. That had been some sort of power struggle between the two.

Store it away. They came close to shooting each other. Over what? Me?

She turned around abruptly at Halliwell's deep hiss as he pushed himself up from the deck. The sudden movement made it feel like her scalp was on fire. The big man pulling her hair—he liked inflicting pain, and it seemed compulsive.

Store that away, too.

Fire spread through her now, breaking up the ice in her gut. When the big man dragged the other corpses into the airlock, she looked away. His sick pleasure in the carnage was too much to bear.

How old had Clark been? Twenty-six? Twenty-seven? He'd been cramming for another shot at medical school. He had a boyfriend back on Kedraal, associated with some government agency or another. A sister, too. What had she been involved in? A systems designer, right? And a niece with a second on the way.

Lopez. Fresh out of training. Still skin and bones, barely any heavier than when he'd gone into boot camp. She'd seen photos in his record of his home on Rungier. Just a simple farm boy, an only child, not even battle tested yet.

Now they were dead.

What else was there to take away from the moment?

They were butchers. Animals. Savages. There was no reasoning with them. They'd been caught up in violence for so long, they weren't just numb to it but addicted. At least that was the case for the big guy and his boss.

Learn their names. Know the enemy.

Gabriel. They called him Vic.

Chung. Quentin. The old man. The boss.

Wong. Jimmy. The old man's nephew. Not smart.

Hurley. The one with the sunken cheeks. The medic. Lazy? Bored? Not the sort of motivated person you'd want at your back.

Rai. Dev. Just as cold as the others but a potential ally.

And the strange one. Penn. Eli. He'd come to the privateers with the idea of kidnapping the executive Carone and joined them for a cut. Was that sort of initiative and discipline normal? Not based on what she'd seen of the privateers. Penn and Rai were the only two who seemed to exhibit control and think more than a second ahead.

Could Penn be something more? Former military? Some sort of cop? He was all business and didn't seem to enjoy the bloodshed like the others did.

Store it away.

With only six of them left, anything that might turn one against the others or even cause them to opt out of engaging in murder was worth exploiting.

Rai pushed Parkinson to the deck and just sort of slid over to Chung. The two of them separated from the rest. They were doing a good job of trying to look calm and relaxed as they strode away, but there was tension in everything about them—their muted voices, their forced-casual stride, even how close they were to each other.

It was the power dynamic. The old man was clearly in charge, but Rai seemed to barely acknowledge that. Instead, the way he acted, he was more like a consultant who didn't really report to anyone. He just did what the old man said.

Most of the time.

It didn't look like Rai would've been in on the execution.

So, was Rai trying to cool the old man off? Did he even have that level of influence? Could he even care?

He cared. She was sure of that. About her, definitely.

Stiles's shaky voice brought Benson around. "Commander?"

"Yes?"

"Could we..." Stiles nodded toward Halliwell, who was having a hard time keeping his arms up.

Benson turned to Penn. "Sergeant Halliwell will bleed to death if that wound's left untreated."

Penn stared at her. He was like a machine: cold. Finally, he turned to Wong. "Hey, go up to the infirmary and grab one of those medical kits."

Wong snorted. "Fuck you."

Hurley shook his head. "I'll fucking get it." He ambled away, muttering.

And she wasn't the only one to notice the lack of urgency. Penn closed his eyes and shook his head.

Not just professional and disciplined but upset by the lack of it in others.

Big, powerful hands settled on her shoulders. "Ho-ho! Look what we got."

Gabriel's hands slid down her ribs and under her arms. His fingertips pressed against her breasts.

Then he had her on her feet, turned to look into his ugly mug with its big, square jaw and rubber-looking nose. What would she endure to see Halliwell turn that face into a red, puffy mess?

Maybe she was about to find out, as the thug dragged her aft.

There were a lot of "private" spaces in the cargo bay, areas out of sight from the others. He could smother her screams in those places and—

"Hey. Hey!" The big thug stopped and leaned into her. "Don't fight me. Quentin wants to talk to you."

Chung? He was done talking with Rai?

She couldn't see either of them anywhere, but Gabriel was dragging her again, taking her toward the engineering bay. His powerful fingers dug into the muscle of her upper arm, pressed against the bone.

And at the hatch they'd locked open after coming aboard, she was able to see Parkinson's little throne room. The scent hit her: metal tools and electronics, the dull chemical tang of lubricant and cleaners, melted solder, motors and dirty work coveralls.

Chung sat in Parkinson's favorite seat. He pointed at the floor in front of him. "Let her go."

Gabriel shoved her forward; she barely stopped herself where the old man had pointed.

Was he going to touch her? The old man?

He scratched the material covering his protruding gut, which shook from a quiet chuckle. "Thank you for your time, Commander."

Defiance was the wrong call. "I've been willing to answer questions—"

He held up a hand to cut her off. "No hard feelings."

She cocked an eyebrow curiously.

"About the killings. My people. Your people. It happens."

Just like that. He expected her to accept it? Was it even sincere? "We could have cooperated from the start. We're search and rescue. The ship doesn't even have weapons."

"Yeah. But this antenna array you got. What's up with that?"

Antenna array? "I'm sorry? Which... We have antennas—sensors, comms—"

She barely caught the old man's nod, then the big hands were on her again, even more aggressive than the big woman had been.

Gabriel turned her around. "You're a pretty lady. Hate to mess up your face."

That was enough. All the violence and abuse.

Enough.

She dug her nails into the big man's cheek. As nails went, the commander's weren't long and sharp, not on a ship where she might have to get involved in repairs or carting bodies or tools around.

But she had *nails* and they sank into flesh just fine.

Especially when she was mad like she was.

The big man's smug smile vanished, and she saw all the white of his eyes.

Then he swatted her arm away and punched her in the gut.

She tried to groan, to let the universe know just how much the strike hurt, but there was no oxygen in her. *None.*

Her knees buckled. It was as if all her muscles and bone had turned to jelly.

The brute caught her by the flight suit neck and pulled her back up, then pinned her against the wall. His right hand was cocked to strike again.

Chung sighed. "Enough with the punching. We need answers."

Gabriel grunted. Then he slapped her. Open palm. It turned the flesh of her cheek to fire.

He slapped again, this time the back of the hand.

She imagined what his balls would look like, then imagined pressing a blaster barrel against them. What would they look like after she pulled the trigger?

Another slap.

Her flesh must have been torn off. There was nothing but nerve endings left. And acid tears were rolling down those.

The bastard was feeding off her pain. He was getting off on it.

She screamed and took a swing at him.

He blocked it easily.

She swung again, also easily blocked.

He guffawed. His horrible, inhuman laugh that twisted his ugly face up and wrinkled his big lump of a nose.

Her third swing was unexpected. It got through. She got the satisfying sensation of the nose giving.

His head rocked back. Not from the power of her punch but the surprise of it.

"Oh-ho!" He ran the back of a hand under the fleshy beak and showed her blood. Instead of punching her again, his eyes took on a wild look. "Oh! Ho-ho!"

Chung snapped his fingers. "Vic. Move away."

The brute did, but he was looking at her hungrily now, leering.

Once again, Chung pointed to the floor just in front of him.

Benson pushed off from the wall and wobbled to where he'd indicated. Her heart was going crazy. She could barely breathe. Finally, she got her legs to handle her weight.

The old man looked away. "Tell us about the antenna array."

"What...antenna array?"

Chung waved, and Gabriel yanked her backward by her hair.

She twisted around, fist raised, but he easily pinned her arm to her side.

Then he slapped her again. Not as hard as before, but this time it was faster.

Slap. Slap. Slap!

Chung sighed. "Okay. That's enough."

The thug lifted her and set her in front of the old man.

There was color in the old man's scarred cheeks, making his whiskers almost glow. He squinted at her, then harrumphed. "She doesn't know."

Gabriel laughed. "Oh, man. We can't be done."

"She doesn't know." Chung pushed up from the seat.

Benson's cheeks felt raw, tingly. She couldn't stop crying no matter what she tried, and she'd learned a lot about suppressing tears from living with her mother. Benson had always believed that her mother's harsh words and stern treatment were every bit as bad as being hit.

That idea seemed horribly naive now. A lot of her views seemed naive when she looked at the monster and his terrifying smile.

"Hey-hey, come on. Don't leave me like this. Give us a few minutes, huh?" Gabriel's wink made her stomach knot.

"Later." The old man tilted his head. "Who would've known about this thing?"

She swallowed. "What 'thing'?" Her voice broke. There was a hatred in her heart for the big man, a hatred like nothing she'd ever thought possible.

"A special antenna array. Anyone in your crew?"

"We didn't have any special equipment installed. I would know."

"Yeah, well, you did have it installed and you didn't know. So who would?"

Antennas? "Commander Martinez should have known everything about the ship. He was the captain. But he should've told me. He would've. We had some minor upgrades at Persephone Station."

"Yeah? Minor upgrades? That's what he told you?"

"Yes. I was his XO—executive officer. We were the only two trained for command."

"I see. Anyone else? Maybe someone you're not thinking of."

"I've known everyone in this crew for years." *Except for Stiles and Lopez.*

"Years, huh? All of them?"

"Well—" She couldn't tell them about Stiles. She was too fragile. If they did to her what they'd done... "Except for Private Lopez. We took him aboard at our last resupply."

"When was that?"

"A few months ago. At Persephone Station."

The old man's eyes lit up. "At a resupply. Is that normal?"

"No. We'd suffered some personnel losses."

"Who hasn't?" Chung's nails rasped against his whiskers. "So this Martinez, how well did you know him?"

"I was his XO for nearly four years."

"I think I heard that somewhere. You two friends?"

"Not really."

The old man's eyes seemed to drill into her face. "Disagreements about how to run the operation?"

"He took chances."

"Yeah. I think you said that, too."

Chung took a couple steps and ran his stubby fingers over some of the equipment. "Vic, we need to get those repairs done."

Gabriel's shoulders slumped. "Aw."

The protestations ended when the old man waved his fingers toward the door.

Once the sound of the thug's boots had retreated, Chung turned back to her. He seemed almost sympathetic. "You going to be okay?"

"Yes." Benson sniffled. "Are we done here?"

There was no way she was going to offer up forgiveness or fall for false connectedness. These were heartless, cold-blooded murderers. They didn't see the value of human life. They really were the product of the Gulmar Union philosophy, even if they'd never had access to wealth like the people in power. Greed still defined their behavior.

Chung nodded. There was at least some professionalism about him. "Take me to the bridge. I want to see everything."

14

It wasn't that the cargo hold was cold, but in the shadows of the forward port corner, Rai was able to find the solitude he needed to cool down. Anger like he was feeling—*real* anger—always triggered memories.

Of his childhood in the slums of Hyberanon. The way the choking smog would hide the blinding morning sun, and his mother's flatbreads would smell so fresh and wholesome with tea and pickled onions.

Of his training at his father Masran's side. The hours spent with guns and knives in the dark basement when his father wasn't hunched over the physical books that tracked the real flow of money among bars and taverns and gambling houses.

Of his mother and sisters dying. The travel they'd done when he grew older to see the sights and visit relatives and the way his father refused to let "the boy" ever go along.

Of the network of lies that defined his life.

"You must always remember who you truly serve and do so with honor and dignity that will transfer to your children and their children, for our people measure themselves through the value of generations rather than the individual."

How was a child to understand those words? Yet Masran had pulled his only son aside at six and begun his training with exactly that.

An edifice had been built on that foundation: service, honor, dignity, history.

But then one day Rai's mother was gone. His sisters, too. An accident.

Crushing for a boy. And the bodies were too broken to be seen. They were burned and their ashes sent to the heavens, where they could rise to their fates.

The thing is, boys become men. And men have not just the curiosity but the wherewithal to dig. And digging produced no accident reports, no death certificates, no records of cremation.

Digging produced a divorce...

A woman who looked like his mother fleeing through the starport with daughters of his sisters' ages...

Without a solid foundation, no building stands long.

Except Rai had by then been steeped in the ways of Masran's people. Vows had been taken that couldn't be broken. After all, the family was judged over generations, and if Rai failed to live up to the expectations placed on him, there would be far too great a stain placed on everyone living and dead and yet to be born.

So fury had been set aside then. A hatred of Masran and of the lies he'd told from the first words spoken was similarly set aside.

And service to Chung was a linchpin to the foundation Masran had built and his father before him. That meant Quentin Chung could shout. He could threaten. He could poke Rai in the chest with a stubby, old, arthritic finger and even spit in his face.

Remember who you truly serve.

Rai exhaled. He shook his shoulders out.

How different childhoods could be. All the things he had in common with the other privateers but didn't actually.

Benson's childhood must have been different, filled with lies of its own.

She couldn't possibly know about those lies. Not like he did.

That brought a smile to his face. *"How would you like to know something? It's something very interesting?"*

Her brow would wrinkle at that. It was a good look for her. It gave her more warmth, made her even prettier, he was sure of it. He imagined her with hair pinned up, revealing her elegant neck, maybe with jeweled earrings dangling from her long, narrow ears. Yes, a good look.

He strode back toward the ghostly echo of conversation where Chung's people guarded the *Pandora* crew.

Gear rattled and clanked, and Gabriel's animal grunts slowly resolved into commands. He was herding the muscular female Marine, the skinny technician, and the pretty nurse around the airlock.

Rai stopped just outside the cargo maze and shoved his hands into his pockets. Penn and Wong watched the two doctors and the engineer. The big Marine was lying down.

Alive, but he looked bad.

At least Chung was finally getting his focus back on the mission. It had taken far too long and cost them far too many people, but they were making progress.

Except he wasn't anywhere to be seen.

And neither was Benson.

Steps clanged on the stairs behind Rai.

"Fucking full-time medic." It was Hurley. He came out of the maze, head down, shaking an emergency medical bag.

"Hey."

Hurley's head came up, and he nearly dropped the bag. "Shit, Dev!"

"Where's the old man?"

"I thought I saw him and the captain heading to the bridge."

"Who's that for?"

Hurley smirked. "The Marine with the hole in his chest."

So Chung still wasn't focusing on getting Carone prepared. "Tell you what, you get him patched up, I'll make sure Carone's really salvageable."

"Oh!" Hurley's eyes widened. He'd been up in the infirmary and hadn't thought about her.

Rai walked to where the others could fully see him and pointed at the drunk doctor. "C'mon."

The doctor blinked in disbelief. "What?"

"Carone. She's thawing. You're running out of time if you're going to save her. And you." Rai pointed at the engineer. "You'll help him move the body around."

They didn't budge until he snapped his fingers. "Move it!"

He kept the two of them ahead of him. Slumped shoulders, constantly turning heads—they were too confused to be real trouble. They were probably expecting a blaster through the back. It was tempting. What he needed was focus, not all the distractions they were causing.

Keep Carone alive, sell her to the highest bidder. Simple. Efficient.

If they were quick about it, Chung could possibly salvage his relationship with the Azoren. No one had to know they'd missed out on buying someone so important.

But everything had been put at risk. Why? How?

Hadn't Chung admitted he thought the drunk doctor really was the one behind the plan? So why not put a blast through his head? What made him so special?

When they reached the infirmary, Rai sent the doctor back into the glass cube where the corpse was. "Make sure she's ready to move."

The engineer tried to cross his arms but couldn't seem to get the hang of it.

"Don't be so nervous." Rai put some warmth into a charming smile.

Parkinson returned the smile. "I-I'm not."

"Hey, this doctor. The super surgeon. What do you know about him, huh?"

"Dr. Dietrich?"

"Yeah."

The guy was all business, sealed up in the cube, dressed in scrubs and gloves again, looking the body over, oblivious to them.

"Well—" The engineer shrugged. "He's supposedly a brilliant surgeon."

"Supposedly?" The guy couldn't just accept someone else's reputation. Ego.

"I mean…yeah. I'm not a surgeon, so how should I know?"

"But you're brilliant in your own right."

Parkinson straightened. "I am. Engineering is every bit as hard as medical school. We don't deal with guessing. Measurements mean something."

"Sure. Not a ship in the galaxy would choose a doctor over an engineer."

"I've said that so many times! But Chuck—Petty Officer Kohn—he wants to go to medical school instead of actually pursuing engineering. He could be something, especially if he studied under me."

"That's the scrawny technician?"

"With the attitude, yes."

"I noticed that."

"And it keeps getting worse. Dr. Dietrich keeps covering for him when he screws up. Commander Martinez was going to torpedo Chuck's request for med school transfer. You don't send a screw-up off to train for eight years."

Martinez. The dead captain. "Not if you're smart. You guys are all smart, aren't you?"

The engineer snorted. He crossed his arms easily. "Supposedly."

"He ever pull off anything a brilliant surgeon would?"

"We don't get that many surgeries. We're mostly focused on stabilizing people who've suffered exposure or severe burns or...y'know. Survivors. Lots of them are in cold sleep when we arrive, like you guys. If we can't fix their ship, we just transfer them and take them to a facility for more extensive treatment."

"What about this drinking problem?"

Parkinson scratched his back. "From what I've heard, he was going through a messy divorce, then his wife was killed in some sort of accident. It crushed him, I guess."

The surgical bay airlock hissed open. Dietrich waved Parkinson over. "She's ready."

Parkinson followed the doctor back inside, and after a minute they came through the airlock with the Carone woman. They set her down on another bed and hooked her up to some machines, then replaced the sheets covering her with a clean one.

Dietrich pulled his gloves off. "I've initiated a transfusion. She should be stable when she comes around, barring complications."

Rai looked the woman over. She *looked* dead. "How long?"

"Three or four hours."

More than enough time to get the ship repaired. "Let's go."

When they returned to the cargo bay, Gabriel had his repair team suiting up. Rai sent the doctor and engineer back to the other prisoners and strolled over to the big oaf, who grinned.

Rai tapped his cheek, mirroring where Gabriel's had a few deep, red gouges. "Shaving accident?"

The idiot leaned in. "Ho-ho! Your girl wanted some action."

"I bet she did." Rai pushed down his rising heart rate. Gabriel was going to be killed at some point. Being the one to pull the trigger, that's what mattered. "Hey, I thought you'd want to know that Carone should be thawed and ready to go in four hours."

"Yeah?" Gabriel straightened. "Oh-ho! Ready for action?"

"Leave it alone, okay? She's worth millions."

"Doesn't break anything."

Rai studied the tops of his shoes. "Can I talk to your pretty nurse for a minute?"

"Talk to her?" Gabriel chuckled. "Sure. Who cares about talking? Hey, Hurley, suit up! You're going with us!"

Rai got the woman's attention and nodded aft. She fell in at his side with the sort of stunned look she'd worn earlier. A few meters short of the engineering bay, he stopped. "I have a couple questions for you."

Her big, dark green eyes studied his.

Oh, yeah. She was a looker. It didn't seem like she was meant for the military, not with the way she was trembling. Not everyone in uniform needed to be a cold-blooded killer, but...

"Okay." That was all she managed.

"You know anything about this Dr. Dietrich covering for Petty Officer Kohn screwing up?"

Confusion replaced fear. "Covering—?" She pressed her palm against her forehead. "Chuck's...a good guy. He doesn't get along with Chief Parkinson, so Commander Martinez rode him, that's all."

Benson's dislike of her boss was making more sense. "A good guy. Smart enough for medical school?"

"Yes. Dr. Dietrich said Chuck was wasting his time on the *Pandora*."

"This was one of the times your doctor was sober?"

Stiles bit her lip. "He's a good doctor."

"You got a thing for this Kohn?"

She looked away. "Is that really why you wanted to talk to me?"

"Nah. It's just this Parkinson guy—"

"He can be jealous. And petty. Chuck's very smart, and Will resents it."

Jealous. So she wasn't hiding from Parkinson that she was fooling around with Kohn.

Rai had to fight back a snort. You pack people into a confined space, you send them out to the middle of nowhere for any length of time, and things happened.

"Thanks." He guided the nurse back toward the others. Kohn and the fat doctor were helping the big Marine into an environment suit. Stiles hurried over to assist, but not before giving Penn a look. He straightened, apparently as vulnerable to her looks as everyone else.

Not a good thing, not with the way everyone was already on edge.

Then Stiles and Kohn exchanged a quick glance that Parkinson noticed. His face turned a bright red.

It didn't add up. An incompetent captain. A drunk doctor. An egotistical engineer.

And a very special antenna array that no one seemed to have a clue about.

Except Nguyen, and she screwed everything up getting herself killed. And now it wasn't just Chung running around trying to figure out what was going on; Rai couldn't make sense of it, either. That was really annoying. If he could just make sense of it, maybe he could calm things down and get them moving in the same directions again.

But the captain and the scrawny Marine—the only people who might've been able to answer questions about the antennas—were dead.

Equipment scraped into the airlock, then the *Pandora* repair crew went in. Gabriel and Hurley watched through the window. After a bit, they put their helmets on and followed.

Someone hissed. Soft. Secret.

Rai turned.

Parkinson looked around. He wanted to talk.

Rai knelt beside the engineer. "Yeah?"

"What'd she say?"

"The nurse?"

"Yes." His voice rose from its whispery tone, and his cheeks grew red. The jealousy ran deep.

"She said you had a problem with Chuck. I didn't realize she was so wild."

The redness deepened. "I can tell you this: We had a lot fewer problems on the *Pandora* before she came aboard! A lot!"

"Was she fooling around with your captain?"

"What? No! Lenny has a wife. Had. He was very loyal to her. His relationship with Brianna was very professional. He was doing everything he could to help her integrate into the crew. She's apparently not used to close quarters like this."

"You don't say. How long has she been aboard?"

"She came aboard with Corporal Lopez."

Rai twisted around to look at the airlock. "A few months ago, right? When the maintenance was done on the ship?"

"Yes. Why?"

"Nothing. It's just not a lot of time for someone to integrate, is it?"

Rai strolled over to the airlock. There was someone still alive who might be able to answer questions after all.

He needed to chat with Petty Officer Stiles again. Soon.

15

THE REALIZATION THAT CHUNG WAS WASTING PRECIOUS TIME ON THE WILD
goose chase gnawed at Rai. At the same time, the crazy situation that had
pulled them all out of cold sleep just kept becoming crazier. Maybe the
old man was wrong to waste so much time on the research, but *some* time
was justified.

Wong and Penn looked bored, neither of them actually watching over
the three prisoners. The doctors weren't a threat. And the only risk the
engineer posed was that he might piss himself.

Rai headed for the stairs. "Eli, come with me."

Penn fell in quickly. His boots echoed in the open cargo bay until
Wong shouted.

"Hey! What about me?"

Rai smiled. "You'll be fine. Unless you need me to tell the old man
you're scared of them?"

That shut the little bastard up.

It was warmer on the top deck. Or maybe getting away from the gory
reminders of the execution made it seem better. There was still a hint of
alcohol in the air from the earlier trip into the infirmary.

At the top of the stairs, Penn grunted.

Rai stopped. "What?"

The younger man shrugged. "Nothing. I'm just confused. What's everyone worked up about? We got Carone. We're almost home free."

"Sure." Rai eyed the hatch that led back to the infirmary. "I think Quentin might see another angle."

"You mean this antenna thing?"

"Yeah. Like maybe someone will pay money to know the Kedraalians had a ship in the DMZ. Maybe they'll pay more to know it had special gear aboard."

The way Penn's cheek twitched seemed to indicate he grudgingly accepted that.

Rai pinched the bridge of his nose. "This what you expected?"

"Expected?"

"When you brought the kidnapping idea to the old man. Were you expecting things to go like this?"

"Oh." The younger guy stared at his boots and adjusted his coveralls. "It could've gone bad from the start. It's a tough job to pull off, kidnapping someone valuable like this."

"It is."

"Everyone could've died."

"Wouldn't have surprised me." Rai cocked his head. Wong wasn't making a stink of things, which was good. "What do you think of the team?"

"You know. They're privateers. You don't expect everyone to be the most disciplined."

"Not like you. You've got a cool head. Where'd you learn what you know?"

Penn sighed. "I worked security for a while, before I got fucked over."

"What happened?"

"You know how it is, someone from the slums can't be trusted, so if something goes wrong, pin it on him."

It was the same sort of story Rai had seen over and over again. Keep the poor people in line. If the opportunity's there to screw them over when something goes wrong, by all means, put it on the guy from the slums.

Rai took a step toward the hatch that would take them to the bridge, then stopped. "Look, I don't want you to take this wrong. You show smarts. But that pretty nurse? The way she was looking at you? She's trouble."

"She is?"

"Definitely. She likes playing men against each other."

"I thought she was just trying to make a connection."

"Sure. Just watch it. Vic's got his eye on her, and he's possessive."

Penn seemed to think about it. "Okay."

Their boots echoed less noticeably in the narrow passageway that ran past the bathroom and the command crew cabins. The dimmer lights were annoying, something probably built into the way the ship handled simulated time passing. It was always a captain's call—let everyone think their shift was during the day or create a day-night dynamic. Dim lights in a spaceship...it just didn't make sense.

It looked like the bridge was locked down, and Rai didn't have credentials, so he rang the buzzer. When the hatch opened, it revealed Benson twisted around in a chair, watching.

She turned away almost immediately.

It wasn't so fast he couldn't see the discoloration on the soft skin of her face.

Gabriel.

The bastard had slapped her around. Hard.

Chung was twisted around in one of the pilot seats, his gut made more noticeable by his slouch. "Dev. Did I call you up here? I forget."

"Nah." As Rai entered, he waved for Penn to follow. "I wanted to chat."

"Yeah?" Chung's eyes darted from Benson to Rai. Suspicious. "Then chat."

Rai leaned against the console Benson was focused on. "What happened?"

Her fingers flew across keys and buttons, but she apparently made some errors, repeating some of her work. Her hands shook. "Nothing."

"Your cheeks just turned red like that?"

"The big guy asked me some questions."

Even though he'd known that was going to be the answer, Rai was furious.

Chung was focusing on Penn now, eyes squinted, head cocked. "You two have something specific to chat about, or you just jerking each other off? Jimmy's pissed you left him down there alone."

Penn looked away; it was a smart move—just signal you're following orders.

Rai rubbed his chin. "I think we've lost our focus."

"Yeah?" Chung scratched his stubble. "We're focused."

"I don't think you are."

"Maybe we should talk alone."

Rai backed up, jerking his head at Benson so that Penn knew to keep an eye on her.

In the passageway outside the bridge, the old man waited for the hatch to close, then scratched the material covering his belly. "So talk."

"We've got to quit with this abuse shit. Are we here to beat up women or get money?"

"Why can't it be both? They're all gonna die."

Ringing echoed in Rai's ears. Arguing about letting them go wasn't worth it, not at the moment. "What matters is how you live. You shouldn't suffer like that."

"Let it go."

"We've got big money coming with the Carone deal."

"Later, sure. But you've got to keep your people happy."

If Rai dropped the old bastard right there, just put a couple shots into his gut, there would be issues. Penn would fall in line. Wong would have to be killed. And Gabriel would be killed even if he wanted to fall in line. Hurley? There was no telling with him.

But Rai knew that just him and Penn trying to make the deal with the Haidakura would be suicide. And Rai wasn't someone to put a team together.

He needed the old man. For now.

Remember your true loyalty. Remember.

Rai gritted his teeth. "Okay, so you let your crew have their fun. But we're wasting all this time digging around for something that doesn't pertain to us."

Chung's focus turned distant; he was thinking. "Maybe it does."

"How?"

"Ask yourself, what's a ship doing out here in the DMZ? And it's got special antennas no one aboard knew about?"

"But someone does."

Chung's attention was back on the moment. "Say again?"

"This pretty nurse. Stiles."

"What about her?"

"She came aboard when the maintenance was done."

Chung laughed.

"What's so funny?"

"Your girlfriend said that scrawny Marine did."

"They both did."

"Yeah, but she lied." The old bastard seemed to enjoy that.

"Whatever. Point is, we have someone we can ask about what happened. She was at the same station this work was done at. Maybe she saw or heard something."

"Yeah. Maybe." But the way Chung was staring said he didn't believe that.

He thinks I'm trying to deflect attention away from Benson. "So what've you two been doing up here?"

"I had her going through all the captain's logs. She's the captain now."

The hatch hissed open, and Penn poked his head out. "Hey, she says she's ready."

Chung's brows arched. "Let's go see."

Benson was still in the pilot's chair. She didn't turn around when they came in.

The big display screen that ran across the entire console separating the pilot's stations from the viewing glass was filled with windows of text.

Chung took the seat he'd been in before. "Show me."

She pointed to the display. "These are all the logs: official logs managed by Commander Martinez, our master audit logs, systems logs—everything. What you're looking at here is the consolidation tool the captain has access to. Everything's gathered into this one view."

"That's what we wanted." The old man leaned on the console in front of him, elbows resting on the narrow area that didn't hold buttons or keys.

"So exactly what is it you want?" She sounded testy.

"Let's say your captain was running a little game. Maybe he was being paid to do something illegal."

Benson shook her head. "Lenny had his shortcoming, but he wasn't that type."

"Yeah? You know him that well?"

"I told you, I served with him for four years."

"Humor me." Chung pointed at the windows of text. "Search for the date you picked up this Lopez kid. And—" He twisted around to smirk at Rai. "—what's that nurse's name?"

The way Benson tensed made Rai nervous; she *had* been trying to keep information from them. *Protecting her crew.* "Stiles."

The bridge was quiet except for the hum of the ventilation system.

Benson finally nodded. "Okay." Her voice was shaky. "That's…easy enough."

She tapped the query in, and the data scrolled past—green letters on a black background. It was mostly meaningless junk if you weren't the captain of the ship, but that's what she was, what she'd been trained to be. She leaned forward as the data in the windows came to a stop.

The old man looked from the data to her. "You see anything?"

"N-nothing." She typed in another command.

Rai reached over her shoulders and gently took her hands in his, pulling them up from the console. "You found something."

"I—" Her hands shook. She was so warm and soft.

"Let me see." He tugged gently, and she seemed to surrender, a few seconds later stiffly climbing from the seat.

The glow of the console reflected a wicked green in Chung's dark eyes.

Rai studied the console for a minute, then slowly tapped through some commands. Finally, he had her search brought up in the history and ran it again. The data scrolled, then stopped.

It looked the same as before to Rai's untrained eyes.

Nothing jumped out.

The old man sucked in the stale air. "You find something?"

"Give me a minute."

Rai poked around. It was gibberish. Meaningless nonsense.

But it couldn't be, not if she wanted to hide it from them.

Not everything was meaningless, though. When he really looked at it, things started to make sense. There were manifests. Cargo. Personnel. There were official transfers. They'd taken on medical supplies along with the Stiles woman. They'd changed out filters, purchased food...all the things a starship would need to do when at a port of call. Sure, a ship could last months in space, but resupply made life easier and better.

There had to be a way to filter out the mundane things. A few taps and pokes, and he had weeded out what wasn't relevant.

But he still couldn't see. Something had caught Benson's eye—

He almost missed it again while scrolling through the remaining data. Almost. But he didn't: There were gaps, periods of time that showed up in some logs but not others.

And the log that had everything in it, some sort of master audit log. A copy of the audit log, something only the captain could see.

Time. Date. Events.

His heart raced.

"See this?" He pointed to a set of codes in the master audit log. "Something happened while they were in the port."

Benson's head was bowed, her hands covering her face. "We had maintenance done."

"Yeah." Rai finally found an entry in the captain's log. The codes. Notes. "You had a new system installed. The antennas."

"Upgrades. Martinez knew about it."

Rai found the note Martinez had left. "He was following orders. What's this? GSA?"

"The Group for Strategic Assessment. It's...the military's intelligence agency."

"Never heard of it. I thought the Republic had the Security and Intelligence Directorate."

"That's the big one. GSA is..." Benson sighed. "It has a different focus."

"Well, the focus here seems to be on starting a war with the Azoren."

Chung snorted. "Starting a war?"

Rai shrugged. "His notes. Assignment to assist Kedraalian ships spy on Azoren assets. Primary purpose: Determine the viability of infiltrating the DMZ."

Benson groaned. "The accident that sent us off course was meant to provide official cover. Commander Martinez knew it. He knew we would be here for days doing maintenance, maybe longer. We were supposed to scan for potential gaps in the Azoren sensor buoy network and to cover for ships attempting infiltration."

"You were spies."

"And he never told anyone."

Rai almost chuckled at that. And then he thought about what she'd said. Covering other ships attempting infiltration.

There could be other ships en route toward their area right then!

16

BENSON WRAPPED HER ARMS AROUND HERSELF DESPITE THE BRIDGE growing warm and stuffy with four people in it. Martinez's scent seemed to have been obliterated already, replaced by the smell of cold sleep gel, and soap. But it was more than the bodies squeezed into the tight space; it was the heat those bodies were generating. Chung was glaring at her. Challenging her. Accusing her. Rai seemed to have lost trust in her as well. And the other one—Penn—seemed to be waiting for things to go sideways.

It was Chung who finally spoke. "Who the fuck are these other ships?"

Rai scrolled through the log again. "No names given anywhere."

"What the fuck's going on here?" The old man squeezed the arms of his chair. His cheeks were red. There was spittle on his lips. "We got Kedraalian ships incoming or what?"

"We do at some point. We just don't know which ones or how close they'll be."

Penn put his hands on his hips. "Don't forget there's an SOS out there. If they come in close enough, they'll respond to that. Ours, too."

Benson flinched but relaxed when no one else seemed to think anything more of the implications. "Um, I...don't understand how this has become what it has."

Rai arched an eyebrow. "Your people looking to start a war with the Azoren?"

"If that's what really was intended."

He tapped the display. "It's right there. See for yourself."

"But it doesn't make sense. The Republic military has always been about defending against attackers, not provoking them. There's a big faction in the Assembly that's been trying to cut back spending for years."

Chung grunted. "Looking to start a war with the Azoren. You sure you want that fight?"

Benson slumped. "I can't see how anyone would go looking for war."

"I'm old enough to remember what it was like."

"War for the Union?"

The old man sneered. "I'd rather watch the Gulmar burn than fight for them. No, I was a smuggler when the Azoren were still actively fighting the Moskav. Thirty-five, forty years ago."

Benson had never heard about war among the other four powers, not with any certainty. "How…long did that go on?"

"Years. Off and on. Mostly little skirmishes on one side of the DMZ or the other. This was before they realized they could hire privateers to do what their warships couldn't—violence without escalation. Not even the Azoren wanted full-scale war."

Rai looked up from the data display. "No one wants war until they're sure they can win it."

"Yeah." The old man's fingers scraped over his whispers.

How could anyone ever think there was certainty in war? The only certainty she had ever heard of was destruction and death. Lots of death. "What was it like?"

"Tension. Fear." Instead of angry, the old man sounded anxious. "Back then, you had to run through the old DMZ to get into Moskav space. Tech wasn't so good. You were only safe going in there because their ships were so slow and everything they did was so backwards."

"Did you ever see any space battles?"

"Afterwards. Ruined ships. Corpses floating in the black." He smiled for an instant. "If you were lucky and fast, you could scavenge cargo and make some good money off it."

"Did you?"

"A couple times. You see all that money they lost, you come to understand why things cooled down."

Benson shivered. "It just doesn't make sense. Why would they do it?"

Rai straightened. "The Kedraalians? Probably for the same reason anyone else would: They want to expand."

"But we have all the resources we could ever need. Seven habitable planets, three times the number of systems. Parsecs of space with asteroids and planetoids and—"

"And a desire for more. It's how the Gulmar sees things. It's how the Azoren see things. Your people are only bordered by two other powers; the Azoren are bordered by everyone."

"We don't want war." Did they? "Why don't the Moskav and the Khanate just expand outward?"

"Just uproot and leave their planets to someone else?" Rai chuckled. "Would you?"

"To avoid war." No. She was lying to herself. Even if the Republic only intended to fight defensively, they *would* fight to keep what they had.

"The Khanate supposedly did." Chung sighed and pushed out of the chair.

Benson blinked. "They uprooted?"

"Fled deeper into the galaxy. Some say. Never heard of anyone checking. Doesn't matter. People will always want more. And that's why there's always going to be the threat of war. And that's why people like me will always make money. If I can survive."

It was an alien way of seeing things, but it put Martinez's decisions in a light that made a little more sense. Either the Republic felt constrained or threatened.

Or both.

They were looking to get an advantage on their worst enemy: the Azoren.

Rai held up a hand to stop Chung as the old man pointed them all to the hatch. "Hold on. That data you were asking for? Ship names, types—all that?"

"Yeah?"

"Looks like it was in the log."

Chung leaned toward the display. "Where?"

"No, it's gone now, but it was there."

"Gone. How the fuck you know it's gone?"

The slender man's fingers danced over the console. "Because even the captain's log she was looking at has data missing. There should be consistent timestamps but—" He pointed to the display.

Benson once again flinched. Had Rai seen what she'd seen?

Chung leaned against the console until his nose was centimeters from the display. "So this guy knew?"

"Or someone knew we might look." Rai glanced at Benson. "They didn't clean up when the data was deleted, just who did it."

"When was it?"

Rai nodded toward Benson. "You'd have to ask her, but I'm guessing the timestamp is after they entered the DMZ."

Chung rounded on her. "You still want to tell me you didn't know?"

She slouched so that she was just a little taller than the old man. "I didn't. And there's no way I could have known. You saw me go through the process of modifying the official chain of command. Until I accepted the role of captain, I didn't have access to that system or any of those files."

"So who else could've done it?"

"Technically? Chief Parkinson. He's good enough and has emergency privileges that would make it possible. But Martinez would've been alerted, and Parkinson's been busy this whole time."

The old man snarled at Rai. "This fucking engineer."

Rai nodded. "Anyone else?"

Benson could only conceive of one person. "In theory, Petty Officer Kohn. He has the ability to elevate his privileges to do some of the work he does."

"But you don't think it was him?" Rai's tone wasn't challenging.

"Chief Parkinson and the captain—Commander Martinez—made a point of blocking Petty Officer Kohn at every opportunity."

"Friction?"

"Just a little. Things were becoming dysfunctional."

Rai turned back to Chung. "So, Martinez is your guy."

Chung made a sound that must have been a frustrated growl. "Shouldn't've had Vic wake up first."

The old man shuffled to the hatch, which hissed open. Penn followed.

Rai set a hand on Benson's elbow. "Hey, Quentin, we can't leave these logs accessible."

"Yeah, whatever. Close them." Chung was already shuffling down the passageway.

"All right." Rai's eyes sparkled as the hatch closed. "He's pissed because he's the one who said Vic should be the first of us to wake up. I thought it should be me."

Benson relaxed a little. "Vic's the one who killed Martinez?" It was hard to be sure given the short look she'd had before the feed died.

"Yeah. The rest of us were still a little groggy. Now we lost our chance to figure out how long we've got. We have to assume the schedule's much more aggressive than we thought." Rai looked to her for guidance as he closed the logs.

The sooner the other ship was repaired, the sooner she and her crew would die. "I'm sorry we caused any trouble for you."

"No. Look, okay? This whole situation—you're not the only people in danger."

"We're just the ones looking down the barrel of guns when we're no longer useful."

"And your career is ruined even if you live; I get it. And I understand you're pissed that your boss screwed you over with this mission, but he was following orders."

"Was he?"

"Well, you're search and rescue. A ship needed rescue. How was he supposed to ignore that?"

"Okay."

"I know you're eaten up about that globe, the things you dreamed about. Who knows, maybe you'll still fly the *Valor* one day. Right? That was the ship?"

Benson smiled nervously and glanced away.

"What?" He sounded concerned.

"It seems so petty and selfish now. With what's going on, I mean—worrying about decorations and rank and title. All I want is to protect my crew."

"You can't give up your dreams."

"When you're faced with death, career just isn't the same."

Rai shut the system down the rest of the way. "We're all the same. Sure, we're individuals, but we all have the same basic functions and needs. We're a product of our biology, but we're also a product of upbringing."

Like years living under her mother? Fighting for a few minutes of attention, rejecting it when she didn't want it? "Even the basics can be different."

"I get that. But you have no idea what motivated your captain."

"He was following orders, just like you said."

"And I get that, too. People can do some terrible things following orders."

"There should be a reasonable limit to loyalty."

Rai's back stiffened, and he ground his teeth loud enough that she could hear it. "You should be careful saying something so broad. You need to walk in the other person's shoes before you judge."

Was she judging Martinez unfairly? He'd put everyone at risk. He'd… He'd what? If he hadn't lied, he'd at least deceived. As captain of the *Pandora*, his first responsibility should have been to his crew, even if the mission was supposed to be dangerous. You don't introduce *more* danger. And he had. Where had he briefed everyone on what he *could* say? The drift that had set them on the course that brought them into the DMZ was something he had to have known about. Why not tell everyone they were on a riskier mission and to be ready for potential problems?

Why not simply refuse the orders?

As she followed Rai down the stairs to the cargo hold, Benson chewed on that idea: refusing the orders.

Would she have? It would have ruined her career as quickly as going into the DMZ and getting crew killed through reckless behavior. That had always been the warning her mother had given about the military:

"You'll never have easy options, Faith. The military is just one set of terrible choices after another."

The idea that her mother could have been even slightly right was annoying.

Were there any good choices facing the captain of a ship like the *Pandora*? Benson couldn't see a way to save her crew. Not even one of them.

But at least Rai and the other privateers hadn't seen what she had in the log: The SOS fired from the *Pandora* had been from the same string of hidden orders and messages in the captain's log.

That was something, wasn't it? Maybe she should take some consolation in that?

After all, it was a whole different puzzle than the one facing them at the moment: Who had set up the whole tasking for the *Pandora* and left them in such a hopeless situation?

What should she even take from it? Was there actually a slim hope after all?

Because if the SOS the *Pandora* had fired off had been triggered by what she'd seen in the logs—at the time she'd seen in the logs—it meant that Martinez was still alive.

And they had an ally out there.

17

THE OLD MAN WAS PACING, THE ECHO OF HIS BOOTS THUDDING ON THE cargo bay deck loud enough that everyone was glued to his movements. Benson wanted so badly to tell the others of her crew that everything was going to be okay.

Would that be fair? Tell them that they were all going to be fine because they just *might* have help from someone who apparently took a laser beam to the face and was bad enough off that everyone had left him for dead? And how long had he been on a ship with radiation leaking from its reactor?

A quick peek at the folks still aboard the *Pandora*—Dietrich, Gaines, and Parkinson—and she realized it didn't matter. She didn't have the people who could make a difference if the time came.

Benson's attention drifted to the dark trail smeared along the deck, leading from her huddled crew to the airlock.

Lopez's blood and brains. She could barely make out the stench of urine.

He'd been a kid, younger than Stiles.

It wasn't right. They should've had a chance to fight back. They should've done what Benson had wanted to do from the start: blow the umbilical and flee.

Her stomach flipped, and the material of her flight suit suddenly felt heavy and rough on her skin. Could she have done that? Could she have lived with it? These were *her* people to care for now. *Her* responsibility.

Being a captain wasn't as easy as she'd thought it would be.

The *thump-thump-thump* of Chung's pacing stopped. His heel squeaked on the deck. "Hey!"

Benson snapped out of her distracted thoughts.

"We need to speed repairs up." The old man ran stubby fingers through wispy white hair. He looked at the three prisoners, then right at her. "Who can do that?"

"I-I can."

He smirked. "I'm keeping you and that engineer in my sight."

Gaines raised her hand shakily. "I've helped with hull repairs and some other simple work in the past."

Benson bit her lip. She didn't want the doctor involved, but there was no rational reason to protest.

Chung waved the youngest of the privateers toward the airlock. "Jimmy, get her across."

"Uncle Quentin, I—"

"Hey! Did that sound like a request? Get her across!"

The kid pointed his gun at Gaines. "Let's go, fatty."

Benson's cheeks burned, but Gaines didn't protest. She accepted Dietrich's help up with a smile, then swung past Benson, stopping long enough to hug her. "We're going to be all right, Captain."

While Gaines and Wong suited up, Chung scratched his scalp. It was nervous energy, same as the way his scarred face bunched and relaxed. "Dev?"

Rai stepped from the entry to the narrow path created by the piled cargo containers. "Yes?"

"These other ships—the ones that could be coming here?"

"Or somewhere in the DMZ. We don't know if it's here."

"Yeah, well, we gotta know. We gotta know soon. This idea that we might have a ship just show up while we're defenseless…" Chung shook his head.

"What can we do? Let's just have everything ready to go."

"Backups. Data backups!" Chung turned to Benson. "Hey. What about backups? Could this data exist somewhere else on your ship? Another system? You gotta have something."

She hadn't given that any thought. "In backup storage. It's offline."

"On this ship?"

"Near the bridge."

That brought a smile to the old man's face. "And the deletes wouldn't copy down to it?"

"N-no." She wanted to get him to consider other possibilities, to give up, but the way he was acting, that wasn't going to happen.

"So we got the data somewhere."

"We should. Transactions are copied to an online storage platform. A few times a day, those transactions are copied down to backup storage. You can recreate any data in any system from that backup at any point in time. The compartment's shielded and hardened. We use systems like that to figure out what happened to a ship after a disaster."

"So check it out."

Rai turned, ready to escort her, but Chung said, "You stay here, Dev. Eli, you take her up."

Penn shrugged. "Sure. C'mon."

He bowed his head as he casually strolled past Rai, but Benson thought she saw something between the two of them. Were they...scheming? Or was there something else going on? She'd seen something out of the corner of her eye when Rai had turned.

Had Penn made a face at Chung? Shrugged his shoulders? He'd done something.

She fell in behind the young man, trying to catch Rai's attention as she passed, but he was focused on Chung.

He's mad about this power play. Chung doesn't trust him. How can I use that?

The way Chung and Rai were acting reminded her of what she'd heard went on between a lot of fathers and sons: a struggle to establish independence and authority.

So maybe Penn had been part of Rai's clique and Chung was signaling his own authority?

As they approached the top deck, she slowed. "What was that thing between you and Chung?"

"Thing?"

"A signal. I couldn't make it out."

"Oh. There's this disagreement going on between those two. The old man knows Dev's sweet on you."

Sweet on me. "Well, that's an odd thing to assume."

"It's not my assumption. I hardly know these guys. When you two stayed up on the bridge so long, it pissed Quentin off."

"That's funny, because Mr. Rai was trying to assure me it was to my advantage to cooperate fully so that my crew could survive."

The young man shrugged. "I'm not involved."

"But you'd pull the trigger if they told you to execute us."

Penn took a few steps into the passageway between the two halves of Officers' Country, then stopped. "I'm just a hired gun. I don't make any money if I don't do what I'm paid to do."

"Including murdering innocent people?"

"That's kind of part of the job."

She punched the panel to open the hatch to the starboard passageway, then waved the young man through. He deferred to her. It took her a few seconds to get through the security prompts using her new credentials, then her access was denied.

Penn leaned forward. "Something wrong?"

She stared at the security panel. "I've never been inside this one."

"Want me to blast it?"

"No."

He smirked. "You sure?"

"Do you even know what you're doing?"

"Actually, I do. I used to work security. I've seen systems like that." He held his hand out.

"What?"

"Your credentials card."

She handed the palm-sized device to him, and he inspected it. "You transferred all the security credentials onto here?"

"Yes. What kind of security did you work that led to privateering?"

"The kind where a kid from the slums gets put in the front ranks when there's any chance something might go wrong and gets blamed for every last thing that does."

Like Kohn, she realized. "You got tired of mistreatment?"

"And the lies and all the inexcusable bullshit." He inserted the key, then stepped aside for her to give a thumb print and scan her eye. "Something didn't take. Who else can get into this area?"

"Offline Storage? I should have been able to. The captain. Parkinson and Kohn."

"The usual suspects."

"What?"

"That's the same group of people you said could get to the log files." He handed her card back to her. "Let's check the bridge systems."

Her card didn't look any different—no scuffs or discoloration. It was a sturdy, gray-green plastic with copper contacts, all ruggedized against demagnetization. It got her onto the bridge fine, and when she slid it into her console, it worked there as well.

Penn looked the card over again. "The tech looks pretty similar. Maybe log in with the captain's credentials and override door security?"

That took a minute.

She yanked her card. "If you were good enough at security, why'd you leave it?"

"I told you."

"But you went into it for a reason."

"Yeah, because my mother insisted I do something more with my life than my friends. Like being born in the slums wouldn't hold me back."

She headed back toward the starboard hatch, noting how he kept a safe distance. Rai didn't seem to worry that she might attack him. Was that overconfidence or was he just that dangerous? For Penn, there was just the caution, although she was sure he could shoot her before she could get him to the ground.

At the Offline Storage hatch, she looked the young man over. Not ugly, not handsome. Wiry. Capable. He just didn't seem as rough and brutish as the others. "Your mother wanted something better for you."

He looked away, lips pressed tight. "She meant well."

"But—?"

"Like my father said, you can't change where you were born. It's all about birth to the Gulmar. Either you have money or you don't. If you don't, you never will. Unless you take it."

"At least you had parents." She shoved the card into the slot, embarrassed. She'd had parents, too, even if she'd never really known her father. And like Penn's mother, Benson's cared. And Benson had never gone without the basics like Penn and Rai made it sound like they had.

But the fighting, the feeling of abandonment—how many days in a typical week would she go without seeing her mother? A maid. A tutor. Automated systems with their reminders about schedules, assignments, expectations.

But not her mother.

She had always been good for the ever-present expectation that the path to the Assembly would be taken.

Maybe that hadn't been such a bad thing after all. Would an Assembly member be facing execution by a group of privateers?

"Still not working?" Penn looked over Benson's shoulder.

"Um. Sorry."

She pulled the card out. She hadn't even seen whether the indicator had gone green, but it had timed out now. On the second try, the green light flashed. And her code, fingerprint, and eye scan worked.

And the hatch hissed open.

The guy really did know security.

Penn pressed between her and the opening, hand covering the door sensor. "Hold on."

"What?"

"How sure can you be that no one else could have accessed this area at some point?" He looked around. "Cameras? Logs that couldn't be tampered with?"

"N-no. Not on a search-and-rescue vessel. We weren't worried about sabotage."

"Yeah, well, maybe you should've been, because you've obviously had some." He glanced into the dimly lit compartment. Steps led down to a small platform with a seat and a console. Light came from that console and the area behind it, which was lower and more shadowy. "This is just storage?"

"And some emergency processing. Backup systems. Spares."

"I don't like it." He pulled his pistol. "I can't see all the way back there."

"No one's in there." Could Martinez have somehow gotten back aboard and sneaked into the compartment? Who would have checked it? No one ever went in there.

Penn glanced past her at the intercom a couple meters away. "Just stay back."

He stepped in, and the hatch closed.

Almost immediately, the questions hit her. Who could have gotten into their systems? How could the data have been deleted? What if the SOS hadn't been sent by Martinez but by whoever had messed around with all the systems? Would they trust her if she told them it wasn't her? Their security was built on trust, and she didn't know who to trust now.

The hatch hissed open, and she backed away, ready to run.

But it was Penn. He still looked unsteady but shook his head and holstered his pistol. "Clear."

She exhaled softly, then squeezed past him and made her way to the console. Her card worked just as well as it had on the bridge. "You were worried about the sabotage. Why?"

"Because if the Azoren ever find this ship, and they get wind of you being involved in spying, this ship, this crew: toast. They won't care if you weren't aware of it."

"How's that different from you and your friends?"

The young man looked away. "It's worse with the Azoren."

"You've dealt with them?"

"Some. Through my security work. They're inhuman and cruel. Some of them are like androids. You know, they look human but don't act human."

They'd always believed in a master race. Had they created one that wasn't even human anymore? "Are they any worse than the Union?"

"I guess. Greed and exploitation has its own way of dehumanizing people."

Was the Republic the only good choice? Had she lucked into the good life? What had he said? *You can't change where you were born.*

She almost challenged the idea. Almost. How much did he really know about the Azoren? What if he was doing like her, relying on what he'd heard through generations of teaching and tall tales?

Still, he seemed worried about them.

The console blinked at her. She'd only trained with the system a few times, but she remembered it being a bit...primitive. She brought up the interface, puffed out her cheeks, then started working through the clunky interface.

Penn watched over her shoulder. "Anything?"

"It won't be that fast. This system is built for robustness not speed. I'm pretty sure they were thinking that a system that was really slow and painful would frustrate saboteurs."

He chuckled.

She twisted around. "What?"

"It sounds like something my father said about government systems: If they wanted us to have money, they would've given us money, just like the wealthy families."

"That's not a bad idea, actually. Start everyone off on an equal footing. That's close to how it is in the Republic."

"Not with the Gulmar, and that infuriated my father."

"Maybe he would've liked the Republic."

"I bet."

She had never understood the reasoning behind people joining the factions they had when the War of Separation had begun. Maybe it wasn't something that *could* be understood.

The console finally popped up an option she could use. She tapped the button, then glanced back at Penn. "Is he still around? Your father?"

"I haven't seen him in years." That produced a look of pain in his eyes.

"I never really knew my father." She blushed at the admission. It just felt so odd hearing Penn talk about his. The man sounded concrete, while she'd created a type of mythological version of her own.

"That's tough, not knowing your father. Then again, plenty of my

friends wish they'd never known theirs. Useless or violent druggies..."
He shook his head.

Maybe it was better being able to make up a fictional version of someone after all. "I guess the Republic is the only place to get it right?"

Penn sucked in a sharp breath. "I guess."

Was that a fair thing to say, especially now that she knew that her government had sent her crew to their deaths? And trying to insert ships into Azoren space? It seemed incredibly devious and dangerous.

Almost as if he could read her thoughts, Penn said, "This spying thing, it's what they all do. The Gulmar spies on the Azoren; the Azoren spy on the Moskav; the Moskav spy on the Gulmar. It's probably all that keeps everyone from going after each other."

"Knowing that doesn't bring back the crew I've lost."

"No, but it's better to suffer a few unfortunate deaths than death on the scale a war would bring."

She bowed her head. It was true but terrible nonetheless.

He pointed to the clunky interface. "So how do we find this data?"

"Well, the query I'm running should take—"

The system finished processing her request. A message appeared on the display: *No data found.*

No data found? How? She'd chosen the period just before and just after the data had been wiped out. There should have been line after line of options to retrieve.

He leaned over her again. "What's wrong?"

"It's saying there's no data found."

She ran the query again.

The message flashed almost instantly.

How?

He was closer now. "What's going on? Why's it saying that?"

"I don't know." She tried another date range.

The message flashed again: *No data found.*

Penn grunted. "You told us that the data was here."

"It should be. It's just..." She tried all date ranges.

No data found.

"There's no data." She pushed up from the desk.

"What's that mean? You said—"

"I know what I said. I'm telling you that the console is saying there's nothing in the backup."

But there had to be.

She took the steps down into the darker area. There were cabinets of storage devices. If something happened to cripple the ship and risk the whole thing blowing apart, this section would blast away and fire off its own transponder. The system was built to last. It *couldn't* be a failure. That just wasn't possible.

She popped a cabinet door open. Then another.

Penn glanced over the console. "What're you doing?"

"Something's been done to the backup storage."

"That's the backup storage? I thought this was."

"That's just the command console."

"I don't understand."

"This is the storage down here—that's just the way you access it."

He came down the steps. There wasn't a lot of space, so he was forced to stay closer to her than he usually did.

She popped open another cabinet door and gasped.

"What?" He looked over her shoulder again.

"This." A device she'd never seen before flashed on the front of the storage array.

"That blinking thing? What is it?"

"Not something that belongs there." She pulled it away from the storage array. "It was plugged into an interface."

"And?"

"And I think it wiped out our storage." She rolled the thing around in her hand. It was just a box, about palm-sized, maybe five times as thick as her card.

He took the thing. "This wiped out the storage? How?"

"I don't know." Her voice rose. She swallowed. "I've never seen anything like it before."

"Well, we're going to have to answer to Quentin just the same. He was expecting the data."

"I wanted to see it, too." But it was actually a relief to have it wiped out. If Martinez was behind all this...

"This place is too easy for a saboteur to get into."

It was.

Penn glanced along the ceiling, then climbed back up the steps. "You sure there's no way you can figure out who's been in here?"

"Yes."

"And who has access to this area?"

"Just Martinez and...Parkinson."

"Seems like a lot of things point to this engineer of yours."

They did. And Benson wondered how much she really knew about Parkinson.

18

Rai followed Chung astern to the *Pandora* engineering bay and into the maintenance bay beyond. The noise of the forward compartment was muted; it was much louder in the maintenance bay. Bad things could happen back there, out of sight in the half-light, with no one to notice even screams.

But Rai kept his hands clear of his holster. There was friction with the old man, but they were still allies.

For now.

Chung patted the bulkhead separating the two compartments, a thumping noise that was barely detectable over the drone of the life support and power systems and all the other machinery. "This place, it's got that lived-in feel. You smell it? Like people been in here, working. Real work. Not like that engineer's place, not like his work."

"I smell it." It wasn't just small talk; Rai really could detect what the old guy was talking about. There was a physical sense, a *feel* about the maintenance area. It was in the grime on the surfaces, the scuff marks on the corners, and the tackiness of the deck beneath the boots. People *worked* in this compartment. "What's on your mind?"

"Right to it, huh?" The old man chuckled. "I know you're pissed."

"You, too."

"Yeah. This fucking thing, it's been a disaster."

"Regretting taking it on?"

Chung's stubby fingers scraped over his wrinkled face, lingering only for a moment on scars and tattoos. "Not if we come out of it with our money. It's a *lot* of money."

Rai smiled. There was still that. "Money solves a lot of problems."

"It does." The old man put on a mischievous grin. "How you planning to spend yours?"

"I don't want to think that far ahead."

"You and your superstitions. You're like your old man."

"Too much so." *Down to my bones.*

Something buzzed in Chung's coveralls. He dug around in the deep pockets and fished out a palm-sized radio, irritated. "Yeah?"

He shifted his weight, stared at the bulkhead, nodded. "How much longer?"

It had to be Gabriel. Who else was there? Wong? Penn? They would've come looking for the old bastard. And Penn wouldn't interrupt over nothing.

Or was this nothing? Maybe Gabriel had screwed something else up.

Chung's features tightened, then relaxed. "No. We got our eyes on the engineer." After a moment, he tensed again. "Because he's a fucking problem's why. Vic, you best remember you don't tell me how things go, understand? Now, how much longer?"

Chung's eyes shot up, and he gave Rai a hopeful look. "And you think the drones can speed that up?"

They must be ready for the hull patch. If they were asking for the engineer to help, that's where it would be. No matter what the squirrelly little bastard said about being a great pilot, hull work was the only thing the drones could do faster and safer than a repair team. For them to be at that stage, that meant the reactor shielding was repaired. The search-and-rescue team knew its stuff. Nguyen had said she could've patched it with help in a few hours, but they just didn't have the heavy environmental suits to take the radiation exposure.

Rai didn't even want to think about how much radiation he'd been exposed to after the blast. He also didn't want to think about what that blast had done to Borino. The way the guy had just…died. Vomiting. Bleeding.

It was another freakish thing that had set them back and prevented them from closing the deal.

"All right. We'll have him go to work." Chung put the radio away.

Something smacked when Rai lifted his boot. He shifted to his right, exiting the circle of a dark stain on the deck. "Everything's done but the hull patch?"

"Close to. And this Kohn guy says the hull patch would take half as long—"

"With the drones. I heard."

Chung grunted. "I thought we could talk privately back here, but now we need to put that engineer to work."

"Jimmy can watch him and the doctor. Neither one's trouble."

"You don't think the doc might have been behind killing Stef?"

"Maybe. He's too scared to do anything more now."

"Yeah. We can chat out in the cargo bay, I guess."

Rai waited patiently for the shift to happen, with Chung quickly snuffing Wong's little fit of histrionics before it could take off. Once everyone was in the engineering bay in such a way not even Wong could get himself shot, the old man came out to where Rai was waiting.

"Kids." The head of the privateers ran his fingers through his white hair.

"So what's your next step?"

"You're really sore, huh?"

"About the way you handled that kid's execution?"

"You've been pissed since we snatched Carone."

Rai sucked air between his teeth. "I told you from the start, Vic was a bad fit."

"We needed his muscle."

"And I told you he'd get people killed."

"We're not talking about—"

"He got your son killed, Quentin. He might have cost us any chance of coming out of this alive."

The old man slouched. "Let's just focus on the next step, like you said." His voice cracked.

"We can do that." Rai looked away. "Your business doesn't have to collapse, you know."

"It won't."

"I mean you don't need to bring in an outsider."

"We'll see." Chung wasn't convinced.

"What about Sharon?"

The old man sighed. "She don't got the strength. She wants to spend her time shopping and partying with all her useless friends."

"So did your boy."

The old man winced. "He was younger."

"She could take over. She just needs to be given a chance."

"You think she could be like this commander? She's tough. You see what she did to Vic?"

"Yeah." A smile slipped onto Rai's face.

"What's your problem with Vic, huh?"

"I told you—there's a time and a place for brutality. It's a very specific time and place, and Vic's too fucking stupid to get that. He's a thug. He doesn't understand that being a blast hose on full all the time, it ruins the meaning of brutality. You lose allies. You kill innocents."

"He had a tough life."

"We all did."

Chung sniffled. "Maybe I got a soft spot for the big moron."

"Why?"

"His father was…bad. Vic don't know any better. It's all he ever saw as a kid."

"Sure, but every kid has a choice at some point to break away from the inertia, to be his own—" Rai stopped himself. The hypocrisy was too much. "Forget about it."

"Yeah. Forgotten. So, this Carone transfer. You have ideas?"

"About surviving the Haidakura?"

"That's the big concern."

"You can't count on a clean exchange."

"Yeah. I'm thinking we play the usual trick: fake pickup site, run them around, work them up really good."

"You don't want to piss these guys off."

"They'll get sloppy."

"Maybe. Or maybe they call it off. Or maybe they decide to hunt us down."

Chung wiped a hand across his lips. "You got other ideas?"

"They need her alive. We show them we want the same thing they do. But we take away their ability to get at us without getting her."

"Yeah. Thanks for stating the obvious."

"You gonna let me finish?"

The old man waved irritably. "Finish."

"We find out who's running the recovery operation. We find out who's on his or her team. Then we snag a few of them. Tranquilizer gas. Darts. Something. We make them a part of the deal. Hand her off, get our money, release these guys when we're ready to disappear."

"I thought you didn't want to piss them off."

"This forces them to back off."

"We'll need to pick up some more firepower."

This was the sort of information Rai needed to learn from the old man —networking, connections, resources. "You got some people in mind?"

"The Yeoh brothers."

"They're no better than Vic."

Chung chortled. "Foster Dunham and his gang."

"They'll double-cross you."

"Cal Bortles. He has some people he works with a lot."

"Bortles can't keep his mouth shut." Rai's blood heated up; the old bastard was being cagey, protecting his secrets.

Or he had no idea how deep he was in with these Haidakura.

The old man scratched the bulge of his belly. "Anyone else is going to bring too many numbers in or be too expensive."

"Better to pay and have success."

"Success is just you and me walking away with our fair share, ain't it? Ain't that how things been since you were a kid? Huh? You wait too long to cut the other guy, he's already cutting you. We always took care of you and your old man, right?"

"You did."

"Cleaned up your debts. Took care of things when your mother died. When your father died. My father made opportunities for everyone, not like the Gulmar."

Ice ran along Rai's spine at the mention of his mother. "I owe you."

"Yeah. Like family, aren't we?"

Like a twisted, diseased, lying family. "So, you planning to whack whoever you hire to keep things quiet?"

A malevolent smile spread across the old man's lips. "This Penn guy, he's the one suggested selling Carone back."

"Sure. Makes the most sense."

"Yeah, well he's got a security background."

"You think he has contacts?"

"None that he trusts. That's why he came to me. But he does have a plan."

"Really?"

"There's a place the Haidakura would be at a disadvantage, operating in Klein territory. It's a good plan."

No details. The trust wasn't there, not like it was before. For either of them. There wouldn't be any seeing eye to eye. Not again.

But Rai could try to get something from Chung. "What about this crew?"

"These Kedraalians?"

"What about letting them go? They're not the threat. This Benson, she really had no idea her captain was involved in this mess. And maybe he was just following orders."

"Just a good soldier?"

"Exactly."

Chung shrugged. "Let me think about it."

"Are you really?"

"Yeah, yeah. I just don't like loose ends. You don't leave someone behind you. That's how you get shot in the back."

"This ship doesn't even have guns."

"I'll think about it, like I—" The old man's pocket buzzed again. He turned away, still digging around for the radio. "Yeah? Uh-huh."

Chung's back stiffened. "You figure out how?"

Long seconds passed, then the old man nodded. "All right. Come on down here."

Rai waited until the radio was pocketed again. "What's wrong now?"

"Someone got into the backup storage room and stuck a device into the hardware. Wiped out the offline backups."

"How could anyone do that?"

"They can't figure it out. Penn says there's no way it was this commander. He had her with him the entire time. He checked the compartment out before she went in."

"And it's all gone?"

The old man whistled, then snapped his fingers. "Gone. Now we got no data, and we got nothing on who did this spy shit or how. And he said there's no monitoring devices. There's no way to know who went in there."

But someone had. "No way to tell when it happened?"

"No data, no way to know when it happened."

"What about this device?"

"I told him to bring it to me. But he pointed something out." Chung glanced toward the engineering section. "Every place we look, all the problems we see—there's one name comes up."

"The engineer?"

"Yeah. Every fucking time."

"And the captain."

"He's a little too dead to be fucking around with us."

"Maybe it was stuff he did before he died."

"Could be, yeah. You know what else it could be?"

"Sure. This Parkinson guy is a spy."

19

PENN WAS SILHOUETTED IN THE LIGHT FROM THE PASSAGEWAY OUTSIDE THE offline storage cabin. He leaned against the open hatch, preventing it from closing while he talked on a small radio. As far as Benson could tell, his attention was mostly focused on the passageway, but she was sure he could see her in his peripheral vision.

What could she do even if he couldn't see her? He was talking to the old man, passing along the bad news about the data wipe.

And what had caused that wipe? In the dim light of the offline storage compartment, the device she rolled around in her hand just didn't seem... enough. It was still warm, and it smelled like the heat had taken a toll on its internals. Obviously, it had been enough for the task, but it looked so compact. There couldn't be a nanometer of wasted space or a single line of unnecessary code stored in its components.

Purpose-built. Something very, very targeted.

Which meant someone had created it specifically to take out an offline storage system. And that meant someone had intended to do exactly that.

Sabotage.

Again.

She tried to imagine how someone could have pulled it off—who, when, and why.

The passageway wasn't monitored. All it did was connect to the gym, and anyone could have been to the gym before they encountered the *Rakshasa*. There was no way to tell when the device had been put into place, either, because the records were gone and that wouldn't trigger an alarm.

Or would it?

It *should* have. She thought about telling Penn that but left it alone. There was already trouble, and pointing out that the saboteur had known enough to disable alarming wouldn't improve that.

She clasped the device tight against her palm. Whoever had built the device had probably installed alarm silencing into it.

Penn mentioned Parkinson on the radio.

Who else could have done something so sophisticated? The little man knew the ship better than anyone, even Martinez. And as the senior engineer, Parkinson had access to *everything*.

Had he been recruited by Martinez? Maybe all along they'd been working—

Her communicator buzzed, causing her to almost squeal. She pulled it out and stepped behind the wall of cabinets just enough to see who it was.

Halliwell? He'd sent a text message: *Still on the* Rakshasa. *We've got an opportunity here, a chance to kill a couple and get some guns.*

It sounded like the infirmary plan all over again. He'd nearly died then. She couldn't lose more of her people, especially not him.

She replied: *Maybe they'll let us live. Dev keeps pushing for it.*

Seconds stretched on and on. Penn was still talking with Chung.

Finally, Halliwell replied: *You really want to gamble on that?*

She exhaled, then replied: *What do you have in mind?*

More time dragged by, then his reply came: *Lure them in to check the resealed compartment, then evacuate the air in an isolated section through an override. Use the plate bolt gun on another of them.*

The gun was powerful enough to send a bolt through hull armor. It would punch through even the armor the Marines wore, and the privateers didn't have anything to match that.

But the idea had a lot of potential to go wrong. Horribly wrong. How would they isolate the privateer? How would they get him to take his helmet off? And it wasn't necessary if Rai convinced Chung...

You really want to gamble on that?

Halliwell was right. She couldn't gamble everyone's life away on Rai. What he was doing could all be a big con, a way to get her to...

What would she do to save her crew's life? Anything. And he knew it.

The privateers were cold-blooded murderers. All of them. Even Rai.

Penn signed off on his radio chat with Chung.

There was no other choice. Benson texted: *Make it count.*

"Hey?" Penn's boot squeaked on the deck.

Halliwell replied again: *Distraction on my signal.*

Distraction? *Wonderful.*

Penn's shadow drew closer. "You ready to go? Quentin—Mr. Chung—wants to talk with you."

"Yeah. I was just looking at the device again." She popped around the cabinet. "The way it was placed...I bet that was just the right cabinet."

He hooked his thumbs around his hips. "Like they really knew what they were doing."

"I know." She bowed her head. Was she selling Parkinson out?

As they headed back to the stairs, she thought more about that. Who did she have on her end once this plan happened? It was just her and Parkinson. And Dietrich. The doctor should be detoxed by now, but would he have the nerve once he was sober? Would Parkinson have the nerve ever? If he was capable of planting the device, then he had some spine.

Could he have been a spy all along?

At the stairs, Penn squinted at her. "You okay?"

"I-I'm just worried. All these things I had no idea about."

"And you were second-in-command. Yeah. I guess that would piss me off."

She smiled. "We go into danger to save lives. But spying...?" She shrugged.

But the realization sank in for Benson as they descended. *We're search and rescue.* She hadn't said "the *Pandora.*" She hadn't said "the others."

She'd said "we."

From the moment Martinez had died, she had started to assume command. The crew was becoming hers, the mission and the way she saw all the political connections—it really shifted things in a painful way. It wasn't just Halliwell she had to worry about but Parkinson and Dietrich. Everyone was her responsibility, even if they were cantankerous troglodytes.

Penn stopped at the landing and looked up. "You worried about something?"

"Hm? Oh. Yes. I'm sorry." She sped up. "Sergeant Halliwell, actually."

"The big Marine?"

"Yes. He lost a lot of blood. Now he's over on your ship putting himself at risk."

The young man's jaw set firmly. "He looks like a tough guy. He'll be fine."

"I guess so. It's just...he can push himself too hard. He worries about Corporal Grier."

"The—uh—big Marine gal?"

Not pretty or petite, I guess. "He's like her big brother. He'd do anything to keep her safe."

"Marines, right? That's how they operate."

"That's part of it. But those two have a lot of history."

Penn glanced down the stairs. "So did some of Chung's people."

How could she tell the young man this was different? How could she point out that being a murdering pirate might give you history, but it didn't give you the sort of connection of someone who had seen friendly artillery rounds pulverize hundreds of comrades? Could a civilian—a criminal—even understand how surviving one disaster after another drew two people together?

And Halliwell didn't even realize that Grier saw him as more than a squad leader. They owed each other their lives, but Halliwell only knew that the two of them were survivors.

And I gave him the go-ahead to risk his life again.

But risking his life—saving lives—was what energized Halliwell. It gave him purpose, and she had to accept that.

She also had to come up with a distraction. What could that be? Grabbing a weapon? Slapping someone? A fight with Parkinson? There was only so much she could do without tools.

Their boots clanged loudly on the cargo hold deck. It sounded dead, empty, devoid of life. She shivered when they crossed the dark blood trail, all that remained of Corporal Lopez. His death had come so quickly, had been so unexpected, that she hadn't had time to digest it. It was going to hurt when she did have time to think about it, though. He'd been a kid, barely out of training. The first loss under her command.

Rai was waiting for them outside the engineering bay, impossibly cool, his dark eyes tracking her the whole way.

Was that jealousy she saw in his look? Possessiveness?

Or was it all her desperate imagination? It had to be.

He stayed outside the compartment with Penn. It felt like their eyes were on her when she came to a stop a meter shy of Parkinson's station. Chung stood a couple steps beyond the station. His eyes were on the engineer.

The little man was hunched at the control console for his drones, VR goggles covering his eyes and headphones covering his ears. He was totally absorbed in whatever he was doing. There was just enough of his display visible that she could see part of what he must have been seeing through the VR goggles. The bigger of the two drones—Roddy?—pressed a patch plate into place on the hull and held it while the smaller drone grasped one end of the plate with a pincer-like protrusion, then ran a bolt gun along the plate edge.

Parkinson was nearly done patching the hull already.

Chung nodded toward the engineer. "Your chief here really is skilled."

"He is. I'm sure he's told you about his awards and decorations."

That put a twinkle in the old man's eyes. "He did. But to see him do it so quick."

"It can be very impressive." She straightened and tried to look proud, even as she wondered what Parkinson's real motive was in all that was going on. "When Chief finishes, I'm assuming you'll follow the usual procedure for testing systems integrity." Did they know what that was?

The old man's eyes darted to the hatchway. "Yeah. The usual."

He didn't know. Not any specific procedure. "Well, if you're going to pressurize that compartment, you'll want someone in there. Chief's probably your best bet to give it a thorough checkout."

"Pressurization check, huh?"

"We like to rely on instruments mostly, but the real test is how it *feels*." Parkinson would protest the idea if he weren't closed off from the outside world. Instruments were the only way to know if a repair had worked.

"And your engineer knows that feel."

"One of his many skills."

The old man scratched his chin. "Many skills. Didn't you tell Eli this little fuck was the only person who could possibly be behind all these shenanigans?"

"Well, that I know of. But unless you have someone in your crew who knows your ship systems well enough to get life support running in the compartment adjacent to the reactor...?"

Chung grunted.

"All right." Benson repeated a mantra in her head: *Stay calm, stay calm, stay calm.* "If not, then Chief Parkinson should run the test."

"Y'know, I've got a better idea."

"Oh, good."

"I'm thinking maybe Gil and Vic can do this."

A hand shot up to her cheek. It was still tender. "Are those two your...engineers?"

"Good enough."

"Well, you need someone capable."

The old man winked at the hatchway. "I got just the guy. Dev, suit up. Give this pressurization test a go, huh? Keep an eye on things."

Rai? *Stay calm, stay calm, stay calm.* "He's your engineer?"

"Sure. You're the engineer with Stef dead, right?"

Rai hadn't moved from where he'd been waiting for her earlier. "I know the systems well enough."

Chung guffawed. "Just like that."

After a few seconds, Rai bowed slightly. "I'll head across."

Had that been a question in his eyes? Did he suspect? Could she let her people kill the only pirate who'd been vaguely human? *Stay calm, stay calm, stay calm.*

Chung put his hands on the back of Parkinson's chair. "Minutes away from completion. They get the reactor online, we could be out of here in an hour."

Her lips felt so dry. It was suddenly hard to breathe. Parkinson's scent was all over everything in the compartment, present even through Chung's body odor. His fingerprints were on every anomaly that had happened since their arrival—since the drift! She'd screwed up and used that knowledge to force Chung to put someone from his own team at risk.

But not Rai!

What about Martinez? Could he still be alive? Could he be hiding somewhere on the *Rakshasa*? Wouldn't someone have noticed if he were still live or if he'd moved?

Stay calm, stay calm, stay calm.

But how could she stay calm? Chung had seen right through her plan. He was trying to turn her against her crew. She could see it in the malignant twinkle in the old man's eyes. There was a challenge there: *You got some sort of scheme, you wouldn't pull it against devilishly handsome Dev Rai.*

Would you?

She would have to answer that. Soon.

20

EVERYTHING FELT *OFF* TO RAI. HIS ENVIRONMENT SUIT FELT TWO SIZES TOO small. The air in the cargo hold tasted stale. His breathing sounded louder than the air filtration system. Shadows seemed larger and deeper in the weakening light around the airlock.

Something had happened. Chung had decided to send someone over to the *Rakshasa*.

Decided to send me.

Rai undid the holster from his hip and let out the belt, then stretched it over the outside of his environment suit. He did the same with his knife.

It was a plot. Or at least that's what Rai had thought. There had been some sort of scheme, some sort of manipulation at work in the way Benson had pitched her idea. Have someone test a compartment once it was pressurized to get a feel for it. That was obviously a signal, a test.

He zipped the suit closed, then pressed the seal over the zipper.

She had to have been warning him. A signal for him to steer clear of the scheme. Or maybe a chance for him to show he was willing to turn against Chung.

Something. It had been something, Rai was sure of that.

The airlock sealed behind him, then sucked the atmosphere out. It should've left him feeling...almost like there was nothing around him, but instead it felt like an immense pressure was building.

Fighting with Chung had broken the balance. Rai hadn't even realized the balance was there. He'd assumed he was in control all along. Any time he wanted, he could just eliminate the old bastard and take over the operation.

But the operation was more than being smarter than the others. Without subordinates to pull off the big jobs, there was no mission.

The *Pandora*'s outer hatch opened, and Rai stepped clear of the airlock and into space.

No gravity, nothing holding him down, just the umbilical framework that stretched between the two ships.

In a sense, it was the freedom he'd wanted since childhood, since finding out about his father's lies and the obligations behind the long-hidden truth. It was an obligation of generations, and soon Rai would have to find someone to give him children and to raise them within the same structure he'd known.

The Benson woman. He could easily see her in that role. She was strong and smart and loyal. Training her to be subservient would be a lifetime endeavor all its own.

A devilish grin played across his lips; it was something he would relish.

Keep an eye on things.

The old man was going to radio his intent. That had to be what was going on.

Rai pulled himself along the cable that ran below the top of the of diamond-shaped framework. There was no need to recall the harness seat at the other side. It was just him, no tools, nothing gangly or awkward.

Halfway across, there was still no radio call.

That sly smile Chung had made when asked if he just planned to kill all the hired help off—maybe Rai was just part of the hired help now.

Or he'd always been part.

Except the connection he'd felt for years, it had almost been familial, like an uncle.

Chung wasn't *that* good at deception. That was Rai's gift. His training.

Whatever was going on with the old man was about his son's death. And Wong. And Vic.

The kids had latched on to the big idiot instead of learning the right way.

This was the perfect opportunity to fix things. Get rid of Vic, see how Hurley reacts, and get rid of him if he looks like trouble.

Wong...

The kid had to go, too. He was a hindrance, a danger to every plan—

The cable seemed to wobble in Rai's hands. He kept one hand on the cable and braked his inertia with a grip on the framework. When he tested the cable, it was taut.

He licked his lips and chuckled.

Nerves. All the stupid drama was eating at him.

What happened, Chung? Loyalty used to go both ways. I backed you, you backed me.

Not anymore.

Rai hurried across, eye jumping from cable to framework. It wasn't as if the cable would give and he'd go spinning off into space. The ribs were spaced close enough that something would catch. Or he could use his oxygen tank to maneuver.

But the sense was there, and it wasn't going away: Something was wrong.

In the *Rakshasa* airlock, Rai let his body adjust to the ship's negligible gravity. He needed to treat it the same as zero-g, because that's what it was for all intents and purposes.

The inner airlock hatch had been cranked closed. He cranked it open and found himself staring into the familiar cargo hold, now lit by several work lamps attached to cargo mount points. But the hold didn't *seem* familiar; it felt strange. He'd only been away a few hours, but something about the *Pandora* was inviting, and something about the *Rakshasa* was wrong. Maybe it was the way the Kedraalian crew seemed to bond together despite all their warts and differences. Or maybe it was the way Benson commanded—not as some bloodthirsty bully who demanded everything and gave nothing but as someone keeping everyone on-target, someone who cared.

Rai's radiation counter held steady in the amber. They really must have succeeded with the shielding after all.

That was promising.

He gave the cargo hold one last look—empty except for the crates of gear brought across by the search-and-rescue team. He shivered at something he couldn't quite put a finger on, then headed to the closed hatch that would lead to the main passageway beyond.

Closed. They were preparing for life support.

He cranked the hatch open. The passageway made an "L," cutting right one way and continuing ahead before cutting left to the engineering compartment aft. Radiation held steady. He skipped down the straight passageway until he could see the engineering compartment hatch. Silvery light escaped. The hatch itself had been warped by the blast but must have been replaced or repaired.

After taking a few steps to stern, he stopped.

It finally hit him what it was that had been bugging him: Martinez. He was the other possibility behind all the strange goings-on besides that chickenshit engineer Parkinson. Sure, it wasn't like Gabriel to miss out on an opportunity to kill someone, but no one else had actually inspected the corpse. People survived the craziest things.

Rai pulled out a light and reversed course, then took the other part of the "L," slowing as he approached the infirmary. It felt like he was putting a "shoot me" sign up—that was the irrational part of his mind talking.

Still, he pulled his blaster.

The light skimmed along the cabin interior: empty. Getting rid of the other corpses he could recall. The captain's corpse...they'd left that in the infirmary, he was sure.

Nerves. You can't let nerves get to you.

He radioed Gabriel, who took seconds to accept the connection.

"Hey, hey! Big, bad Dev. How's it going?"

Rai squeezed his eyelids shut. "Where'd you put the corpse of the guy you lasered?"

"The captain? He's floating around in the infirmary. I thought that'd be nice. Can you hear the sound he'll make when we turn gravity back on? *Thump!* Nice!"

Nice would be a hole through the big idiot's head. "He's not here."

"So? Someone moved him. We moved a lot of things around. Unless you believe in space ghosts? Ho-ho! Woooo!"

It was so easy imagining the pistol pressed against the man's head. "Did someone push him out into space?"

"Nope. Must be a space ghost!"

Rai killed the connection and checked his pistol: charged.

Blasters had a little recoil. He needed to remember that, even if they were inside a ship, it could present problems. Mainly, it could mean having to maneuver around for a second shot. That could be the difference between life or—he almost said *space ghosts*.

He so wanted to shoot Gabriel.

Retreating back down the passageway to the corner of the "L" seemed to take forever. Rai's light couldn't drive away anywhere near enough of the darkness. It wasn't that his mind was playing tricks on him or anything, telling him a body was waiting just around the corner, but...

His back bumped against a bulkhead: The passageway had ended.

He blew out a relieved breath, turned the light off, and put it away.

Gabriel connected over the radio. "Hey, you coming in here or what? We're ready to test this. Reactor's coming online already."

"Gimme a minute."

Reactor coming online. They were moving along quickly. Maybe they could get the *Rakshasa* out of the area before more Kedraalian ships showed up after all.

Rai started to head aft, then stopped, his thoughts tumbling to what had looked different in the cargo hold. He cranked the hatch open again and dog-paddled along the deck to the crates Benson's crew had brought over. Several of the containers were open. Foam outlines indicated the absence of tools that had been removed for repair work: the work lamps lighting the cargo hold and passageways, the crank tool used to open the hatches, sealant tubes, testing tools.

And bolt guns. There were two empty shadows.

He connected to Gabriel again. "Vic—"

"Ho-ho! Somebody need help back there?"

"Fuck you."

The big clown laughed. "Where are you?"

"Cargo hold. Hey, how many bolt guns did you guys use to work on the hull?"

"One. Why?"

"Nothing. You got your eye on everyone in there?"

"Yeah. They're all beat down." He chuckled.

"I'm on my way."

Rai put his pistol away and searched the nearby area, but there was no sign of the missing bolt gun. He sealed the hatch behind him, then kicked along the passageway. His pace seemed a little quicker than normal as he headed aft, but that was okay. This was important.

The engineering bay hatch had indeed been repaired. Some of the soot had been scraped away, and the hatch itself had been straightened. Everything looked far better than it should have.

Professionals.

Gabriel stood in the center of the big open bay beyond the hatch. Work lights painted everything a silvery white, distorting shadows. Ladders ran up the bulkheads aft, port, and starboard, to catwalks and structural beams that created a wide lattice. There were open hatches port and starboard, and between the two to Rai's right, the Kedraalian repair team members were clumped together maybe eight meters away. Hurley and Wong bracketed the *Pandora* crew, pistols drawn.

Rai counted again—the big Marine with the bolt gun, the muscular Marine woman, the fat doctor, the skinny tech…where was the pretty nurse?

He turned back to Gabriel. The big oaf had the nurse behind him; she struggled to get out of his beefy hands.

One bolt gun; there was no sign of the other.

Rai stepped into the big space. He felt far too exposed with Gabriel and Wong. Hurley wasn't a concern; he'd been solid for years and knew not to fall for Gabriel's shit. "Vic, quit fucking around."

The big man turned around. "Hey, fuck you. I'm just setting up a date. Maybe take her home to mom."

"Your mother's dead."

"She can't complain then, can she? Ha-ha!"

Hurley's voice creaked over the radio. "What the fuck? Are we getting out of here or what?" His big eyes bugged out as he waved his pistol at the doctor and technician. "Shut it, you two."

The voices of Benson's people leaked through Hurley's connection. They were complaining about the way Gabriel was treating Stiles. The pretty nurse.

Something about the fat doctor's voice...

Rai pushed off and floated toward Hurley. "What's got the doctor all worked up?"

"How the fuck should I know? Maybe it's dinnertime. She's bitching about—"

"Yeah, I heard. Connect me in with them."

"Sure. Just remember, you asked for it."

And like that, their voices were there. The big woman's shouts had a definite quaver.

Rai waved as he came closer. "Hey, Doc, you got something you want to tell us?"

"That monster—" The doctor pointed at Gabriel.

But it was a distraction. Rai spotted it almost too late.

The big Marine pushed off from the bulkhead, launching himself at Hurley, bolt gun coming up.

Rai drew his pistol, too fast, panicking, forgetting all he knew about maneuvering in zero-g.

The Marine floated gracefully, and Hurley just seemed to stare. "What the—?"

Wong took a shot, missing badly and getting knocked back and off balance.

The female Marine went after him. She knew her shit, kicking off with even more grace and power than her partner.

Dangerous. Fucking dangerous Marines. This was their element!

Rai finally had his pistol out. He aimed, positioning himself so that his back would bounce off the deck.

The big bolt gun approached Hurley's face mask. The damage that thing could do—

Rai fired. He'd miscalculated, but he hit the Marine in the leg, sending him spinning and drawing a hiss from the big guy.

Wong howled. The female Marine was on him, twisting him around, locking her legs around his narrow chest. If she'd had a knife, Wong's environment suit would already have been compromised.

"Fuck!" Gabriel. He was trying to get a clean shot on the woman but couldn't.

That was how they trained. And she didn't even have the gear she normally would.

A shadow drifted down from the ceiling.

Another person in a Kedraalian environment suit.

The fucking captain! His helmet was patched but gore- and vomit-spattered.

Rai tried to adjust to get a shot but overcompensated and twisted away.

Martinez dropped straight down onto Hurley, who was wasting his time trying to get a bead on the wounded Marine.

Rai took a shot and missed. "Hurley!"

The lanky man looked up...

Just as the bolt gun reached the face of his helmet.

The bolt shot out, sending Martinez back up and away in a fluid spin while the bolt pinned Hurley's head to the bulkhead. Blood misted out on the leaking atmosphere.

Rai fired at Martinez again and missed.

The technician and doctor hunched low—they weren't threats.

Blasters were supposed to be an advantage, but not if you couldn't handle yourself in the non-existent gravity. A laser would have been better, but they had so many limitations.

Martinez hooked an arm around one of the beams, reset the bolt gun, then dove toward Gabriel.

Wong screamed. "She's going for my gun! Help!"

The female Marine had the kid locked in a hold he wasn't about to escape. Their intertwined bodies were floating just above the deck.

It wasn't really much of a choice between helping Gabriel or helping Wong.

Rai got a hand on the deck and started skimming along it, then launched himself at the woman.

Gabriel's curses flooded the channel. The big man wasn't ready to face a guy who was in his element.

And that bolt gun...fuck!

Rai hit the Marine-Wong bundle and grabbed whatever he could. Initially, all that mattered was latching on. And he had a handful of the Marine, he was sure of it—firm but feminine. Not like Wong's scrawny frame.

Almost immediately, the woman shifted her grip, keeping her legs wrapped around Wong and twisting her torso so that she could get an arm wrapped around Rai's throat.

He twisted before she managed a good lock around him, but her powerful hands kept probing and found his left wrist.

But his right wrist was free, and if she had him, he had her.

She began applying pressure on his arm, pressing up with one hand while the other had his wrist locked. In a different situation, she'd have his elbow dislocated in no time, but locked up with Wong and in environment suits...it was amazing she could inflict so much pain so quickly.

Rai brought his pistol around to where she could see it. "That's enough."

She froze.

"Let go."

She did.

Rai wrapped an arm around her throat and brought her around like a shield while he searched for the big man. "Don't move, please."

She made an excellent brace.

Gabriel was pressed against a bulkhead. Martinez had the bolt gun aimed at the bigger man's gut. There was an awkwardness to the captain's movement, as if the energy he'd expended had been too much.

The man shouldn't even have been alive.

"Fuck! Dev, kill him!" Gabriel's voice was shrill, full of panic.

Letting the captain kill the big oaf would have been a form of cosmic justice, something that appealed to Rai.

But he had a mission and needed Gabriel for a little while longer.

Rai aimed. And put a blast through the captain's head.

21

Rai had seen some pretty glum people in his lifetime, but the crew of the *Pandora* pretty much topped what he could remember. Twice, they'd come close to pulling off an escape. Now they were awaiting the inevitable execution. He was cooking in his environment suit, but after what had nearly happened on the *Rakshasa*, he didn't feel safe taking the suit off. If the female Marine had gotten hold of Wong's gun or the captain had managed to kill Gabriel...

Benson was at the front of her crew, arms pinned to her side. She'd refused to drop to her knees and lock her hands behind her head. Instead, she glared at Chung, defiant.

The old man had positioned Penn behind Benson's people, who had followed their captain's lead and refused to go to their knees. Even the big Marine was up, leaning weakly against his fellow Marine.

And all of that was eating at Chung, whose breathing was a booming rasp.

Gabriel was just behind his boss, fingers rubbing the scabs covering the scratches Benson's nails had left on his cheek. "Let me do it now, Quentin."

"Not yet." The old man rubbed his chin.

"They killed Gil."

Chung's head came up, and he glared at the big brute. "That's funny. Way I heard it, the dead captain came back to life and killed Gil. Damn near killed you, too. You wanna tell me how the fuck a dead man does that?"

"He should've been dead."

"Well, he wasn't."

"I burned away half his head."

"Yeah? Not the part he needed, apparently."

Gabriel's shoulders slumped. "Wasn't my fault."

"The fuck it wasn't." Chung twisted around and glared at Rai. "Stay here."

"Sure." Gabriel went back to rubbing his cheek.

Chung stomped over to where Rai stood. "You make sure the guy was dead this time?"

"I put a hole in the part of his head he *was* using. The vacuum did the rest."

"Sounds like Vic talking."

"He's dead, Quentin."

"How the fuck can you know?"

"I know dead."

"So's Vic."

"Apparently not. Look, the guy probably turned off his resuscitation when he got wounded. Pop some stimulants and painkillers and hide out, you can go a couple days with your jaw cooked away like that. But with your brains blown out, it's over."

"Yeah, yeah."

"The ship's ready. Everything checks out—power, integrity, radiation levels are safe. We load up some food and transfer some water, we can go."

The old man's craggy face bunched up. "We ain't done here yet."

"Why? We got the guy who was behind all the spy crap. We got our prize in cold storage again. All we gotta do is collect our money now."

Chung stared at the airlock. "You thinkin' this Martinez guy was the saboteur all along?"

"Who else could it be?"

"Yeah." The old man chuckled. "Not the fucking engineer."

"He's a chickenshit, just like you said."

"Good with those drones, though."

"He is." Rai glanced back at the little man, who cowered behind the doctors. "Maybe he'd take a job with you if you offered him something."

Chung laughed, wet and raspy. "Wouldn't make it a week."

Rai smiled. "He wouldn't."

"What if this Martinez managed to transmit any data? He was on the ship alone for how long?"

"Not too long. And with all the radiation leaking—"

"He was dying. He wouldn't have cared about radiation."

"Fine. Our systems didn't have any power."

"There was still some battery power. He could've gotten into the systems. He knew ships."

"He didn't."

"But if he *did*, we're fucked. Just sending out our transponder information with the navigation logs—"

"He didn't send anything out. Quentin, we're okay."

"Someone puts us in the area of the Carone kidnapping and the DMZ, that'd be enough. Even the Azoren could put together we were double-crossing them."

"Now you're turning paranoid."

"Yeah, could be." Chung laughed nervously. "Fucking lost half my team."

"We've got enough to get back to Gulmar space. We'll be fine."

"I was thinking, maybe we make a run for Moskav space, hide out for a while. There are planets there the Moskav don't bother with."

"Moskav space? You crazy?"

The old man's eyes darted around. "Cautious, that's all. Take all the food and water, take whatever the fuck they got in those crates, use it for trade. Spend a year or two just living, staying out of sight."

Rai sighed. The old man was rattled. He'd been right about assuming there was an ambush planned by Benson's team, but he'd completely misjudged his own team. And he'd fallen for the pretty commander's distraction—an argument he should have seen through.

Rattled, definitely.

Running into Moskav space wasn't going to solve anything. In fact, it would guarantee an end to their Azoren charter.

But there was no protesting it. Not yet.

Chung turned at the sound of his nephew's scraping boots. The kid moved stiffly and there was a sober look in his eyes. It was different thinking maybe you'd come close to being drilled in a shootout and *knowing* you'd come close to having your blaster pried from your hands. The scrawny kid was even more rattled than his uncle.

The old man sneered. "You about ready to start loading?"

Wong nodded and bowed his head. "What should we load up?"

"You make sure Carone was sealed up in cold storage okay?"

"Yeah. She had vitals before we put her in, then we juiced her up and slid her in the primary slab."

"Good." The old man swept a hand to indicate the crates in the cargo hold. "Then take all of it."

The spoiled kid's eyes widened. "All of it? That's too—"

"Too much, yeah." Chung rolled his eyes at Rai. "Get Penn to help."

"O-okay, Uncle Quentin."

"Start with that caged-in area to the fore."

That left only Gabriel guarding Benson's crew. Malevolence twisted the big oaf's face when he turned around to watch Wong and Penn enter the maze of crates.

Rai's gut twisted. He knew the crazy look. The big man was looking for an excuse for violence. And that was his doorway to...bad things. The way Benson and her crew looked—broken but defiant—was just a tease. They'd patched up the big Marine, which had just made things worse. The female Marine body-shielding her sergeant only antagonized Gabriel more. He had his need to terrorize, and a wounded enemy was ideal.

"Hey." Rai tapped the old man's elbow. "Let's just grab the best shit and go."

Chung twisted up his face. "Nah. We want it all."

"They're gonna need something to survive on."

"No they don't. I made sure this thing's gonna blow when we're done."

There. The old bastard had said it. He'd set charges. They were dead, whether or not he pushed them out the airlock. "All right, fine. But tell Vic that's where it stops—killing them. I'll buy him some whores when we get back. Leave the women alone."

Gabriel growled something at the *Pandora* crew, then hurried over to Chung's side. "Hey-ho, after what happened, I need something to relax." He breathed in deep, like a chef might while taking in a master dish. "Y'know? Before we go. He-he!"

The faintest hint of disgust crossed Chung's face. "Sure. Before you do that, we need to send a message. Separate the ladies."

"All of them?" The big guy's lips twisted into a pout.

"Hey, do what I fucking said. You'll get what you want."

A chill ran down Rai's back. He felt powerless. The opportunity was there. Shoot the ogre in the back, put a round into the old bastard, hunt down Wong and give Penn a chance to join up.

But that left the problem of not having contacts to put together a team to sell Carone. That money meant everything.

"You going soft on me, Dev?" Chung was giving the sort of sideways squint he gave when he was judging merchandise.

Rai looked away. "It's all pointless. You're going to kill them. Do it."

"I told them—don't fuck with me, things will be okay. They still did it."

"You don't have to sell me, y'know. I know what you planned for them."

Chung's boots scraped on the deck. "Good. Then this ain't a surprise."

It became harder to breathe as the old man marched over to his pet monster, and Rai found his eyes drawn against his will to where the two stood, maybe a meter away from Benson and her people. It was on their faces, too, the realization that this was it, the end. The pretty nurse just slipped into something like shock, staring into the distance like she had the previous time.

Gabriel pulled the pretty nurse aside. "You ladies, form up around her."

At first, Benson didn't move, then the big man pressed his blaster against her cheek. "Or I could just shoot you right here."

The fat doctor—Gaines—wrapped her arms around Benson. "There's no need for more violence. We've seen so much death, so much. Please now, let's set aside the gun and seek peace and healing."

Benson patted the other woman's hand, and the two joined Stiles.

"Hey!" Gabriel pointed his blaster at the muscular female Marine. "Move!"

"Fuck you." Muscles stood out on the woman's neck and along her jaw.

"Sure. You're not so bad." He put the pistol against her cheek. "But you gotta do what I said, or I'll fuck the hole in your head."

"I'm not leaving him."

The big Marine squeezed the woman's shoulder. "We stay together."

Chung snapped his fingers. "Leave her."

Gabriel twisted around. "But you said—"

"Leave her. I got what I want."

Rai licked his lips. What did that mean? Was Chung going to shoot the Marines first?

Benson's eyes slid from her people to Chung, then to Rai, before flying back to Chung. "Quentin, you and your crew could walk away. Right now. Take whatever you need and go. There won't be any repercussions."

Chung scratched the material stretched over his gut. "Yeah?"

"You suffered casualties. We suffered casualties. It's just the terrible part of war."

Gaines nodded vigorously. "It's true. All this violence, the killing, it never should have happened. No more killing, please. Let me tend to your wounded and you can go."

Chung bowed his head and rubbed his chin. It was a really convincing play at thinking about the proposal. "You're right."

The fat woman reached a hand out toward him. "Bless you. You understand."

"I do. War's terrible."

"It leaves scars not just on the flesh but the soul. And it makes us less than human. But there's always redemption."

"Redemption sounds good." The old man grunted.

Gabriel cocked his head. There was confusion in his dull eyes. He was never any good at following the old man's cons.

Chung nodded toward Gaines. "Let's find some redemption, Vic."

"What?" The brute's brow twisted.

"Shoot the fucking bitch."

Gaines gasped, but she didn't seem surprised as the pistol came up. "Your soul—"

Gabriel cackled. "Don't need one of those."

His pistol whined, and the doctor staggered back. Her eyes rolled up, as if she might be trying to make sense of the hole between them.

Then she shivered, and her body hit the deck.

Chung shook himself. "The ladies are all yours."

"Ho-ha!" Gabriel threw the pretty little nurse over one shoulder, then grabbed Benson around the waist. "Keep your claws in, or I'll brain you."

The female Marine pushed the big Marine back and spread her legs about shoulder width, readying for an attack.

Gabriel guffawed. "You think—ho-no-no—that—" He shook his head. "You're okay, sure, but I got what I want."

He headed toward the maze, tugging Benson along despite her trying to drag against his grip. She turned toward Rai, and the challenge was there in her eyes: *Are you going to let this happen?*

The question slammed around in his head. There was no doubt the big Marine would have died fighting Gabriel for the woman based on the tension in his wounded body. And that answered Rai's question about just what sort of relationship existed between the commander and her Marine sergeant.

But her question had been to Rai. She hadn't looked back at the wounded man.

And the question was in Chung's eyes, too. The whole thing was another of the old bastard's loyalty tests. Worse, Chung was too cagey to read. There was always the small chance that he was on to all the other factors influencing Rai's actions, no matter how unlikely that was.

One shot. A quick pull from the holster. A blast that would perforate the old man's gut and leave him in so much pain he could only scream until he died.

Rai would be committed. His life would take an entirely new direction.

The lifelong vow would be broken or at least put at risk.

All he had to do was commit. Accept that he could find more happiness in life with Benson than he'd ever known and commit.

He relaxed, letting his hand drop slowly.

And the old man saw it. The cagey old bastard saw it all developing.

"Hey!" It was Wong. The voice bounced around inside the dim maze. "Hey, check this out! Uncle Quentin!"

Chung cocked his head: *Do we have a truce?*

Rai strode toward the maze.

The old man fell in, matching each step. He snickered. "Being the fastest guy around's always going to be your solution?"

"It's a good one."

"Yeah." Chung's eyes drifted up to the stairs, where Gabriel wrestled with Benson. "Hey! Hold off. We got something down here."

The towering thug wrapped a beefy arm around the commander and lifted her off the floor. "Fuck. I'm all worked up!"

"Tough. Put them back."

Put them back. Like they were just more merchandise.

Wong was in the far forward port-side corner, inside the cage. He had a couple of the containers open and was smiling from ear to ear. Penn peered into one of the crates in the shadows, frowning.

Chung slowed as they neared the corner. "What's all the shouting about?"

"Some crazy stuff. You gotta see."

The old man's pace picked back up. "Better be good crazy stuff. You just pissed Vic off."

Wong's eyes jumped to the dark maze. "Is he coming here?"

"Soon."

Rai peeked over the old man's shoulder as he dug into the crate that had been unstrapped and set on the deck. Instead of foam cutouts, a hard frame network held the contents in place: carbines, grenades, devices that Rai couldn't quite figure out.

Wong smiled. "See?"

Penn scowled and backed away, fists on hips.

Rai twisted to look at the other man. "What?"

"Strange cargo." Penn shrugged. "For a search-and-rescue ship."

Chung stroked his chin. "They weren't search and rescue. Not all of them."

"It's assault gear. Who else could use it but those Marines?"

"Yeah." Chung straightened. "And why didn't they? Huh."

Rai tested the chain cage. "It was secured. Not for them."

"Yeah, maybe."

A quick look into another crate revealed armor that the Marines could have worn. Rai ran a finger over the black material. It was smooth and gave like a gel. "They had no idea about this."

"I get that." The old man grunted. "Looks like we're back to the problem of those other ships, huh?"

"And the accelerated timeline."

"Yeah." Chung slapped the side of one of the crates. "Okay, we'll load this first, then the food and water. But I got something else to do first."

He hooked a finger at Rai and headed back into the maze. "That just bought your pretty captain a few more minutes."

Rai swallowed. An interrogation would mean looking into her eyes.

And looking into those eyes was certain to destroy his control.

22

THE BIG THUG'S GRIP WAS AN IRON CLAMP ON BENSON'S FLESH. SHE fought for breath and thought her ribs would crack at any moment. Her flight suit was sturdy, meant to handle all sorts of wear and tear in her daily duties, but when she'd fought against Gabriel at the base of the stairs, he'd yanked her so hard that the material around the zipper had torn. Her skin was raw where the material had strained against her.

Now the privateer's voice boomed in her ears as he dragged her back to the rest of her crew. "This ain't over. Ho-ho-ho-no! You wait! I'll make up for lost time! You're gonna regret this!"

As if it were her fault his twisted reward had been canceled.

What was going on? Was this all just part of an elaborate torture? She'd caught something in the strange exchanges between Chung and Rai, some sort of test of wills.

And Rai hadn't acted to save her. Or had he? She'd been spared. For now.

Gabriel—Vic to his fellow thugs—set Stiles down like a precious porcelain doll. He wasn't so gentle with Benson, howling and driving a shoulder into her face.

She staggered back, nose aching, and someone caught her.

Dietrich. The last remnants of the alcohol was leaking out of him, mixing with his sweat. His eyes were still bloodshot, but it looked more like that was from crying. How close had he been to Gaines? She'd been like a mother to everyone, the peacemaker and bridge builder. How many times had she covered for him and no one even knew?

He seemed to spot the T-shirt exposed by Benson's torn flight suit. "You all right, Captain?"

"Yes. Thank you." It hit her again: She really was the captain.

My crew. My responsibility.

It was all so crazy, all so impossible.

That was a normal feeling, of course. Her training told her to step back and look at things logically, coolly.

How do you react after something tears apart your sense of self and competence?

Crazy. Dehumanized. Ashamed.

And that was what was rushing through her now: shame.

Shame when she noticed Halliwell's fragile stare.

Shame when Corporal Grier turned away, muscles standing out on her neck and clenched jaw.

Shame when Petty Officer Kohn's lips quivered at the sight of the almost catatonic Stiles.

Shame because they'd been on their way to a session of rape, then murder.

What could have been more wrong? Benson felt as if she'd betrayed Halliwell, and he probably felt as if he'd failed her. In her bones, it seemed as if she'd let the entire crew down.

I'm an absolute failure—powerless, incompetent.

But her training told her that wasn't true.

Believing that it was her fault...that was giving all the power to the privateers.

Benson was done giving *anything* to them.

She bunched her flight suit together where it had torn. It wouldn't hold, but it was an act of defiance that the big monster would see. There would be no easy surrender to him and his comrades. She and her crew had nearly won out twice. If a third opportunity came, they would finish the pirates.

Dietrich was crouched at Stiles's side. "It's as if she's gone into shock."

Benson glanced down. "She doesn't seem to handle this sort of stress well."

The young woman stared straight ahead, only occasionally blinking.

Dietrich ran experienced fingers along her throat, jaw, and cheeks. "Did he hit her?"

"No. It's as if she knew what was coming and just shut herself off."

"She showed exceptional calm in medical crises."

Gabriel snorted. "Yeah, well, women sometimes aren't ready for a crisis like me."

A knife. A jagged piece of glass. A rock. A heavy section of pipe. Benson would have been happy with any of them, with anything. She just wanted a chance to strike back at the animal. He was so big, so much stronger than any of them except maybe Halliwell.

Panic threatened to overwhelm her.

How do you kill someone so much stronger than you without a weapon?

Maybe she should have listened to her mother's recommendation upon learning that her daughter was going into the military.

"You're going into the military, Faith. A paid killer—that's what you've chosen to become."

The delivery had been dismissive and scornful. That was Sargota Zhanya's favorite method of communication, whether in an effort to dress down a fellow member of the Assembly or when telling her only child she'd made a bad choice.

"That outfit makes you look absolutely horrible, Faith. Or did you mean to dress like some common peasant? You're the child of a senior politician and that calls for some modicum of dignity. Do remember that."

"Did you seriously elect to take another semester of physics, Faith? We discussed this, don't you recall? Your rhetorical skills are barely comparable to a freshman's."

"I want to serve the Republic." Faith blushed at the memory. What could have been worse than reinforcing her mother's views than to flash some clunky, anemic rhetoric?

"Oh, do stop. Collecting recyclable waste serves a higher purpose than the

military. If you just want to fly around the galaxy in a dreadful ship, sign on with one of those disgusting merchant operations. You can get all the ridiculous hormonal energy out of your body at the same time. Most of the diseases you'll contract can be cured easily enough."

"I'm going to command a starship, Sargota, and I'm going to do it my way." Faith had offered that comeback with her head thrown back and her chest thrust out. She liked the way she towered over her mother. What better way to say this woman is her father's daughter?

"That seems like a pleasant fantasy, of course. You do realize that you'll be facing threats that require more than a sharp mind, which I still question you even have. There's no value being soft and feminine in this role. You'll need to become a murderous ape, just like the rest."

"I want to be a leader."

"Nonsense. Undergo the gene mods. Take the hormones. You'll see how ridiculous the idea is within four years and abandon this silly phase of your life."

That was her mother's solution, to become a man for a few years and get the nonsense out of a youthful, confused mind.

Without a doubt, the transformation would have helped in many ways. Bulked out, trained for more physical combat, she would have taken a different course in her career, maybe pursuing a career in the Marines. And she would have been able to stand up to someone like Gabriel. In fact, he wouldn't have had any interest in her.

But that wasn't Benson.

Her identity—her desire—was that of a woman. She would succeed or fail as who she was, and no callous monster was going to change that.

Anyway, the idea of undergoing physical transformation to achieve her goal was another "logical and practical" solution, the sort of thing Assemblywoman Sargota Zhanya would embrace. Realistically, it was probably meant to scare her daughter away from military service.

Benson didn't even want to think about how her relationship with Halliwell would have been affected.

The sad truth of the matter was that after millennia of human development, things still came down to the brute being able to win out. That wasn't something worth giving up her own identity over.

She needed something else to deal with this particular adversary.

Next time the choice is between upsetting someone and saving my crew, I'm making the right choice.

And if she survived this, she would need a gun. One that she could hide from anything but the best detectors. Something built to the body's contours. Usually, they were reserved for senior officers and special operatives, but she was going to demand one. Maybe even one of the ones that could be surgically implanted. All she would've needed was one shot, up close, right into the side of the big bastard's head, and all his strength wouldn't have meant a thing. She could kill him with her own hands while his brains were scrambled.

And she'd enjoy it. One less scumbag in the universe.

If she lived, she'd explain all of that to Halliwell. It wasn't his fault.

Chung exited the maze, smirking. Rai followed, head lowered and eyes averted—ashamed.

She'd been a fool to hope he would intervene. How could he? It would've been the end of his career, if pirates had such a thing.

But...there seemed to be something going on around that already. His fights with his boss, his...had Rai been flirting with her? Whatever. Unless it had all been a ruse, it seemed like he was done with the privateering life and ready for something new.

The old man slowed, then stopped. He had a strange look on his face. Scheming.

He was scheming, plotting.

That couldn't be good. His twisted thinking was behind everything that had gone wrong—Martinez's death, the execution of Private Lopez and Dr. Gaines, and Halliwell's injuries.

Chung considered Gaines's corpse. "Vic, toss that out the airlock."

That. As if the woman hadn't been a mother, a doctor—a *healer.* As if her years of service, of giving and caring and reassembling bodies and *saving lives* didn't matter. As if the man had any right whatsoever to talk about someone as gracious and loving as Eve Gaines!

The brute sneered at Benson, then grabbed the doctor's body by the ankles and dragged her over the deck, leaving another track of dark gore in his wake.

He enjoys that. *It's like a wild animal marking its territory.*

Once Gabriel was away from them, leaning against the bulkhead next to the airlock, Chung moved close to Benson. His eyes drifted to her torn flight suit, then he stretched onto his tiptoes so that they were almost at eye level. "You want to avoid what almost happened, maybe you should cooperate with me."

"Cooperate?" She swallowed. "Why would I do that?"

"Because there are worse things than what Vic was going to do to you."

Worse things.

It was so typical of a thug, a promise wrapped in a threat served up on a tray of deceit. The old man had no intention of protecting her from Gabriel.

Chung turned without another word and headed into the maze. Rai jerked his head at the old man's back; she needed to follow him.

To where? For what? Would Rai do anything to help her if Chung tried to...

Just give me your gun, dammit.

Dietrich looked at her with sober, concerned eyes and shook his head. "Don't."

"I have to." Benson lightly patted Stiles's shoulder. "Take care of them."

The path through the piled cargo crates felt so much darker and tighter than before. When Gabriel had brought her back through, it had almost been like being freed from prison. Now? What story had she heard as a kid? Something about a hero entering a labyrinth with thread? Some sort of monster had been deep inside, hiding within the twists and turns, and the greatest threat wasn't the monster but getting lost. That was how the monster ended up killing its victims.

She wasn't about to get lost. Her crew—her people, her *family*—would be her thread. They would guide her back from whatever this was, and she would do everything in her power to save them.

Would it be enough, though?

It had to be.

23

Two of Chung's people stood in the restricted storage area—Penn and Wong, Benson realized. They had several crates open and looked excited. Well, Wong looked excited. Penn looked more annoyed than anything else. It was possible that was just a trick of the light in that area. It was darker there than other parts of the lower deck. No one was supposed to spend any time inside the restricted space, after all. It even managed to have a fresher scent to it, probably the result of a less-overworked intake vent.

Or her imagination.

That imagination would probably be necessary to figure out how going into the restricted area involved cooperation. What did the old man want?

She turned to Chung. "That area's off-limits."

A wry smile split the old man's face. "Don't say."

Heat spread through her cheeks. Why had she thought Republic security would matter to a pirate? "I mean..." Her voice wasn't so ridiculously loud now. "Well, the only people who ever went into there were Martinez and the security team that loaded the crates."

"Uh-huh."

He couldn't care less. This was loot. Plunder. Part of the prize he obviously intended to take. "If it's proprietary medicine, you're not going to be able to sell it for much."

"Proprietary medicine, huh?"

"Pharmaceutical companies have rights to certain medicines. We transport those to wherever they're needed as part of our patrol."

The old man turned to consider Rai. "Proprietary medicine."

Rai grunted. "Sounds like the Gulmar."

Did it? "We have businesses, too. We just don't let them run things."

"You don't?" The slender man nodded toward the crates. "How much would they charge for this medicine? Do people die because they can't afford it?"

"Of course not. They make a profit, but it's not criminal."

Chung held up a hand and stopped a meter shy of the secure area. "Not really like the Gulmar, then. But this ain't medicine."

And a quick glance confirmed what he said. The opened crates held... weapons. Armor.

She tried to process that. "Guns?"

"I thought maybe the Kedraalian Republic might have an appreciation for dark humor." The old man smirked.

Benson moved closer to the crates. "But..."

"You've never seen this stuff?"

"These..." She squatted beside the closest crate. It held what looked like assault weapons, the sort used by select Marines and other special units. "Counter-terrorism. Tactical assault."

"So you *have* seen it."

"Not on *our* ship. We have our own small armory. It's meant to deal with—"

"Pirates?" Chung chuckled. "Well, maybe you need to upgrade."

They did. But she didn't just need weapons, she needed a plan. Killing Gabriel was the key. Kill *him*, and she had a shot at killing all of Chung's people. And that was the only way she could save her people.

She ran fingers over the barrels. "These weapons are brand new."

Rai moved a little closer. "Or well-maintained."

No. She'd seen well-maintained weapons. These had the smell of cleaning oil, fresh paint, and sealant. Halliwell took good care of his guns, but scuffs and scratches were inevitable. These weapons had been produced recently. For whom?

She glanced up at Rai to correct him, but she froze at the look of fury in his eyes. His body was stiff, his fingers curled.

Is he mad at me? Why?

And then Rai glanced toward the old man. The fury transformed to hate, but it was a look that was only there for an instant, something Chung wouldn't have noticed with his focus on her and the crates.

Why would Rai hate his boss? Was it—

Rai's attention turned back to her, and his look softened. She caught a hint of remorse and imagined he might even be signaling something close to self-loathing.

For not helping her earlier. For the whole mess.

But he wasn't telling her he would protect her, just that he felt bad not being able to.

She was on her own.

Benson patted the weapon barrels. "On my first assignment, I was aboard the *Constellation*."

Chung grunted. "What was that?"

"Well, I guess it was a light destroyer, but they were designating it a heavy frigate under the newer designations. It was an older ship. It was slow as could be. They'd sort of repurposed it as a tender. We hauled things around, moving among a few systems."

"Huh." The old man was distracted, probably calculating the value of the haul.

"This one time, we had some people come aboard at a port." She pointed to the armor. "They had gear like that. It was a special team."

Chung sneered. "Not like your Marines."

He wouldn't have said that if he'd seen Halliwell's team in action instead of being ambushed. "I guess not. I asked about them and was told to let it go."

"Secrets in the military." The old man shook his head.

Was there more to the military than what she knew? Of course there was. She was just a lieutenant commander working the fringes.

What could she do with these weapons, though? Enough. A few

rounds into the big brute, a burst into the old bastard. That would be all the others needed. Grier could kill the Wong kid with her bare hands.

Penn pulled a device out of one of the crates. "You ever see this before?"

Benson reached for it. "A grenade?"

"A stun grenade." He rotated it just out of her reach, but kept it close enough that she could make out the pin. "I've seen something like it before when I worked security." He casually dropped the grenade back into the crate, not securing it like it had been.

Wong bounced up and down on the balls of his feet. "It's worth a fucking bundle!"

Chung looked the weapons over. "Worth a lot on the black market."

Rai pulled one of the guns out of its crate. "A pretty good amount."

He rotated the weapon around and hefted it, getting a feel for the design. "These carbines—automatic." He handed it to Chung. "They have a better rate of fire and range than pistols. They'd be ideal for tight quarters."

The old man sniffled. "So how'd this get aboard? You're search and rescue. Isn't that what you like to keep reminding me?"

Benson sighed. "The crates were loaded when the system upgrades were being done."

"And you didn't know?"

"I told you, it was restricted access, so no one looked at it."

"No one? Crates get loaded and you don't look?"

"Normal crates, sure. That's part of my job—inventory management. These aren't part of inventory."

"You said Martinez went in here."

"He was in charge of the transfer. He's responsible for all restricted items. Everyone else...we just assumed it was proprietary drugs, like I said. There are disease outbreaks at some of the outlying stations."

"But not worth much." He cocked an eyebrow.

"Well, they *can* be worth a lot, especially if you'd be willing to sell them to a rival corporation to reverse engineer for...piracy."

The old man grinned. "I like this haul better."

Money. It was all about money for Chung and his privateers. They weren't loyal to the Azoren in the least, and he couldn't care less about the implications of these weapons being sneaked onto her ship.

People were smuggling weapons on her medical ship. Assault weapons.

Someone could have staged attacks from the *Pandora*. The same people who were planning to enter Azoren space through the DMZ.

Lenny, what did you sign us up for?

Chung's nails scuffed across his white whiskers. "Okay, yeah, load it up now."

Wong whooped and pushed past Benson to pull the top crate from the stack with a crash. "Big money!"

Penn hurried over to the crate and put a booted foot on top. "Hey, wait. I got an idea."

"Yeah?" The old man shot a look at Rai that said ideas weren't expected from someone like Penn.

Benson duck-walked to the other open crate on the deck.

"What about this?" Penn tapped the front of his boot on the crate top. "Instead of selling these, we should use them for the Carone handoff. The grenades alone give us all the advantage we need."

Wong glanced around, confused, and his uncle's scarred face twisted in irritation. Benson wasn't sure what was going on, but it was an opportunity she wasn't about to miss.

She slipped a hand into the crate with the loose grenade and fished around for it.

Chung fixed a hard stare on Penn. "We got good enough guns to take care of this Carone thing."

Penn bowed his head. "Not from what I can see. There's, what, five of us?"

Benson's heart pounded as she slipped the grenade out. *Don't look at me. Don't look.*

They weren't going to. The young privateer's behavior apparently was being treated as something of a challenge of authority. Why? He was making a good suggestion. But maybe Chung didn't care for suggestions, good or bad?

The old man swatted the younger man's leg, nearly knocking it from the crate top. "I'm fucking telling you we're good enough. We're selling the weapons, and that's it."

Rai crossed his arms. If things got ugly, would he get involved?

She slipped the grenade inside her torn flight suit. *Can they see it?*

Chung snapped his fingers and pointed at her. "You—"

Blood pounded so loudly, she wasn't sure she could hear him. "What?"

"Help get these crates to the airlock." The old man glared at Penn. "And I don't want to hear any other suggestions from you, okay? This Carone thing, that's a big enough headache."

Rai followed the old man away after nodding at Penn. Had that been a signal of support? Approval?

Penn grumbled under his breath. "What an asshole."

Wong laughed. "He's used to running things the way he likes."

"Yeah, well, Carone's worth a lot more than these weapons."

Chung's skinny nephew shrugged. "Easier money, though."

The old man shouted something, and a minute later, Gabriel came jogging out of the maze. "Ho-ho! Sweet weapons, huh?"

Wong pointed to the crate Penn had put his boot on. "Yeah. Help me carry this one, okay?"

Penn waited until the two of them were headed into the maze, then jerked his head at the crate Benson had originally examined. He sealed the lid, then glanced at her. "Ready?"

She took the handles on the nearer end and the two of them worked their way through the shadowy piles of cargo. If the privateer saw the grenade, he didn't react. The thing rubbed against her belly and slid around as if it might find some way to pop out of her flight suit.

But it didn't.

Just outside the airlock, the other four privateers stood, hands on hips, glaring at Penn and her.

Still stewing over being challenged? Or did they suspect what she had in mind?

Penn muttered, "Idiot."

They set the crate down a step short of the first one.

What was the blast radius of a stun grenade? Ten meters? Fifteen?

She backed up, looking for all the world like she was anxious to grab more crates. Her crew watched, confused as she felt. Halliwell's eyes reflected anger, self-loathing.

It's not your fault. She wanted to shout that out. She wanted to hug him.

If the opportunity arose, she would.

The privateers were grumbling. She thought Chung had said something about "necessary."

Gabriel growled. He turned toward her. "No!"

The old man held up a hand. "Sorry, Vic, but we gotta finish them off..."

His nephew reached for his pistol, as did Chung.

That was it! They were going to kill them now. Just like that.

Benson reached into her flight suit and grabbed the grenade. It slithered from her fingers and dove down into her right leg. She dug after it.

Chung's eyes lit up. "Hey—!"

He knew! They all knew!

She got a couple fingertips around the weapon. Her thumb pinched along the tube. She yanked the grenade out just as pistols started clearing holsters.

The pin came free easily, and she tossed the weapon.

Not too hard. Not onto the crates. Not into someone's hands.

The privateers reacted instinctively, backing away from the thing rather than grabbing it. They weren't worried about shooting her anymore. A grenade had bounced off of them and onto the deck.

Benson threw herself flat, away from them, away from the grenade, eyes closed. She thought maybe one of them had done the same.

And then the stun grenade detonated.

Loud, with a concussive force that shoved one of the crates around and felt like an intense burst of air washing over her. Her ears rang, and her head throbbed.

But she got up. Wobbly and uncertain but up.

The privateers didn't.

Penn's head came up, then dropped again.

Somewhere far away, boots stomped across the deck.

It was Grier. She was among the privateers, stomping, then backing away with two pistols. She tossed one back to the others; Halliwell caught it.

Had she kicked the other pistols away? She had.

"Commander?" Grier sounded dull and distant.

Benson stumbled forward and waved for Kohn to follow. "Airlock."

The technician hurried to help her. They dragged Gabriel in first, with her taking just a second to kick the big man in the side of the head, then Chung went in. Benson wanted to do a slow decompression for just the two of them, something for her team to see and appreciate, but it wasn't the time for that.

Grier rushed forward, staying wide of the other privateers. "Let me shoot them, ma'am."

"No. Space." Benson waved the Marine and technician away.

"What about them?" Grier pointed the pistol at the other privateers.

"Prisoners." Benson typed in a normal cycle. Revenge was a luxury she couldn't afford. This was simply doing the job right.

Chung's head came up.

Behind her, Rai muttered something. "Bum."

Bum? The system started sucking air from the airlock compartment.

The old man dug inside his coveralls. He didn't seem panicked.

Rai tried to sit up. "Char…"

Chung got to his knees. He was smiling. He held something up uncertainly.

What was he saying? His mouth was moving slowly, forming words clearly for her.

Intercom.

No. She wasn't about to do that. There was nothing he could say—

He waved the thing again, then he tapped a button.

The oxygen was nearly evacuated.

Rai shook his head. "He—" The slender man rubbed his forehead. "Bombs."

Bombs?

Something rumbled back in the engineering bay, and the lights flickered.

Parkinson screamed. "The reactor! He blew the reactor!"

Benson halted the process. She hit the intercom "What do you want?"

Chung looked around, then found the intercom. He was struggling to breathe. "Open…the fucking…airlock."

Her finger hovered over the button. One push, and he would be sucked out into space with the last of the air. Well, there wasn't enough air to suck him out, but he would die. In how long? Seconds. No more than a minute.

But that was too long. "Why? So you can kill us?"

He waved the detonator again. "Let us…back in, or I…press the buttons."

Buttons. Bombs. Detonating all the bombs.

She turned on Rai. "Is he telling the truth? Did he set other bombs in here?"

Rai nodded. "Charges. Multiple charges."

Could she risk it? Exposure to space wasn't instant death. Had she missed their only chance…?

Grier had the pistol leveled at the hatch. "I'll put a round right through his fucking head."

Would that prevent the detonation? Benson glanced at Rai and the other privateers. They weren't going to do anything.

She nodded. "Be ready."

Chung leaned against the window, detonator where she could see it.

She reversed the evacuation cycle and stepped back. They were back to a standoff.

Chung and Gabriel stumbled in. The giant was gasping. "Fuck it! I'll kill her right now! I'll—"

Alarms sounded, and everyone's heads snapped up.

Parkinson covered his ears. "That's a hard scan alarm!"

It was. Benson kicked the rest of the pistols back toward her crew.

The old man growled. "You forget I've got—"

Benson scooped a pistol up and pointed it at him. "You understand that's a hard scan alarm? Maybe you forgot that we're in the Azoren side of the DMZ?"

Chung grunted. "Still have a detonator."

"Fine. Chief, get me information on what that is."

Parkinson dashed back to the engineering bay, and several seconds later leaned his head out. "Something's incoming, all right. Fast. Big. It's a warship."

A warship. "One of ours?"

"No." Parkinson ducked back into the engineering section, then a moment later returned. "They're hailing us."

"On the intercom."

Benson turned back to her crew. Were they any better off now?

The intercom squealed for a second, then a deep voice boomed. "Kedraalian Republic warship, you are in Azoren Federation territory. Surrender immediately or you will be destroyed!"

Not better. Worse. Things had somehow gotten worse.

24

"Here's how this is gonna go." Chung waved the detonation device for Benson to get a good look at it. His raspy voice slithered through the open space of the cargo hold. "It starts with your little Marine girlie dropping that pistol."

Grier squinted—not angry but sighting in. "I can put a hole in his ugly fucking face, Captain."

"Could be. Don't mean the charges won't go off."

The military is just one set of terrible choices after another.

Benson's head pounded, and her throat tightened. She'd always wanted a command of her own. This was the sort of thing she'd trained so hard for. But there were never supposed to be only such hopeless options, were there?

Chung snickered. "How's it feel to be the one dead in space? That big, bad ship coming, and you can't do a thing about it."

She held up a hand. "We've got options here. Everyone can walk away alive."

Grier didn't lower her gun. "He killed Danny, ma'am. And Commander Gaines."

"We killed some of his people."

"Not enough, ma'am."

Gabriel laughed, but stopped when swatted by the old man.

Chung licked his lips. "There's animosity. I get that. Might want to remember there's a big ship inbound. Nobody gets along with the Azoren."

Benson didn't want to test that theory. "So what's the deal?"

"Put the blasters down."

"We can't do that. Not with you holding that detonator."

"Then we trade. You like trades?"

"Depends."

"You'll like this one. We take our guns and your cargo. You get the detonator."

They wouldn't take the time to gun her crew down, would they? Just getting across the umbilical with crates was going to take minutes. The incoming ship wasn't a half hour out. Every second counted. Then again, he'd already taken their reactor offline. What else could he do with the explosive charges?

Plenty.

But she had them dead to rights. "You get your guns after we get the detonator."

"Counteroffer, huh?"

"Counteroffer."

He chuckled. "Guns and detonator swap at the same time, and we get the cargo."

"One crate of food, those two crates of weapons, and we swap guns and detonator at the same time."

"No deal." It came out mirthless, impatient.

He's feeling the approach of the Azoren. "I'm not bluffing, Quentin."

"I see that." The old man scratched his chin. "All right. Deal."

"Petty Officer Kohn, you and Dr. Dietrich find a crate of food they can have."

Grier lowered her gun.

Chung handed the detonator to his nephew. "It's a good decision."

It was the exact proposal Benson had made before things had gotten so out of hand.

The young man stepped away from the other privateers and set the detonator down; Grier kicked her gun toward the privateers; Halliwell skipped his across the deck plate.

The scrawny privateer grabbed the two pistols, then backed up.

Benson's radio buzzed as she plucked the detonator from the deck: It was Parkinson. "What is it, Chief?"

"This reactor. The blast damage. It's not that bad. The blast shattered a control panel and a section of the coolant reservoir. It's repairable. There's no radiation leak."

She lowered her voice. "Good news."

"Yeah. He obviously doesn't know reactors, not like whoever blew the reactor on their ship."

"That was intentional?"

"Or the luckiest explosion ever. From what I saw through the drone, the blast shredded the shielding. That's the quickest way to a shutdown, and it's not that hard of a fix if you've got a shielded drone to do the work."

That sounded freakish and convenient. "Give me an estimate."

"Fifteen minutes. With Kohn's help."

"Don't wait for him." She disconnected. Fifteen minutes. Would that give them enough time to escape the destroyer?

Kohn and the doctor set a crate in front of the airlock, then backed away, hands raised. The big thug seemed to enjoy the moment. Apparently, being on the edge of death was just a minor distraction, a part of his day.

Chung muttered something to his team, and Gabriel and Wong began suiting up, while the old man and Penn kept Benson's team covered. Rai had recovered his pistol, but he just watched.

Was he considering staying? It looked like he might.

"Hey!" The old man pointed his gun at Rai. "Suit up."

Rai's lips twisted. He really was thinking of at least something if not abandoning his team. Then the moment was past and he began pulling his environment suit on, but his eyes kept drifting to Benson.

What was he thinking? Was he considering...more with her? Something serious? Was that even possible? He was a criminal.

Once Gabriel was suited up, he cycled the airlock and started dragging crates inside. Wong covered the *Pandora* crew while the others finished suiting up. The young man was about Lopez's age but had none of the discipline and respect of the Marine. How much had their backgrounds played into such differences? Everything, probably.

Chung holstered his pistol, then before putting his helmet on, turned to Benson. "You should be proud of your crew. Most would be dead by now."

She bowed her head. It was probably as close to a compliment as he could manage.

The airlock closed and began to cycle. Benson ran to the viewport. The pirates were hauling the crates into the umbilical.

Minutes. They could secure the crates and power on, but they couldn't get far. The destroyer could track them down eventually.

She studied the detonator as Grier squeezed next to her to get a look at the retreating pirates. "Wish we had an external gun, ma'am."

"We're alive. That's what matters."

"Not all of us."

Benson handed the young Marine the detonator. "Any way you can figure out where the charges are?"

"I can check with Petty Officer Kohn. He might be able to rig up something, but it's going to take time."

And they needed to get the reactor online first. "Disable the detonator."

Grier wandered over toward Halliwell, whose brow was wrinkled in frustration. He was a man of action, someone who gained validation from protecting others, so being unable to contribute was going to eat at him.

Kohn shuffled up to Benson. "Commander Benson?"

"Yes?"

"The privateers?"

"They're gone."

"I-I know. But…"

"What is it?"

"Well, I thought we'd be, y'know, dead by now. So, I left them a…surprise."

A dozen images flashed through Benson's mind: something frightening, something dangerous, something that would anger them. "What sort of surprise?"

"Their reactor's working, but it's going to shut down once they engage the engines."

That fell into the anger category. "As in they'll have to power it back on?"

"If they can figure out what I did." He smiled mischievously.

"And can they?"

"I think they said that lady was their engineer."

Rai knew technical things. Would he be able to figure it out? "Thank you for telling me."

"I-I thought we'd all be dead, so it would be revenge."

Benson squeezed the younger man's shoulder. "Sometimes, people need a little revenge."

Kohn relaxed. "Thanks, Captain."

"Now we need to prepare for that destroyer. Can you help Chief Parkinson?"

"I—" Kohn winced, then slumped. "Yes, ma'am."

She would need to work out the kinks between the two of them. If they lived. That was still a big if. And if she hoped to increase their odds, she needed to talk to Halliwell.

He was looking the detonator over with Grier, who was leaning in close to him.

Benson fought back a momentary surge of jealousy. The muscular woman had her eyes on Halliwell, but it was more complicated than just sexual interest. They'd both come aboard the *Pandora* with baggage, but the one thing that was clear was that they were tight. When things were at their worst, the two of them were inseparable. Benson wouldn't have it any other way.

She stopped a couple steps shy of them. "Sergeant Halliwell?"

He looked up, and there was a hint of pain in his eyes, as if he were conflicted between wanting to jump to his feet and show he was still whole and wanting to hold her. "Yes, ma'am?"

"This destroyer. How big of a Marine contingent is it likely to have?"

"Too big for us to deal with."

"I don't think they're going to ask us if we'd like a different option."

His eyes shot to Grier, who seemed to tense, then back to Benson. "If you're seriously considering fighting—"

"If they try to board, we don't have much choice."

Halliwell swallowed. "Surrender." That was little better than a whisper.

"That's an Azoren ship. I'm not sure they'd accept surrender."

"They're demanding it, aren't they?"

"If you wanted to get aboard a ship to kill the crew, what would you do?"

"Tell them to surrender." His voice was even softer.

"So we have to stop them somehow."

"Even if we stop a boarding party, the destroyer will just blast us apart."

"I'll take my chances. I'm not putting you all at risk again."

He seemed about to challenge her on that, then nodded.

And he would've been right. Wasn't she putting them at risk with a plan to ambush any boarding party? Kill them all, and then what?

But if he'd been in the situation she and Stiles had nearly been in…

We have to try to outrun them. We can make it into Fold Space if everything goes right, and we'll lose them that way.

If they don't blow us apart before then.

But the *Pandora* had the sensor-dodging system installed, didn't it? That was what had put them in such peril in the first place. If they could figure out how to activate that…

Halliwell shrugged. "Two squads."

"What?" Benson had let herself become distracted. "How many would that be?"

"Probably close to a dozen." Halliwell considered that, then nodded, apparently convinced. "They'll have twice that aboard the ship, easily."

"So they'll have twenty to thirty?"

"As many as fifty."

"Why so many?"

"Pirates. They aren't going to try to take a destroyer, but from the sound of it, piracy's even worse in Azoren space than ours, so the destroyer is going to be used to dealing with boarding actions."

Like what he had trained for.

"Okay. Twelve people won't be able to come through the airlock at the same time, not with armor and gear."

"No. And they won't make mistakes like pirates might."

"Meaning?"

"No easy kills. They'll tie off on safety hooks. They'll have fast-release lines connected to each other. We'll need to consider them experienced boarders."

"Armor? Weapons?"

"Heavy armor, at least for the first group. And probably boarding weapons."

She'd seen those in the Republic fleet: shotguns with armor-piercing rounds. They wouldn't penetrate hulls, but they could penetrate personal armor and more importantly, they could shred environmental suits.

Grier scanned the cargo hold. "We don't have any hard cover down here."

The closest thing they could use for would be the engineering bay, and that was too far back to be of use. A boarding party could get into the cargo crates and get cover of their own if gunfire was only coming from one source. And a single grenade could take everyone in the engineering bay out.

Benson turned back to the stacked crates. "What about those?"

Halliwell shook his head. "They won't stand up to a good boarding gun."

"Stacked a couple deep?"

"Maybe. We'd need to get them set up fast."

"We can do that."

Grier stood and waved for Dr. Dietrich. "Doctor, if you and Petty Officer Stiles could help me?"

Halliwell's face twisted. "They'll have stun grenades, just like what we used."

That meant cover wouldn't be as beneficial.

Benson turned toward the cargo crate maze. "I'll see what we can get from those other restricted crates. There were more grenades in there."

"That stun grenade seemed pretty effective. It could get through armor."

She hurried to the airlock, retracting the umbilical, then called Parkinson. "Chief, put some distance between us and that privateer ship."

"How? We don't have main power."

For a brilliant chief engineer, the man had no imagination. "Maneuvering thrusters. Figure something out."

Benson rushed back to the restricted area and began looking through the other open crates.

Armor. Weapons. It was enough for her depleted crew. She pulled out a vest for her and the Marines. After a second, she grabbed a fourth for Kohn. They should have the reactor back online before any boarding action, so if he wanted to help...

Ammunition. The weapons were slug throwers, like boarding weapons. She needed magazines, bullets.

She popped open another crate.

"What the—?" Not ammunition. Not weapons or armor.

Another crate was similar to the first. Then another. She found loaded magazines in the fourth, but the other things...?

Electronics gear? Explosives? They'd been carrying around explosives that weren't clearly marked?

It all looked exotic, high-tech, made for very specific purposes.

Benson piled guns on top of two of the armored vests and hurried back to Halliwell. She helped him into one of the vests. "There's gear back there that's...different."

"Different?" He loaded one of the carbines.

"I think it's more assault gear. Like breaching charges."

He froze. "I don't think they were sending Marines in to test the DMZ."

Something odd was definitely going on. "Who, then?"

"Spooks. SAID or GSA. Something."

Benson glanced around. Being used by the military was bad enough, but an intelligence agency? "I need to go get more weapons."

She jogged forward but slowed when someone called her.

Grier. She caught up about halfway into the maze. "Clive—Sergeant Halliwell said I should give that gear you found a look."

Benson let the slip go without reaction. Of course the two of them would be close. *I don't own him.* "I'll show you what I saw."

Dietrich and Stiles were setting crates out—two deep, two high. The doctor looked winded already. At least he'd drawn the nurse out from her catatonic state.

We have a small chance.

Benson set out the armor and weapons, then pointed to the odd crates.

Grier poked around inside. "Thanks, ma'am."

"I'll take these back to Clive." There. The look from Grier said that she understood. They both had their sights on him.

As Benson approached, Halliwell readied another of the guns. "Any luck with more grenades?"

"Not yet." She jogged back to the crates. Her legs felt spongy. Sweat dampened her brow. Was she really planning to lead her team through a pointless fight against a boarding action?

Grier held up one of the devices, her lips pursed. "Impressive. Cl—Sergeant Halliwell and I had training on this sort of stuff once. Not this nice, but the same concept."

Benson began opening more of the crates. "What is it?"

"It's meant for heavy ship assaults. Hull-penetration charges."

"What? You put them on the hull and blow them?"

"Inner hull, Captain. You ride a breaching pod in. Like a very small, very fast attack craft."

Benson had heard of breaching pods. "Those have lasers?"

"Yes, ma'am. Just enough to get you through the outer hull. There's an umbilical that seals up around the cut area, then the insertion team goes through and blasts the shit out of the inner hull with these. Or if you don't want to actually capture the ship, you set a few of these in key places, and—" She made a sound like an explosion.

"That seems...dangerous."

"It's all sort of suicidal, really. Point defenses tend to make short work of the assault pods. Unless you can overwhelm the enemy with a whole bunch—send in more pods than they can blow up. Even then, you're going to lose a lot of people."

"Unless you sneak them in outside of battle."

"That'd be the best way."

"Too bad we don't have some of those people on that destroyer. It would be a nice way to get rid of the threat."

Grier chuckled. "It would. With the right placement, you don't even need charges this big."

Benson didn't want to think about what the casualty rate would be like on an assault using the pods. And she didn't have to; she'd found a crate with more grenades inside. She took four out and stuffed those into her flight suit, then grabbed more magazines.

Grier set one of the breaching charges down and examined one of the electronic devices. "Unless they have some crazy electronic countermeasures to hide the ships from targeting."

"Those breaching pods you're talking about—they have ECM?"

"Yes, ma'am."

"Something like the thing they installed on the *Pandora*?"

"You think that's what it was for? Some sort of insertion and assault?"

"We'll have to remember to ask someone at headquarters if we survive."

They hurried back to the others.

Halliwell had already taken up position behind one of the crate walls. He was pale and sweating.

Benson set the magazines down beside him. "You and Corporal Grier are going to be our best hope."

Halliwell grabbed her wrist. "It's not too late."

"Clive, we don't have a choice. They either fly in weapons blazing and we're dead before we know it, or they try to board us. If they try to board us, they want this ship. And now that we know what we know, we can't let them have it."

His eyes widened. "Oh."

It had finally dawned on him: They would be executed as spies if they surrendered.

Benson helped Grier and the others set out more crate walls. When they had four set up, the commander waved Stiles over and gave her three of the grenades. "Petty Officer...Brianna, how are you doing?"

The young woman looked down at the weapons. "I'm okay, ma'am."

"You checked out on us a few times."

"I-it's the fighting."

"All right. Well, we're going to have a little more."

Stiles nodded. "I-I know."

"But all I'm going to need from you is one little thing. You won't even be in danger." She hoped the young woman didn't sense the lie behind that. "When that airlock cycles, some people are going to come through. Sergeant Halliwell, Corporal Grier, and I, we're all going to try to keep them pinned down."

Another nod. "You want me to throw this?" She held up a grenade.

"Just pull that pin and toss it toward the airlock. It's really easy."

Stiles stared at the grenade.

"Can you do that, Petty Officer Stiles?"

"I shouldn't be killing anyone."

"Those are stun grenades. They're not lethal."

"But you'll shoot—"

"In self-defense." She brushed hair back from the young woman's face. "They don't have any problems killing us. You understand?"

"I do."

"All right."

Benson hurried back to Halliwell to help him get an environment suit over his armor. They wouldn't put their helmets on, but having the suit on and helmet nearby gave them a chance if the Azoren breached or things went awry.

When she was sure no one could see her, she kissed Halliwell, then moved to the next crate wall over, where Grier was hunched low.

The corporal looked her weapon over. "You ready, Captain?"

"I don't think I have any other choice."

Grier's nose wrinkled in a smile. "That's the attitude."

Benson settled to her knees and hefted her weapon.

And waited.

25

The umbilical framework felt like unstable wood to Rai's fingers. Any second, one of the crates was going to slip free of someone's grasp and shatter the ribbing, and he and the others would lose their grips as the whole assembly came undone.

Dying in space wasn't the worst way to go, just floating until your oxygen ran out and you slipped into unconsciousness. He'd talked to someone who'd come close once, rescued after blacking out.

"Beats a blaster shot into the gut." That's what the gal had said.

He believed her, too, but he didn't want to find out for himself.

So he squeezed the frame tight. Better it cracked in his grip than he somehow slipped between the frame.

Gabriel's crazy singing was a faraway sound that couldn't be silenced any more without shutting contact off from everyone else. Although, *that* idea had its own appeal, too. Aside from Penn, there wasn't a one of Chung's team Rai wanted to hear from. As far as he was concerned, they could all go spinning away into the black of space, lost among the glittering sparkle of distant stars, never to be seen again.

But there was the oath. The damned oath. The reason for his life.

He'd come so close to throwing it all away for the chance to stay with Benson. It was something he couldn't quite fathom, but the attraction was real. It was visceral. And passing up on her was going to haunt him for as long as he lived.

Rai's breathing calmed as he approached the airlock. He cranked the volume back up on his speakers. "Quentin, you want me to go in first?"

The old man wheezed. "Yeah. Check the systems. We gotta get the fuck outta here."

They did. They were cutting it close if they hoped to outrun the destroyer.

Rai cycled through the airlock and hurried into the cargo bay. With power restored, the lights made the space seem much smaller. Yet it was empty. The food they had stored inside had been spoiled by the radiation. Useless. So they'd tossed it before going into cold sleep, relying on the shielding of the infirmary and the cold sleep gel to keep them from lethal doses of radiation from the reactor.

It didn't slip past him that they'd been nothing but lucky to date—the radiation hadn't killed anyone that wasn't already dying; they'd been in cold sleep for a very short time before rescue; and the rescue had come despite the outrageous odds they'd faced by losing power in the DMZ.

What mattered was keeping the luck going.

He hurried into the passageway outside the cargo hold and turned hard right, happy at the lights and the gravity. It was a good start.

Halfway to the infirmary, he popped open the hatch and took the steps up to the top deck, where the bridge awaited. No space ghost waited for him.

That drew a chuckle. "Fuck you, Vic."

Rai settled into the pilot seat. The *Rakshasa*'s bridge was about half the size of the *Pandora*'s—two seats, and an emergency space for a third. That reduced space was reflected in the smaller consoles that held simpler control systems.

Those systems weren't necessarily diminished, though. He pulled up a readout on the approaching ship. It was close enough for a passive scan, registering its own signals, heat signature, and the profile it presented against the background of space.

Azoren. Destroyer. One of the older ones but still deadly.

Rai snatched up the station headset and listened over the radio.

"Gulmar commerce vessel, you are in Azoren Federation territory. Surrender immediately or you will be destroyed!"

It was almost exactly the same as the message the *Pandora* had received.

Automated. Or close to it. The crew was probably busy preparing for all contingencies.

And it was closing fast, which meant it would be doing a hard burn closer in. The one upside to that was that non-essential crew would be in cold sleep chambers or acceleration couches. Either way, they wouldn't be ready to hop out and jump into combat immediately.

They had to be responding to the SOS, which meant they had to have been patrolling the DMZ on the Azoren side. Which also meant they knew the way through the mines and didn't care about their own sensor buoys activating.

Combat-proven, too. They had to be.

All of this was good to know, something to store away for future use. Except it wouldn't help if there was no future to use it in.

Chung connected from the cargo hold. "Whatcha got?"

"Azoren destroyer. Older model. Coming in *fast*."

"Yeah, yeah. Patrol ship."

"Has to be. I thought they were all frigates this close in."

"Yeah. Could be worse. We're gonna be okay. Ready to launch?"

Rai tapped the launch sequence on the console. Systems flashed to life: green light after green light. "Looking good so far. When do we want to engage the drive?"

"As soon as fucking possible." Chung's breathing was heavier now. He was moving through the ship's normal gravity, probably coming up the steps.

His booted steps and labored breathing echoed in the entry.

Rai checked through detailed readouts. Everything looked good. They could spin the drive up anytime, but—

Chung lumbered through the entry. "What the fuck are we waiting on?"

Rai turned the chair around. "I've been thinking."

"Yeah? I told you to quit doing that."

"Why not just stay here and bluff them? Tell them what happened, but don't say a thing about planning to sell Carone back to the Gulmar."

"And give up the money? You nuts?"

"It's only money. We live long enough, we can make it back."

"We launch now, we'll live. We stay here, we'll never have a chance to make that sort of money again."

"But if they've already figured out who we are—"

"Did they identify us?"

Rai tapped the headset. "They called us a Gulmar commerce vessel."

"So they don't have anything but the SOS ID."

"They can track that identification back to our charter."

Chung shrugged. "We'll log a fucking new Gulmar ID. They're cheap enough to get."

"But it runs the risk of—"

"Dev, listen to me. The Azoren ain't big on people showing initiative. This wasn't their assignment. They're gonna see through any explanation we give."

"Meaning what?"

"At best, they'll take Carone for themselves and send us on our merry way."

"Fine."

"Fuck that. We make a run for it. We put that Kedraalian ship between us and them and go."

Rai frowned. That wouldn't serve the oath, but neither would blasting a hole in the old bastard's gut. "We have everything locked down?"

Chung squeezed past Rai's seat and plopped into the other one, pulling the headset on after fidgeting with it, then keying into the intercom. "Vic, you hear me?"

Gabriel's voice buzzed in Rai's headset. "Ho-ha! Hey, boss-man!"

"You got those crates locked into place?"

"Food, yeah. Still looking the weapons over."

Chung muted the intercom and lowered his face into his palms. "For fuck's sake."

Rai smirked. "You're the one who put the crew together."

"Don't remind me." The old man let out a long, slow sigh, then reconnected to the intercom. "Vic?"

"Yo!"

"Seal those crates up and lock them down. All of them. Now."

"But the weapons—"

"Lock the fucking crates down!" Chung disconnected and slammed his headset down.

Rai pulled his headset off. "I'll go make sure we're getting it done."

"Don't be long."

Rai's boots clattered against the steps, then on the lower deck. If time mattered, Gabriel was the wrong person to count on. He lived in his own reality, unconcerned for anyone else. It didn't register for someone like him that the Azoren were a threat. The big guy's pea brain couldn't see anyone as a danger.

When the cargo bay hatch opened, Rai's suspicions were confirmed: Gabriel was taking his sweet time loading the crates up.

The idiot still had one of the carbines in his hand, like he was imagining he was about to repel boarders. "Hey! Dev, check this out, huh?" The brute swept the barrel across the airlock hatch. "Pew! Pew! Killed 'em all!"

"You're pissing Quentin off." Rai strode across to the crate farthest from Gabriel and snapped a finger at Wong. "Load it up."

The kid had two of the guns in his hands. As if he could handle the recoil. Disappointment spread across his face as he handed the guns to Rai, who pushed them into the braces. When everything was back in the crate, he slammed the lid shut. "Lock it into place. Now."

Gabriel finally seemed to get the message. "Yeah, sure. He-he-he." After a second, he pushed the weapon into its brace and closed the crate. "Tell Quentin we're good."

"I will."

When they moved the last crate toward a tie-down, Rai spun on his heel and exited the cargo hold.

Penn fell in close behind. "Hey!"

Rai stopped shy of the hatch that opened onto the stairs. "I don't want to be a jerk—"

"Nah, I understand." Penn glared back at the cargo hold hatch. "It's just these guys. Quentin's gang."

"I know."

"All this chaos, the lack of discipline. You can't do business like this."

"Not for too long. Most pirates are like that. People like Chung have never known anything but violence and disruption."

"But it's not how you run a business."

"Not a long-term one, no. But they don't believe they can think beyond a day, or they'll die."

Penn pinched the bridge of his nose. "That sounds like the Union."

Rai laughed. "It sounds like humans. Most people think about themselves and how to better their situation in the next few minutes and little more."

"I get that. It's what makes it easier for people who think bigger, y'know."

There was a look in the younger man's eyes that left Rai unsettled. Penn was…different. He couldn't be some punk from the ghetto. He was too slick, too *educated*. People just didn't think that way. Not in the Gulmar Union, especially not from the slums.

And Penn seemed to be signaling that he saw the same thing in Rai.

Could the kid be a spy? For the Azoren? That would make sense. If they wanted Carone all along, why not plant someone like Penn? Put together a team of privateers who had no idea what they were doing, make it look like a criminal operation.

It's what Rai would do.

And Chung was too fucking stupid to ever suspect anything like that. All he cared about was the money.

Penn shrugged. "Forget about it. I'm just stressed, I guess."

"Sure. Everyone is." But Rai still felt the same oddness about the other man.

"I'm gonna go strap in."

"We can talk later, okay?"

"That'd be good." Penn waved and headed toward the cabins.

You're being paranoid. He's just a scared, pissed-off kid who sees a couple idiots putting everything at risk. Not everyone's as stupid as Gabriel and Wong.

Plus, Penn was right: Chung's crew was epically dysfunctional. That wasn't a brilliant or deep observation. It had been easy to ignore the fact because it had been advantageous to work for Chung, but the guy was too self-absorbed to realize how stupid he was.

Rai rushed back up the steps.

Chung's face was red, and his lips quivered. "Planting a garden or something?"

"What?"

"They're getting closer!" He nodded toward the view screen.

On the sensor display, the destroyer was closing still, but it was clearly decelerating now.

Rai settled into his seat and strapped in. "We've got time."

"Sure. All fucking day!"

"Everything's locked down except for Vic and your nephew." Rai smiled wickedly. Just how pissed was the old man? Bad enough to turn the two morons into paste?

Chung keyed the intercom. "You've got one minute to get your asses into an acceleration couch!"

He glared at the console display where the destroyer was closing.

Rai ran another check while the minute passed, then he brought the engine online. Hard acceleration was called for, and that was what he was going to give them. "Full burn."

He brought the engine fully online and set it to climb to full power in as short a time as was possible.

And nothing happened.

Then power shut off.

Rai stared at the dead console in front of him. "What the hell?"

Chung turned around, eyes wide. "This ain't full burn, Dev."

"We've got no power." Rai tapped the console. Nothing.

"Those fucking assholes!" Chung smacked the console. "Blow 'em to pieces!"

"We don't have power. Understand? No. Power." Rai unbuckled. "The reactor."

"Yeah, I figured it was the reactor, thanks. Get it running. Now."

Rai grabbed an emergency lamp and stomped down the steps. It was possible the reactor had simply stopped feeding power to the ship systems. Shutting down outside of an emergency situation, that took a while. Going offline while still running made more sense.

Stef would have known what to do. Without her, they didn't have a real tech.

After making sure radiation levels weren't changing, Rai hurried to the engineering bay. It was pitch black, and quiet other than a distant hum. Like the reactor was still working.

He peeked through the viewport. There was some light inside the reactor room—the consoles. Everything *looked* okay. There were no fires, no signs of damage.

Benson's people. It had to be. Their own little taste of revenge. He laughed.

Emergency lighting slowly clicked on—the last of the battery power.

He made his way over to the intercom, still chuckling. He composed himself, then keyed the intercom. "Quentin, it's all good down here."

"What the fuck do you mean it's all good? We're not moving!"

"And we're not going to. The reactor's working, but it's not putting power out. We'd need a qualified tech to get it online anytime soon." *And you got Stef killed with your little adventure against the Kedraalians.*

"So what the hell do we do?"

Rai looked back toward the cargo bay. "You want to fight them?"

"No."

Of course he didn't. Five of them? They wouldn't stand a chance. "Then we need to prepare for them to board."

"I'm not fucking letting them on." Chung sounded ready to snap.

Rai waited a few seconds before keying the intercom again. He wished he could see the old man's face at that moment. "Quentin, we don't have a choice. We have to surrender."

26

A SHUDDER RAN THROUGH THE DECK OF THE *PANDORA* CARGO BAY. BENSON exchanged a look with Grier, the same sort of look the new captain imagined had been exchanged a million times in the moments before a million battles. Mouths would go dry, guts would tighten, hands would tremble.

Do we have the right tactics? Do we have the right gear? Do we have the right personnel?

Benson knew for certain they didn't have the right personnel, or at least she knew that they didn't have *enough* of the right personnel.

She rolled her shoulders, trying to adjust the armor that was so snug against her. It compressed her chest, making it hard to breathe.

Nerves. Just nerves.

Why couldn't the crates have held the lightweight environment suits the armor was meant to integrate with? Maybe they did. They didn't have time to pop all of them.

What mattered now was being ready for whatever came through the airlock. Would the semicircle of piled crates be enough cover for her and her crew?

Once again, she checked her weapon, then sighted on the hatch.

Grier stretched and adjusted Benson's grip. "They're going to have some recoil. Target center mass." The Marine had a cool, reassuring look of confidence, the sort of look that said they were going to be just fine.

Benson squeezed the grip tighter. "Thanks."

Grier nodded. "You ever train for boarding action, ma'am?"

"Trained, yes. This is my first live one."

"Remember your training."

"You ever do any live fire boarding actions, Corporal?"

"A few. Pirates. Clive led me through two of those."

"He's a good squad leader."

"They don't make 'em better." The younger woman smiled—bright, warm. It was a good look for her.

Benson glanced toward the crates Halliwell was hidden behind. "You've served with him most of your career."

"Enough to know he's the best. Don't matter what his records say. The best."

"His records reflect someone overcoming impossible odds, same as yours."

Grier's stone-faced confidence cracked for a moment. "We all should've died on Dramoran."

"But you didn't."

"Should've." The Marine's voice cracked. She swallowed. Her strong jaw shook. "My fault."

"You weren't running those artillery batteries, Corporal."

"But I was on point. My team was scouting. We—I—made a bad call, took everyone into a valley with narrow exits. Bottlenecked everyone."

"I've seen the report, Corporal. The problem was with the artillery."

Grier shook her head. "A good scout would've diverted the unit."

"The entire area for kilometers around you was hammered."

"Don't matter, ma'am. And if it weren't for Clive, my career would be over. He...got me off the bottle before the hearings. He'd been trying to get me to, y'know, grow up. Wasn't until the battalion got wiped out that the message sank in."

There hadn't been a thing in Grier's record about alcohol abuse. What had been in the record was the sloppy failure of the Dramoran regional commander who had failed to properly log the live fire situation.

Describing an attack that took the lives of a thousand Marines as "a failure of communications systems" wasn't just inaccurate, it was a bald-faced lie. The Dramoran had the same comm systems as the Marine contingent.

Benson managed a shaky smile. "You could have been blackout drunk, and it still wouldn't have been your fault, Corporal."

"I failed my comrades."

"The military failed your comrades." And the entire Dramoran chain of command was complicit, but how could Benson let that information out? It wasn't official. It wasn't acknowledged beyond whispers and mutters behind closed doors. General Narisah Gullaly had failed to communicate anything at all to the lower echelon about the artillery barrage.

Was it malevolent? No. But it was incompetent, and that should have cost several officers their careers.

But no one was going to go after Gullaly. Benson knew through her own mother just how important the Dramoran officer was. Now the head of one of the biggest Dramoran businesses and a major contributor to the Dramoran Freedom Party, Gullaly and her family were then and now the key to keeping the planet loyal to the Republic. A thousand Marines dying was nothing compared to an entire planet's loyalty, especially one as vital as Dramora.

Benson turned to the younger Marine, but before a word more could be spoken, an alarm sounded.

The Azoren were at the airlock.

They had seconds. The outer hatch would be overcome. A squad would come in. Heavily armored, probably.

"Chief, status on the reactor?"

Parkinson grunted as something rattled and clanged over his communicator. "Almost there."

"Almost doesn't cut it. How long?"

"Another minute."

Too long. Benson needed more bodies, more guns, and she needed them now. "Hurry."

The airlock control panel flashed red. The outer airlock hatch had been compromised. If there had been an opportunity before to surrender, it was gone now. The Azoren Marines were committed.

Center mass. Just keep firing. Armor can't last forever.

Benson glanced at Stiles. The young woman was crouched down into a ball, clutching one of the grenades. Maybe she wouldn't freeze up. Maybe they had a chance.

Were there boots thumping against the deck now? Could she actually feel that?

The lights flickered.

Were they hacking? They couldn't be hacking. The systems were too robust for that. No one could connect through the limited airlock—

Parkinson cackled. "It's online! Reactor online!"

Benson sighed in relief. "Get out here, Chief. You and Kohn. Now."

Kohn connected. "On my way, Captain!"

Now she heard boots certainly. Kohn.

Parkinson's voice raised an octave. "I'm not a combatant, Captain."

It was the sort of nonsense Martinez had put up with but not her. "You are now."

"Captain—"

"Get out here and grab a gun!"

Kohn skidded to a stop behind Grier. His eyes blinked rapidly; his head jerked around. "Where's a gun?"

Grier jerked a thumb over her shoulder toward Halliwell's position. "Back there. Armor up if you have time."

The young man nodded and flashed an anxious smile, then his eyes drifted over to Stiles.

He wants to contribute. He wants to show her that he matters.

Parkinson stumbled out—gasping, almost sobbing. He was worse than Stiles. At least she seemed to want to contribute. The chief was a blubbering coward.

Benson set her gun down and held out the last grenade. "Chief!"

He shuffled closer. "Captain, I—"

"Take it. Get behind cover. No, not over by Petty Officer Stiles." Benson pointed to where Dietrich was hiding. "Pull the pin and throw that grenade at the hatch when it opens."

"I—"

"Dammit, Chief, man up! Just stay out of sight until they come through. And don't hit one of us."

He clutched the grenade to his chest and staggered behind Halliwell until stopping next to Dietrich, all the time mumbling.

The airlock panel flashed red again, and the inner lock opened. The air didn't evacuate—the Marines had sealed the outer hatch again. At least there wouldn't be the chaos of depressurization. No one benefited from that.

Parkinson shrieked, and his grenade arced over the cargo crates, then bounced off the bulkhead about a meter forward of the airlock.

The grenade didn't even detonate.

Then the chief dropped to the deck.

Benson hissed and wished she had the time to kick the little coward. "Ready!"

Out of the corner of her eye, she saw Kohn stop wrestling with his armor and grab his gun. He was trying, showing resilience when it was needed.

A form clumsily rushed through the airlock hatch—deep gray, with thick, black stripes along the side. The helmet and shoulder pads were black as well, and the faceplate a reflective silver.

Armor. It wore heavy armor, just like Halliwell had warned.

Something arced over the front rank: grenades.

Right toward the spot where Parkinson had dropped.

A horrible popping noise, a flash of light Benson was aware of more by reflection than direct sight.

Her ears rang, and she could only imagine the people close to the explosion were blinded and deafened. She wanted to check on Halliwell, to know whether or not there was a reason to even go on.

But she had a target. And another. And another.

So she fired. "Now!"

The gun had a kick all right. Her first shot was no more accurate than Parkinson's throw, and the burst nearly knocked her off-balance.

But one of the Marines dropped, and it looked like he clutched low.

His legs? Had Grier hit him in the legs?

Benson got her gun back down just as the Azoren Marines realized where the women were. The big armored forms brought blockish, stubby weapons around and fired. Chunks of crate flew past. Something oozed from a hole.

But she returned fire.

And Grier did the same, even when a shot from one of the boarding weapons hit her in the chest. She winced but kept going.

A second Azoren fell.

They needed the stun grenade. Now. But Stiles was still hunched into a ball.

"Stiles! Grenade!" Benson couldn't take the time to make sure the nurse followed through.

The Azoren weapons continued tearing away chunks of the fragile cover.

Benson pulled back from the fire and changed out a magazine. She poked her head around to get a look at the others and spotted something off to her left: Halliwell. On the deck. Bleeding out.

Had he survived the stun grenade only to be shot?

Her heart cracked. A weight sank deep into her.

She fired into the Azoren, and one stumbled back. They were seeking cover along the bulkhead to the left of the airlock.

They needed to make room for the others. Draw fire, provide cover.

It was exactly what she couldn't let happen!

Kohn seemed to realize it too. He popped up and edged toward Dietrich, angling for a better shot.

The Azoren turned their fire on the technician as he reached the outer crates. The containers seemed to just disintegrate under the continuous barrage of their weapons, and a moment later, Kohn fell onto the deck, bloodied.

A shot knocked Grier back, but she got up with a groan. "Just those three, Captain."

"I know. And if Stiles would throw her grenade…"

"Combat shock." Grier put a burst into one of the enemy Marines, and he dropped.

Two. It was just two of them. And they didn't have real cover.

We can do this!

Benson tried to sight in on one of the last two, but the airlock cycling again made her pull back just before the crate in front of her split in half under the thunder of enemy fire.

"Second team's coming through!" Benson poked her head around and took a quick burst at one of the remaining pair. "We don't stun that second team—"

Grier fired at the two Azoren who had edged closer to the crate maze, dropping one of them. "Go for the grenades! I'll cover!"

Fear seized Benson. It was hopeless. They were dead.

No! It wasn't. The resuscitation systems would keep people alive. If they could hold out, she and Grier could get everyone into cold sleep. They could fly away.

We can do this!

Benson steeled herself. *One. Two.*

The airlock flashed red again. The second team was coming in!

Grier spun to fire at the airlock. "Go!"

Benson lunged from her position. She stumbled, regained her footing. Sparks lit up the airlock. Forms stumbled out from inside. There was a vague sense that they might be smaller, the armor lighter.

Another couple steps, then the second Azoren team was in.

They turned toward her, boarding guns raised.

She dropped as they fired. The pellets or whatever they had in the weapons pinged and rattled off bulkheads and who knew what else.

For an instant, she had a complete view of the battle: the two Azoren squads, almost half of them dead; Kohn and Halliwell's dead eyes; Grier falling back from more gunfire that was making short work of the last of their cover.

And Stiles. Eyes locked on Benson. Head shaking.

She wasn't going to throw the grenade. She wasn't going to do anything to risk herself.

More gunfire, then Grier screamed, and a weapon clattered off the deck.

This was what it was to be in command. Benson had to save her crew. She *had* to save them. It was all she had left.

She got back up and ran for Stiles. One grenade. That's all they needed—

Gunfire roared, and something knocked Benson to the deck.

Fire. How had it become so hot? And her limbs just wouldn't respond.

Somewhere far away, a familiar voice screeched. Parkinson. It was Parkinson. She saw him in a blurry, hazy motion. He had a gun in his hand.

And he was holding it wrong, like she had.

He pulled the trigger, and pretty sparks lit the area over the airlock.

The Azoren returned fire, but their rounds didn't produce sparks. Just bloody mist.

Parkinson dropped.

Benson tried to crawl closer to Stiles but discovered lead had replaced what should have been arms and legs. "Goddamn you, Stiles. Goddamn you."

An ice-cold pinprick hit the captain. At the base of the neck.

The resuscitation system. It had detected blood pressure dropping down to life-threatening levels. Death was oncoming, and the drug would delay that.

Someone shuffled up to her. A young man. Blond-haired. Pale-eyed. Heavy browed.

An ugly man.

He pointed his boarding weapon at her face.

Do it. Erase me. Save me from this world where pirates murder and my crew —my family—has died.

But the brute had seen or heard something. Had turned. He said something guttural and rough.

Someone cried. Sobbed. Begged for mercy. Stiles.

How the hell could she be the one to live?

It wasn't Benson's concern anymore, though, because the world went black.

27

RAI BRUSHED DUST FROM HIS COVERALLS AND DID HIS BEST TO CENTER THE
hem. The material had an unfortunate lived-in odor, something
inevitable in their line of work. One thing he'd learned about the Azoren:
They loved their uniforms. The sharper, neater, and more intimidating,
the better.

Especially intimidating. They'd rather have someone freeze or sweat
to death than not look sharp.

To his left, Chung scraped at a stain with his thumbnail. The cool of
the cargo hold couldn't keep sweat from beading atop the network of
wrinkles of the old man's brow. "Let me do the talking, okay?"

It wasn't really a question. Rai shrugged. He had no reason to talk.

Penn stood off to the left, closer to the airlock, cool to the point of
boredom. Farther back in the near-empty cargo hold, Gabriel and Wong
leaned against a bulkhead. The message seemed to have gotten through
to them to *shut the fuck up*. Rai had almost asked Penn if he wanted to bet
on whether the two idiots could maintain silence. If they didn't, though,
Rai wasn't likely to collect on the wager.

Something rapped against the external airlock, a metallic, hollow
clang.

Chung waved Penn forward, and the younger man opened the external airlock hatch, then stepped back.

Forms moved around in the small space. The viewport was too small to make out details from where Rai stood, but he had a sense of gray and black. Along with red, those were the Azoren military's favorite colors.

Rai shoved his hands in the coverall pockets, then pulled them back. "What do you think's going on with the *Pandora*?"

Chung's head swung around. "Pfft. You serious?"

"They had a chance to escape if you hadn't blown that charge."

"Fuck 'em. Bitch tried to kill me."

"You were about to kill them, Quentin."

The inner airlock hatch scraped open, revealing several tall, thick bodies in the sort of gray-and-black heavy armor the Azoren favored for their front-line Marines. Silver-coated faceplates completed the black helmets. For weapons, there were the bulky boarding weapons—specialized shotguns.

Rai's hands were away from his body, palms toward the Marines.

Chung had his right hand up, waving. "Welcome aboard."

One of the Marines separated from the rest, weapons dropping slightly. The faceplate rose, revealing a craggy-faced man with dark, golden hair and light green eyes. He looked the cargo hold over once, then turned back to the old man. "What does a Gulmar merchant vessel do in the demilitarized zone?"

"Check your records, Sergeant. We're not a merchant vessel. We're a privateer chartered by your Silver Lightning intelligence agency."

The Marine squinted, then stepped away, faceplate dropped again.

He would call the information in to his command, and there would be a back and forth over the credibility of the claim before someone even asked to see documents. That was another thing the Azoren loved: documentation. If anything, it was a fatal flaw for them. Someone could probably slip a nuclear bomb through security so long as documents said that was okay.

After a bit, the sergeant turned around, faceplate once more raised. "Don't have any record of a Gulmar Union registered privateer."

Chung smiled. "Wouldn't be very good for that to potentially show up in records the Gulmar might access, now would it?"

The sergeant's dour look was testament to his thoughts on that.

"I have documentation." Chung waved the forms he'd pulled from his left pocket when the Azoren had reached the airlock.

That drew the sergeant's attention, but it didn't motivate him to move. "Such documentation being forged is punishable by execution."

"They aren't forgeries."

"Judgment falls to me, not you." The grumpy Marine took a step and waved for the papers. When he had them, he turned away again and paced toward the forward section of the hold.

He would be able to confirm the secret watermarks, the identifying elements of the paper, and the signatures and titles, but he would also have to run it up the chain of command. If there was something the Azoren loved as much as sharp uniforms and documentation, it was their chain of command.

Minutes passed, then the sergeant returned. "Your papers have been confirmed."

Chung held his hand out, keeping his body language just shy of smug.

The Azoren sergeant didn't budge. "Captain Keller asks what you are doing in the DMZ."

"Well, Sergeant...?"

Cold, green eyes stared at Chung, but the sergeant didn't respond.

Chung chuckled. "Just Sergeant is good, I guess. It's a matter of a job gone wrong. We had arranged to purchase information on a potential port to raid. Rumor was, there would be some advanced weapons prototypes being transported for testing. Unfortunately it was a spy, and we barely escaped. You can see the repairs to our reactor, if you want." He nodded toward the hatch.

The sergeant waved one of the other Marines forward, muttered something, then turned back to Chung as the designated Marine hustled toward the hatch. "Go on."

"Well, we made a run for it just ahead of these spies and drifted into the DMZ. When the radiation leak forced us to shut down, we came to a stop and went into cold sleep. Apparently, our emergency transponder was damaged in the attack. It only fired off once."

Rai was fairly skilled at reading people, but the Azoren sergeant was as inscrutable as an android. That seemed to be what the Azoren valued.

Finally, the fair-haired man grunted. "How fortunate the *Hammer of Heaven* heard your call." It was delivered deadpan. "And now Captain Keller would host you aboard our vessel."

"Actually, if we could get a technician to look our reactor over, we'll be on our way."

"The captain awaits you."

No amount of talking was going to change the invitation.

Chung turned to Gabriel and Wong. "You heard that. Suit up."

There was a second Marine squad waiting outside the airlock for them. Rai and the others were kept between the two Azoren groups, and there was no question they were being treated as prisoners, at least for the moment. They'd been disarmed, and a quick pat-down conducted.

An upside to the Marines having so much confidence was that they couldn't conceive of someone else being a legitimate threat.

Once across the umbilical, they entered a hangar bay full of smaller scout craft and gunships packed tight. Pale white light revealed gray-painted surfaces that had no visible scuffs or cracks. Rai had gotten a look at the destroyer on the way across—big, angular, somewhat ugly in its midnight gray blandness. The smaller vessels were like babies awaiting birth from the destroyer's womb.

The sergeant led them through the hangar and to an adjoining open space with racks of tools and panels and all sorts of other things Rai imagined the *Rakshasa* could use.

After chatting with a young man in grimy coveralls, the sergeant led them into a passageway and stopped. "A team of technicians will inspect your vessel to…see what can be done to assist."

And to review your logs and test your story, Rai thought.

But Chung had thought of that. Nothing remained to betray his claims. If they were lucky, no one would think to check cold sleep, and they'd come out of this with an operational ship.

Rai wasn't one to believe in luck in such situations. They had run out.

Boots stomped down the passageway, and someone in a much less impressive uniform of pale gray cut around a bend and ran toward them. It was another young man—a sailor, less imposing than the boarding party, much like the technician. The sailor came to a stop some meters away, and the sergeant went over. The two exchanged a whispered conversation, with the sailor studying Chung's crew a few times.

Just when Rai was sure the conversation would go on forever, the sailor jogged back the way he'd come and the sergeant returned to them. "Captain Keller awaits us outside the starboard cargo bay."

This time, Rai could make out something more in the other man's demeanor than before: tension, irritation.

Something was wrong.

The sergeant barked out orders, and the lighter armored of the two squads hurried back to the hangar deck, apparently acting on whatever had the sergeant upset.

Then he had them moving down bright passageways—headed forward, then to starboard, then to stern, twice up stairs, once down. It probably wasn't meant to confuse the privateers, but that was the end result. Rai had a decent sense of how he could retrace his steps, but the others looked hopelessly lost.

Except for Penn.

Somewhere in all the hurry, he'd disappeared.

Dread sank into Rai's gut. There was no way the Marines would have lost track of one of their prisoners, so Penn was either dead or...

A spy.

Or the Marines were truly distracted by whatever had them worked up.

Even if that was the case, it wouldn't explain Penn simply wandering off.

It wasn't something Rai was going to bring anyone's attention to, either.

The sergeant slowed as they approached another wide passageway. A tall, lean man in bright white coat and pants stood outside a hatch talking with someone in a uniform similar to the group of Marines who'd been waiting outside the *Rakshasa*. A naval officer and another boarding party

Marine. The man in the white uniform was older, probably in his late forties; he had a sharp nose and thick eyebrows. His back was straight and his neck long. The Marine he was talking to was about the age of their escorting sergeant but smaller and slightly darker of skin.

Rai was putting it together: the opposite side of the destroyer, an Azoren Marine, an officer...the *Pandora* crew hadn't surrendered.

The officer waved them in, and their escort gave a hushed briefing, after which the white-suited man turned to them. "Welcome aboard the *Hammer of Heaven*, Mr. Chung. I am Captain Keller. Apologies are in order for this unfortunate situation."

Chung scratched his environment suit where it stretched over his belly. "It's business."

"Ugly business, unfortunately. You are familiar with the Kedraalian ship?"

"The *Pandora*? Yeah. We had, uh, appropriated materials and assistance from them when they came upon us."

The officer's bushy eyebrows arched. "They responded to your SOS?"

"Never could figure out how they got to us so quickly, but yeah."

Rai realized the old bastard hadn't noticed Penn was missing. If he was an Azoren spy, Chung's deviations from the truth were going to be trouble. Then again, everything felt like trouble at the moment, and that left Rai missing his pistol.

Better to go down fighting.

Captain Bushy Eyes cleared his throat. "This Kedraalian ship decided to attempt to repel my Marines. I lost good people."

"They were a pretty strange group."

Gabriel snorted but quickly bowed his head.

The captain frowned. "Fortunately, we overcame the enemy, and I have teams crawling through the ship, trying to understand what they were doing in the DMZ. We've brought across everything from their cargo bay for inspection."

Chung's eyes brightened. "Well, we did what we could to lessen the threat. We took some of that cargo for ourselves, and you'll find a few of their bodies floating in space."

"Yes, we have."

"And I managed to plant some charges on the ship."

"Charges?"

"To make sure they didn't escape the DMZ. We were going to report them to our contacts when we got our systems running. You want to know where those charges are?"

"Please."

"Sure." Chung accepted a data pad from the darker-skinned Marine and typed into it. "That should be all of it."

"Your assistance will not go unmentioned."

"Thanks."

All the preening and fawning was getting to Rai. There should have been some panic about Penn, but everyone was too busy kissing each other's ass. If *Penn* was a spy, it would be Chung and his close circle who would be in trouble. Rai had never done anything to make himself look like a traitor to the Azoren.

Unless Penn had seen something when they talked.

There was a commotion from beyond the open hatch, and a few seconds later, two more Marines appeared holding the pretty nurse up between them.

Chung's eyes widened. "I thought you said they'd fought your Marines."

The Azoren officer's nose wrinkled in disgust. "Not this one. A simpleton, apparently."

Rai fought the instinct to correct the officer. Having a problem with violence hardly made the young woman a simpleton. Then again, from what little he'd seen of the Azoren, they held their few women in such low regard, they probably would equate panic to mental deficiency.

Alarms rang, and the Marines searched around until the captain reached an intercom panel. "Commander Gunder, what is this alarm about?"

"Captain Keller, we are experiencing systems failures. We have personnel investigating, but you should move to a safer area."

The sergeant who had been escorting them stiffened and cursed. He'd finally realized that Penn was missing. He shook Chung by the shoulder. "The other one, where is he?"

Chung's brow furrowed. "Huh? Penn? Shit. I don't know."

Not a spy, then. Rai relaxed slightly. "He was with us earlier."

The sergeant turned red. He hissed something at two of his men, and they dashed back along the way they'd come. When the captain was done with the intercom, the sergeant bowed his head. "One of the privateers has gone missing."

The captain frowned. "Find him." He waved at Chung. "The rest of you, follow me, please."

He led them to a room not far from the cargo bay apparently connected to the *Pandora*. There was a desk, chairs, and a wall-mounted table with pitchers and mugs set on top.

"Help yourselves to some refreshment. Your ship should be repaired soon. I must return to my office to interrogate this—" The officer sniffled. "—woman."

When the hatch to the room closed, Chung began to pace while Gabriel and Wong settled into chairs. No one talked for minutes.

Rai searched for cameras or other possible spying devices. He couldn't shake the feeling everything they were seeing was authentic, that the Azoren were as confused as he was, but…something felt wrong.

Chung ran a hand along the outer bulkhead. At the far corner, he turned to Rai. "What about it?"

Rai poured himself a drink—something steaming and aromatic. "What do I think?"

"Yeah."

"I don't like it." The fluid was tart but sweet. He took a few sips, then set the mug on the table.

"Yeah. Nothing to like." Chung returned to pacing.

"It feels like the sort of situation where troublesome people are disappeared."

"Yeah, yeah." The old man paced for a while longer, then rapped a knuckle against the table. "You think they killed Penn?"

"No."

"When did he disappear?"

"Could've been anytime. It wasn't my turn to babysit him."

Chung grunted. "It's a big ship."

"Lots of twists and turns."

"Yeah." Chung paced the compartment again.

A distant rumbling seemed to vibrate through Rai's boots. "Did you feel that?"

"Hm?"

"Like a tremor."

Another rumbling—more pronounced—shook the fluid in the mug Rai had set down earlier.

"There, you—"

The lights overhead flickered, then died. Emergency lights clicked on.

Gabriel straightened in his chair and glanced around.

Chung spun around slowly. "Explosions?"

Rai smiled at the confusion on Gabriel's brutish face. "Feels like it."

"Can't be the Kedraalian ship." Chung pressed an ear to the hatch. "They didn't have a weapon."

The hatch opened, revealing Penn, an unfamiliar pistol in hand. "We need to go."

Gabriel jumped from his chair. "Fuck yeah!"

The old man held up a hand. "Hold it. Go where?"

"The *Rakshasa*. It's repaired, but it's going to be rigged for towing, and we're going to be sucking vacuum if we don't go. Now."

More than before, Rai's instincts screamed something was wrong, but it was the same feeling he'd had while they were talking with the Azoren captain. "I think we gotta go, Quentin. The guy kept your charter."

"Yeah." Chung's nails scraped through his stubble. "He did."

"I think we're an inconvenience right now."

"All right. You get us back to the ship, kid?"

Penn smirked. "Easily."

The young man was as good as his word, retracing the path better than Rai could have and evading sailors like a real professional. As they ran, power flickered off and on multiple times.

Gabriel cackled. "Ho-ho! Love it!"

Penn shushed the big man. "The primary and secondary power couplers are blown. They'll be a while fixing them."

A ship the size of the *Hammer of Heaven* would have multiple channels and probably multiple power sources. To take those down would have required a *lot* of skill.

"Ho-ha!" Gabriel fell in beside Penn. "You did this, huh?"

Penn shushed the bigger man again. "Yes. When the Marines were split off, I sneaked away."

"Oh, nice!"

The former security man glared back at Chung. "We're coming up on a junction."

Chung shrugged. "Almost there, right?"

Rai grabbed the old man's shoulder. "Just tell Gabriel to shut the fuck up."

"I'm not gonna—"

Someone shouted from around the junction point ahead, then a Marine stepped into view, boarding weapon at the ready. "Halt!"

Penn brought his pistol up and fired, blasting a hole in the Marine's unprotected head.

Wong sprinted forward. "I got it!"

Before Rai could shout a warning, another Marine stepped around the corner and fired.

Chunks of Wong's guts flew clear of his environment suit, spraying the passageway a deep red, and the scrawny man went limp, falling to the deck face down.

Penn dropped the second Marine, then waved Gabriel and Rai forward. "Get the guns!"

Gabriel hunched low and grabbed the closest gun, tossing it back to Rai, then hurried forward to grab the second.

Chung dropped to a knee beside his nephew. "Fuck, kid, why'd you have to be so goddamn stupid?"

Penn waved for everyone to hurry up. "The gunfire's going to draw more people."

Rai took the lead. He recognized where they were now. It wouldn't be far. After the junction, they had another turn, then the hangar bay. That was going to be a problem all its own. Better to keep moving and deal with the problems when they arose then stop and plan, though.

At the hatch, he waited. There had been technicians in the hangar bay. They weren't likely to have weapons, but it was always a risk.

Penn came toward them, dragging Chung along. "Open it!"

The hatch opened.

And two Marines stepped out. They seemed just as surprised as Rai felt.

He fired, blasting the face off one of them, but Gabriel somehow managed to miss the other, who kicked the big brute in the nuts and fell back.

Rai popped around the hatch to finish the Marine off, but pulled back just as the other man fired his boarding weapon. Pellets clanged off the bulkhead, hatch, coaming, and passageway.

The gunfire had Rai's ears ringing, or he might have heard the Marine charging up behind Penn and Chung before it was too late.

The Marine fired, and the old bastard's guts erupted out the front of his environment suit.

Penn dropped with a groan.

Rai brought his own boarding weapon up. "Vic, hangar bay!"

He didn't wait for Gabriel's response but opened fire on the Marine who'd killed the old man. The first shot drove the Azoren back but didn't drop him.

Rai racked another round in and ran after the retreating Marine.

Blood had been drizzled on the deck, bright red. There was only one place the Marine could have fallen back to: a corner that Rai thought might lead to another passageway.

He jogged up to it, quietly, straining to hear.

In between distant weapons fire, he could make out the wheezing of the wounded man: soft but unmistakable, just around the corner.

Rai stomped a booted foot, and the Marine came around the corner. Rai brought his boarding weapon down like a club, braining the Marine.

The wounded man fell, and Rai stomped on the exposed throat.

Chung's corpse was still in the passageway outside the hangar bay, but Penn had pulled himself up to the hatch. Rai gathered the wounded man and hauled him into the hangar bay.

There were bodies everywhere.

And at the airlock hatch, Gabriel was pulling on his helmet. When he saw them, he picked up a huge weapon that was leaning against the bulkhead next to the airlock. "Lookie what I found! Oh, and your weapons—" He pointed the gun at guns, knives, tools, and their helmets piled on the deck. "Right here."

Between that pile and the airlock slumped an unconscious female in a gray uniform. She was young, baby-faced, with dull brown hair. Blood trickled from a flattened nose to a jacket that had officer insignia on it. An environment suit had been pulled partway on.

Gabriel laughed. "Got myself a present."

Rai set Penn down and checked his environment suit. It needed patching. "Leave her."

"Uh-uh. Ho-ho-ho! No way! I gotta know."

"Know what?"

"This shit. All this shit, man. I gotta know how it happened. Ho-ho-ho, she's gonna talk! For a while, at least."

It was the wrong time and the wrong thing to argue over. Rai patched Penn's suit, then got their helmets on while Gabriel finished suiting the ensign up. The big man sang a song about throwing a party and draped the suited-up woman over his shoulder.

And then they were through the airlock, into the umbilical, making a run for the *Rakshasa*.

Rai could only hope that Penn's estimate was right and they had some time before repairs could be completed. Otherwise, they were dead.

28

THE OFFICE WAS BRIGHT; THE AIR THICK WITH MASCULINE SMELLS. A CRISP, white light came from overhead brass fixtures that seemed incongruous with the otherwise modern and sleek aesthetic. For furniture, there was a desk with a built-in display for a surface; a smaller desk attached to the main one, the surface covered with a silver tea set; two chairs bordering on ostentatious with their dark leather and worked wood frame. One chair sat behind the desk, the other chair across from it, braced against a wall.

It was in this second chair that Petty Officer Brianna Stiles had been seated. She now wore only a dark T-shirt and shorts. Her flight suit had been taken from her.

Keller muttered her name while lowering himself into the chair. Her image and other data occupied the top left third of his desktop display. His eyes were drawn to her face, and that made his own face pinch tight and his lips purse.

"Sergeant Preminger?"

An older man—white hair, stocky, short—stepped through the open hatchway. "My Captain!"

The captain wiped at something—a smudge or fleck of dust—that had settled on the display, then plucked a stylus from the right side of the desk. "Commander Gunder has not reported in lately. Please ascertain the status of my executive officer, Sergeant."

Preminger bowed. "Of course, Captain."

Keller opened a drawer and put the stylus away.

Neat, precise—there was a place for everything and everything had to be in its place.

The officer studied the data, but every few seconds, his eyes would drift back up to Stiles's face. Most of the time, there was a sneer, but the more he stared at her, the less intense the sneer was.

He muttered. "Subhuman."

That was the sound of it, despite the drone of air recyclers.

The sergeant returned. "Commander Gunder is ready to speak to you, Captain."

That seemed to calm Keller. He shrank the window with Stiles's image and opened a new window. A younger man with a weathered face appeared. He was the sort with a perpetual shadow of whiskers made worse by a deep cleft in his chin and folds around the corners of his mouth.

Keller glanced up at Stiles, then back at Gunder. "Commander Gunder, I was looking for a status update."

"Of course, Captain."

"I must tell you, this privateer disappearing is a problem."

"It is, Captain."

"How are we to interrogate—" Keller's eyes drifted up, then after a quick assessment of the young woman fell back to his XO's face. "—these men?"

"Perhaps they offer nothing of value to begin with, Captain."

"The technicians found nothing in their logs?"

"Completely blanked, Captain. An act of sabotage, there is no doubt."

"Hm." The corner of Keller's mouth twisted up as he looked Stiles over again. "Perhaps honey with this group."

"Honey, Captain?"

"They seem a group of miscreants, backwards and inbred. The dark one might be the brightest. He has a devilishness to his eyes."

"An animal's craftiness, no doubt, Captain."

"Craftiness can kill, whether it's an animal's or a human's."

"As you say, Captain. What of the other dark-skinned one? The one taken from the Kedraalian ship?"

"She is in my office. I look at her right now, in fact."

Gunder recoiled. "I apologize that you must endure this, Captain."

"We all make sacrifices for the Federation. What about the systems failures?"

"I have assembled a team of technicians. We have reduced the likely source to one area and are searching that now, Captain."

"Good. I expect prompt updates."

"As you command, Captain."

The connection to the XO ended, and Keller sighed. He pulled folded papers from a pocket and set them down with a sneer of distaste. "Privateers, indeed."

Keller unfolded and flipped through the papers using his stylus as much as possible rather than touching things himself, as if dissecting the corpse of a hideous monster that had crawled out of the sewer. Every few seconds, his eyes would flash to Stiles, sometimes squinting, sometimes simply staring and maybe swallowing.

"It isn't right that someone subhuman should be so appealing to the eye." It came out muttered but once again louder than the air recycler.

The woman stared at him with dull, dazed eyes that barely blinked.

Green eyes so dark they drifted toward brown. How could those eyes draw his gaze to them, what with her being inferior? His people had gone through generations of eugenics and genetic enhancement, yet there he was, noting the fullness of her lips, the swell of her curves, the straightness of her regal neck.

"Sergeant Preminger!"

The stocky, old man was in the hatchway almost immediately. "Captain?"

"See if you can communicate with this...woman. Offer her refreshment."

"As you command, Captain." Preminger knelt at her side. "She is quite attractive for her people, isn't she?"

"Her people lack the purity of ours. They are mongrels. It is what will help us to rise above."

"Perhaps the captain could avail himself of her pleasures after so long away from home?"

Keller's cheeks flushed. "We are not savages, Sergeant."

"We are not, Captain. My jest was improper. I apologize."

Keller stretched toward her and snapped his fingers. "Can you understand me?"

Stiles nodded slowly.

"So you are trained well. Or maybe you are...more than we're led to believe." He swallowed loudly, and his attention returned to the paperwork, but only for a second. "Would you like water?"

She nodded. "Thank you."

Preminger disappeared, and the desktop flared to life again with Gunder's face. "Captain, good news!"

Keller sighed. "What is it?"

"We believe we've found the cause of the system attacks, Captain." The XO held up a strange device. "This was inserted into a data access terminal near the forward primary power coupler."

"What is it?"

"Something I am not familiar with, Captain." Gunder turned away, and when he turned back, the device was gone. "I have one of my men looking at it now."

"Update me immediately upon—"

A deafening squeal preceded the connection going dark by less than a second.

The captain recoiled, then ground the heel of a palm against his ear. He tried to raise Gunder again but had no luck.

"Sergeant Preminger!"

The stocky old man returned, handing Stiles a cup of water. "Captain?"

Keller tapped the darkened display, as if that might convey meaning to his assistant. "I cannot raise Commander Gunder."

"How odd, Captain."

"Yes. He was at the forward primary power coupler. Go to him with haste. I need an update immediately on the device he found."

The old man bowed and hurried out.

Keller ran a finger along his jawline as he stared at the Kedraalian captive, as if her drinking water was somehow captivating. "Perhaps—"

A noise rumbled through the deck, and the lights went out.

Stiles whimpered and her cup clattered to the floor.

"What is this?" The captain stood, a shadow in the faint light coming from somewhere outside the office. "Silence, woman."

She did as he asked.

The faint light grew brighter, and he returned to his seat, jaw set. "Such outrageous failures. This will reflect poorly on Gunder."

Stiles stretched out to retrieve her cup, and her T-shirt rode up, revealing the smooth skin of her belly.

Keller stared for a moment, then looked away. "This...this has been one disaster after another. Entering the DMZ over some pointless emergency signal, losing Marines to your people. None of it will sit well with headquarters."

"I'm sorry, Captain."

His brows arched. "Yes. Well. It is my promotion that concerns me, you see. I will need to find some way to deflect all these problems to someone else, or it is my command that will be questioned."

"We never meant any trouble." She scraped a thumbnail along the rim of the cup.

"Killing Marines..." He cleared his throat. "It's a diplomatic mess. You understand that?"

"Commander Martinez knew that was a risk."

"Your captain, this Martinez?"

"He was. The privateers killed him when we tried to assist them."

"Ah. They lured you in."

She nodded. "We're search and rescue. Unarmed."

"Hmph. I have several dead Marines who would disagree with such an assessment."

"We took the weapons from the privateers."

Keller blinked. "And how would you do that, exactly?"

"They were more concerned with...raping us than anything else. When they were...distracted, we took their weapons."

"And didn't kill them?"

"We wanted to leave in peace. We sent them back to their ship, then you arrived. You saved us. Except they told us they would tell you to kill us."

"I see." Keller's voice softened.

"Commander Benson, she never wanted any of this."

"The female officer?"

Stiles bit her quivering lip. "We tried to flee, but the pirates had set charges in our ship."

"Unfortunate."

She brushed tears from her eyes. "I'm sorry. I'm sorry about your career and your Marines. They were so afraid of dying. Commander Benson and her crew. The Republic is terrified of war with the Azoren."

"Yes." Keller straightened. "As they should be. But the Azoren Federation doesn't seek war."

Something whistled—an intercom. "Captain Keller? This is Sergeant Preminger."

Keller twisted around and pressed a button on the wall. "Go ahead, Sergeant."

"There has been an explosion at the forward primary power coupler. Damage control teams are just now forming."

An alarm whined strangely, and Keller spun around, lips quivering. "An explosion? Did someone sound general quarters?"

"From the bridge, Captain. I sent a runner. The intercom suffered damage from the blast. The bridge has been cut off."

A commotion had been audible through the last bit.

Keller stood. "I need to be on the bridge." Keller's eyes settled on Stiles. "Where is the commander, Sergeant Preminger?"

"Dead, Captain. His entire team was caught in the blast."

"Dead?" Keller snatched up the paperwork and shook it. "I want those privateers put in the brig. Immediately. If they resist, kill them."

"As you command, Captain."

Keller shuffled from around the desk, eyes staring into the distance.

"Gunder was a good man. He'd been selected for DNA preservation. Engineered offspring."

Stiles took the captain's hand. "That sounds like an honor."

The Azoren officer stared at her hand but didn't pull away. "It is. But his death will not be a waste. It was his responsibility to oversee both boarding parties."

"And he was killed searching for the cause of the problems?"

"Exactly so. And his death, every failure falls to him."

"That sounds sensible. Are the Azoren like that? Logical and sensible?"

"Yes." Keller licked his lips. "Everyone understands how it is. Logic must prevail. The strong must rise. My promotion—"

"Would it strengthen your promotion if you had the people behind all of this in your custody?"

"The people…" He glanced down at her.

"The Union. The Gulmar."

"They were behind…" His eyes locked onto the paperwork in his left hand.

"I can tell you what I heard. Maybe you could find more details by interrogating the pirates. You said you were going to interrogate them, right?"

"Yes."

"Then I'll tell you what they said and what I heard. If that would help your career. And help to make up for all the unfortunate death."

Keller squeezed the young woman's delicate hand, admiring the warmth and smoothness. "Yes, please. Tell me all."

Stiles nodded. "What you hear should see the right people punished."

"Good, good."

"And maybe it will help us all to deal with our losses."

29

KELLER LEANED AGAINST THE FRONT OF HIS DESK. THE KEDRAALIAN PETTY officer—Stiles—stared into the empty cup gripped tight in her golden-brown hands, as if drawing strength from it. She'd spoken a moment before, but the words had been lost in the unsettling echoes coming from the passageway outside the office. Emergency lighting only magnified the beauty of her profile and lent an intimacy to their huddled space.

Before she could begin again, a staticky squeal buzzed through the intercom, then the squeal was replaced by Sergeant Preminger's voice. "Captain Keller?"

Annoyance flashed across the captain's face. He pushed off from his desk and slapped the intercom button with unnecessary force. "What is it, Sergeant?"

"An update, Captain."

Keller sighed. "Go ahead."

"The privateers?"

"Yes?"

"Marines found the office they were in empty."

"Where was the guard?"

"Dead, Captain. They broke his neck, and his body was stuffed in a storage closet."

"The room was sealed. How could they break his neck?"

"We wondered the same, Captain. Is it possible the door was compromised when power failed?"

"It is, but then he would hear them opening it."

"And he would have shot them. Yes, Captain. So we have been confused by this."

Stiles raised her head. "You said one of them was missing?"

Keller's eyes widened. "Has there been any sign of the missing privateer?"

"None, Captain."

"Then order everyone to full alert."

"But the communications are not work—"

"Use runners. Warn everyone. These men are to be shot on sight."

"As you command, Captain."

The Azoren officer stepped away from the intercom, obviously distracted. "You suspected this of these privateers?"

The young woman nodded. "I'm a medical technician, a noncombatant sworn to care for the wounded, but they were willing to kill me."

"And defile you, yes. They are savages by trade and coming from the Gulmar..."

Her chin shook. "And I think our captain might have been in league with them."

"You can explain this?"

"I think so, Captain Keller. I'm not an educated officer like you, but I know what I heard and saw. Maybe it'll make more sense to you than me."

"No doubt it will." He patted her firm, youthful shoulders to reassure her, then leaned against the desk again. "Tell me what you know."

"It began when I came aboard the *Pandora* a few months ago. I had just completed advanced training and had drawn what looked like a choice assignment."

"A search-and-rescue vessel?"

"Those and high-end medical ships are what you want. Search and rescue gives you a real opportunity to save lives for people out on the frontier in rugged conditions, and the medical ships have all the most advanced systems and best surgeons. You learn so much either way."

"And you had no fear of pirates or...insurgents?"

"We have an armistice with everyone who split off after the War of Separation, and—"

"The Struggle for Independence, please."

"I'm sorry. My education isn't very sophisticated."

The Azoren officer shrugged.

"When we were coming aboard—Private Lopez and I—there was a lot of activity on the ship. I didn't pay it any mind, because I already had priority assignments waiting for me: instrument sterilization, medication resupply, and surgical chamber decontamination."

"There were no other people to do these tasks?"

"Oh, there were. Commander Dietrich believed in testing new personnel. The way he saw it, our ship would never have ideal moments for training and testing, so he didn't wait."

Keller harrumphed. "Training is a discipline that requires formality."

"Our school had the same philosophy. Dr. Dietrich was a surgeon with years of experience in emergency rooms. His views were unorthodox but respected. I'd been warned about him."

"So this activity you saw, was it special?"

"It must have been. There were crates brought aboard that had security teams guarding them. And there were things being installed. I heard from Chief Parkinson—the senior engineer—that the systems were top secret."

"Top secret? On a search-and-rescue vessel?"

"That's what frightened me. And I didn't realize why until today."

The officer folded his arms over his chest. "Go on."

"Well, Commander Benson and I were getting ready to come on to the second shift just a few hours ago, but something strange happened. An alarm—like the one you just had—went off. It turned out that while we were in Fold Space, our systems had malfunctioned, and we'd drifted parsecs off course."

Keller's brow furrowed. "Impossible."

"I know! And Chief Parkinson—the engineer? That's what he said, too. But he had an explanation."

"Which was?"

"The systems installed when I was picked up. Someone had inserted a modification that would override all the safety systems and redundancies that should have taken us out of Fold Space at the first safe opportunity and warned the command staff about the error."

"What sort of modification?"

"Well, I'm not an engineer, Captain, but Chief Parkinson said it was something tied into the core software. And he thought it would have to have been approved by Commander Martinez."

"Your engineer, he saw this modification?"

"He saw indications it had been installed, but what he said was more important was what he saw when they were trying to do a post-mortem: Someone had deleted logs. Everything that would have pointed to exactly that sort of modification they'd done—all of those logs were gone."

The tall man leaned forward so that he was closer to her eye level. "And that somehow points to your captain and the Gulmar?"

"I think so, Captain. You see, right after we came out of Fold Space, we got the SOS from the *Rakshasa*—the privateer ship. And when Commander Benson tried to get Commander Martinez to ignore the signal and do a full burn for the Kedraalian side of the DMZ, he refused."

"That could easily be the work of a dedicated search-and-rescue commander."

"It could, sir. And we all thought it was. Until he refused to call the rescue off after seeing the ship itself."

"And that matters how?"

"We identified the hidden belly turret. And we found the ship's registration that clearly indicated it was Gulmar, just like the SOS had said."

"Hidden weapons are no guarantee of piracy."

"Oh, no, Captain Keller. But Commander Martinez did two things that showed he had to have been complicit: He left all radios running after saying the *Pandora* had to undergo diagnostics, and he knew the ship."

"What does that mean?"

"He identified this Gulmar ship based on profile and registration data. No one else knew anything about it."

Keller waved a hand dismissively. "A good captain knows such things."

"Would he have gone aboard a potentially hostile ship without a full complement of Marines? Because Commander Martinez left his most experienced Marine behind and sent the most experienced Marine he had with him to check on the reactor instead of taking her with him. And then he checked on the infirmary without anyone to back him up."

The Azoren captain tapped his chin. "I fear that this is hardly conclusive."

"Would you change your mind if you knew that the captain had a special device installed in our offline storage area that wiped out data that could have proven his involvement with the Gulmar?"

Keller's back straightened. "A special device? You saw this?"

"I have it, Captain Keller. In my flight suit right thigh pocket."

The Azoren captain headed into the outer office where Preminger had laid out the petty officer's flight and environment suits, returning a moment later holding a small device that fit comfortably in his palm. His pale eyes were locked onto the compact thing, which he eventually held out to her.

She took it and examined it quickly. "That's the one."

"There is an unmistakable resemblance to what Commander Gunder found."

"Wouldn't that make the case?"

"That your captain and these people worked together?"

"Not all of them. Since he was killed by one of them the second they met, but there was someone in that crew who was supposed to meet with Commander Martinez."

"You are sure of this?"

"Yes. Chief Parkinson told me something he didn't tell anyone else. He and Commander Martinez were very close. They'd served with each other for years, on the *Huntsman* before the *Pandora*. Before going across, Commander Martinez asked the chief to use his drone to transmit a code into the *Rakshasa*. It was low power, a very specific frequency, and directional, right into the interior, where only a radio inside could pick it up."

"And this was abnormal?"

"Chief—"

The intercom buzzed, then a more normal tone slipped out of it, and a second later, Sergeant Preminger's familiar voice came through. "Captain!"

Keller groaned. "Excuse me."

The look on the officer's face said it all: It was odd feeling irritation at the interruptions of the job, but he absolutely was. The day-to-day duties of a captain were important. They established routine and consistency that enabled a ship to survive losing many of its staff officers. But emergency duties and keeping a calm head when facing emergencies—that was what made an officer most valuable.

"What is it, Sergeant?"

"Captain! There has been an attack! The privateers have killed several people. Many technicians were killed in the hangar bay."

Keller's back stiffened. "Have you found these privateers yet?"

"Not yet, Captain. We think they might have returned to their ship."

"Then ready a boarding party!"

"The Marines are still aboard the Kedraalian ship."

"Pull them back! Wait. Do we have functional weapons?"

"In perhaps thirty minutes, we will have the ability to use point defense and close-quarters defensive weaponry."

The captain raised his face to the ceiling. "Recall the Marines. Have them board the privateer ship and eliminate these vagabonds."

"I will see to it, Captain."

Duty wrestled with curiosity on the tall captain's face. He studied the documentation taken from the privateers for a few seconds, then returned to the front of the desk. "You propose your captain and one of these privateers worked together."

"After we lost contact with the commander, Chief tried to hack the code of the message, but he never had time."

"If I am to understand you, you propose that your captain worked in cooperation with the Gulmar, possibly as a spy."

"After all that's happened, Captain, that's what it looks like to me."

"Off of no more evidence than this device, the system modifications to your ship, and this encoded message."

"And the fact that we ended up here just in time to receive the SOS."

"It still is less than a compelling case."

Stiles bowed her head. "Commander Benson knew something was wrong."

"And this was the XO?"

"Yes, sir. She took over once Commander Martinez was killed. She would've told you about her suspicions except she was afraid you would've thought she was part of it."

"But she wasn't."

"No one else was, but they all died because of it. And I would have too, if I hadn't been so terrified. Killing people is something Marines do. I was trained to *save* lives."

"It is a noble profession." Keller rubbed the smooth surface of the device, then set it on his desk. "I will admit that there are many things about this matter that leave me perplexed. Coincidence is believable when data supports it as exactly that and the frequency stops short of absurdity."

"I hadn't thought of it so deeply, but I agree."

"It is something I am prone to do in my free hours, thinking about the ways of the universe."

"I—I wish I could do something like that, just…think."

That brought a smile to his thin lips. "Not everyone is so inclined, even when their genetics provide the aptitude for such a thing."

"Then you think this…goes beyond coincidence?"

"To an educated man, credulity is stretched beyond anything reasonable. And if one cannot credibly explain something, it is incumbent upon them to examine the more obvious alternative."

"What is that, Captain?"

"As you say, the probability of some conspiracy."

"That makes me wonder, sir: Does that mean you and your ship were brought here as part of that conspiracy?"

The tall man seemed to sink at that, and his chin jutted out, and his cheeks reddened. "Excuse me." He stepped out of the room and returned with her flight and environment suits, which he handed to her.

She stared at them, eyes blinking in disbelief. "I—"

"You are free to go, young woman." He set the suits down on her chair. "Quickly, though."

"Free?"

"From your story and the events that have transpired since our arrival, I gather that you are not the threat. In fact, you and your comrades would seem to have been victims."

She stood, shapely legs and arms trembling. "And your people as well, Captain."

"Yes."

"I'm sorry."

"That is kind of you. Thank you."

She lowered her head as she pulled the flight suit on, fumbling with the zipper a few times before closing it and pulling the environment suit on. "I—I'm not sure how I can get the *Pandora* out of the DMZ, sir."

"You needn't worry. We will provide you a solution to your troubles."

"Thank you. Would you have someone you could spare as an escort, sir? This ship is so big that I was lost almost immediately."

"I will take you on my way to the bridge."

The passageways seemed a little brighter than his office, with lights occasionally flickering. The repair crews must have been making progress.

At the cargo bay, he waved her toward the hatch. "It is unfortunate that our peoples were unable to find a peaceful resolution to what separated us."

Stiles bit her lip. "It was a pleasure meeting you, Captain."

He bowed. "Good fortune."

And then the hatch opened, and she passed through, boots clanging on the cargo bay door as she headed for the airlock and the *Pandora* beyond.

30

MOTORIZED HARNESS OR NOT, THERE WAS NO WAY THEY WERE GETTING across the umbilical. At least that's how it seemed to Rai. The thing was just a skeletal framework of struts and beams now telescoped out to its full length from the Azoren destroyer, to the much smaller *Rakshasa*.

But what *really* didn't help Rai's mood was the way Gabriel kept cackling over the radio connecting them.

"Ho-ho! And now, see, I got this fucking plasma cannon, right?"

He was a big man—tall, with an enviable "V" to his beefy frame, but the plasma cannon was longer.

Ka-klak!

That was Gabriel slapping a fully charged battery pack into the huge weapon. When Rai twisted around in the front seat of the harness carrying them to the *Rakshasa*, he could see Gabriel had braced the gun against his environment suit and helmet.

Thus the sound of the battery making it through the comms.

"Now—ho-ho—now—" Gabriel sucked in a breath as the whine of the big gun priming sang through the shared connection. "*Now* we get to see how—"

"The fucking gun can't penetrate the hull, Vic."

The harness crawled along the umbilical spine at caterpillar speed.

"I—" Vic twisted around, sneered. He made sure that sneer was visible through the faceplate of his helmet. "I fucking know it can't penetrate the hull, asshole. But those antennas? Up on the dorsal? Yeah."

"You're going to blow through the umbilical framework."

"Nope."

Crawling. Slower than caterpillars. Those could have sped past them.

At least the motor was running. If the destroyer's power systems were online, they could use that to move the harness.

Then again, if the destroyer's power systems were online, Rai and Gabriel would be dead.

"Whup! Whup!" The big idiot brought the gun up and sighted on the antennas.

Rai clenched his jaw tight. He was too old for this. Not older than Gabriel, not by much. They were both in their thirties. Gabriel was a bigger guy, and Gabriel threw that size around; he intimidated people.

Other people.

Not Rai.

He was too fast for Gabriel's idiocy to work and too smart.

It was Rai's mind that had gotten them through the deathtrap of a destroyer when no one else had made it. No one but Penn, who was strapped to the harness at Rai's feet, occasionally groaning.

Tough guy, Penn. Tough luck, taking the boarding weapon blast in the back.

Better that than what happened to the others, though.

Rai doubled over in the harness until he was looking at Penn's bloody, patched-up environment suit. At least the blood wasn't all the kid's.

It was fair to call him that. He probably wasn't thirty yet. But the kid knew his shit. He had connections and recommendations. That got him on the *Rakshasa* for the big job, and it probably accounted for him being able to do what he did.

Before the blast of the boarding weapon hit him.

"You're gonna be okay, kid." Rai patted Penn. "You'll make it."

"Y-yeah." Penn sounded like he believed it.

And they could make it, if Gabriel didn't get them fucking killed with his stupid toy.

Rai twisted around again. "Vic, put the gun away."

"Ho-ho-no!" Gabriel continued targeting the antennas. "Gonna be spectacular!"

"You're gonna blast a hole in the umbilical, you hear me?"

"Nah. It'll go right through the gap."

"We're moving, you—"

The asshole wasn't listening. Rai knew because he heard the whine of the gun building its charge before firing.

Wheeeeeeeeee-ummmmmf!

And a brilliant blue gob of superheated gas wrapped in a white-and-gold magnetic bubble launched straight out from the big gun.

Two things happened almost simultaneously.

Three.

First, Gabriel's voice climbed up to a full-on roar. "Ho! Ho! You see that?"

Second, the harness rocked and the motor seemed to give out, because the gun still had to propel the payload, and most of the recoil went into Gabriel's beefy shoulder, which transferred the energy to his body and to the harness.

And then third, the plasma completely melted away a good three meters of the umbilical framework.

Including the spine.

Somewhere in the seconds after that, two other things happened.

One of them was that Gabriel's laugh tapered off. It went sort of like, "Oh! Ho! Ho-ho-ho! Oh. No. No-no-no. Fuck."

Because the harness came to a complete stop and the umbilical just sort of sagged.

And the other thing—

This didn't really matter to Rai, because he was doing the calculus behind just putting his Graynard LP-7 blaster pistol against the back of the big mook's helmet and blowing his tiny brains all over the battered, skeletal framework.

Anyway, the other thing was that the plasma round hit the antennas and sort of melted some of them. Sort of melted them quite nicely.

But Rai still wanted to send Gabriel's brains into the vacuum. A whole new vacuum for them to live in.

"What the hell?" Gabriel spun around. "You see that?"

"The part where you blew a hole in the umbilical and fucked up our ride?"

"Oh, yeah. That. But, no. No! The antennas. Melting. Ho-ho-ho!"

Rai undid the restraining strap. "Y'know, we're on a clock here. They'll get power back eventually, and when they do, they'll blow the shit out of the *Rakshasa* if it's still here. And since I'll be in it, I don't fucking want that."

"Yeah, yeah. Don't be a baby."

Penn groaned. "What happened? We stopped moving."

"Big Brain here wrecked the umbilical." Rai undid the younger man's restraints. "Don't worry. We're close. We can make it."

Especially if Gabriel carried—

Rai almost dropped Penn. "What the fuck are you doing now?"

Gabriel held up another bundled, bloody environment suit. "What? I'm not leaving her behind."

"Leave her. You carry Penn."

"Fuck you. You carry him. I got her." The big man squeezed around the harness, giant hands effortlessly hauling him and his bundle along the framework. "I gotta know."

Rai almost went for the pistol stuffed in his environment suit belt. He could deal with the recoil. It would be worth the trouble.

Penn pulled himself along the bottom of the umbilical. "I'm okay."

This guy. Rai grabbed a loop on the back of Penn's suit. "I gotcha."

It was slow. Slower than the harness they'd had to abandon. And it was definitely inconvenient. And if Gabriel wasn't going to be helpful getting the *Rakshasa* ready in time, Rai would've done what he should've done a while back, when things started to go bad in the first place.

Except he wasn't so sure it would've mattered.

As he tugged Penn along, counting the seconds to the airlock, wondering how long the power would stay offline, the question gnawed: What had they done wrong?

No. They'd done *everything* wrong. From the second the job actually started to the *Pandora* showing up, and then the destroyer...

He couldn't imagine the *Pandora* still being intact on the other side of the *Hammer of Heaven*. If they had never gotten involved with the *Pandora* in the first place...

Lots of thoughts ran through Rai's mind when he thought back to that mess.

But things had been off the rails before it showed up.

Maybe Gabriel was right to think they should figure out why. When they had time. And they didn't have time, not right now.

"I'm hurting, Dev."

Penn wasn't pretending like he could help get them to the ship anymore.

"Don't you worry. Nothing lethal. I've seen worse." Rai *had* seen worse. Bodies mangled by a straight-on, close-range boarding weapon. Armor usually just transferred the energy to the body. The kid had been lucky to be wearing the exact thing to suck up the worst of the blast. "You're just sore. Painkillers'll fix you right up."

"Yeah, thanks."

Gabriel was at the airlock, waving. "Security, right? They change the code?"

Rai hoped not. "It's not working?"

"No. You know any special way in?"

There was the basic code and the override. Security had been Nguyen's thing. Before... "Try the override."

"Yeah. Yeah! Okay. Override, he-he!"

Rai slowed and tugged back on Penn's environment suit as they neared the airlock. The umbilical rocked from their momentum. But they came to a stop against the hull without too much fuss.

"Hey! Hey-hey!"

The airlock console flashed, and the hatch opened.

Lights kicked on inside. Real lights, not emergency ones.

The Azoren techs hadn't disabled power. Rai hoped they'd actually fixed this ship, too.

The big oaf tugged the bundled form behind him, cackling low and soft. There was gravity now that they were inside the ship, but the big guy held the bundled person without the least bit of effort.

Rai sighed. If life was about having no regrets, then he couldn't understand life. Everything was a regret at the moment.

The outer hatch closed, and they cycled through. Another eternity.

Gabriel howled and tossed the bundled form onto the metal grating of the cargo floor. "Yeah! You ever want to get one of these fucks, Dev? Huh?"

"Sure. In a gunfight. Like we did already." They'd left how many dead on the *Hammer*? "What're you planning to do?"

The big guy unsealed his helmet, then his suit. "Find out what the fuck went wrong, that's what."

"Yeah, I got that. Thanks for the clarification." Rai set Penn down and helped the young man get his helmet off, then unsealed his own. "I mean we got a timetable, okay? I need your help getting the *Rakshasa* ready for launch, understand?"

"We got time."

"We don't. They get power up—"

Out of the nowhere, a knife—a *big* knife—was in Gabriel's hand. "We got time, Dev."

"Sure." Rai held up his hands. "We got time. But we'll have more time once we get out of here and get into Fold Space, right?"

"Won't matter if we don't figure out what fucking happened. They'll just be on us again. They'll just fuck us over like they were trying to do when they showed up. You saw that, right?"

"Sure, I saw it."

Gabriel dragged the other form into a corner and took the helmet off, revealing short, brown hair and a chubby face. A kid, younger than Penn. Red lips, a broad nose that trailed blood down a double chin. She couldn't keep her head up.

Rai's stomach turned. "It's a kid, Vic."

The big guy cut the woman's environment suit away, revealing a gray uniform jacket darkened by her bloody nose.

Penn whispered, "What's going on?"

Rai held a finger to his lips: *Shhh.* "Shit, Vic, she's an ensign."

"Yeah." Gabriel paced around her, knife blade flashing through the air. "Yeah. Ensign. Officer. They know what's going on, right?"

"Not an ensign. They don't know their asses from a shitter."

"Yeah, well..." Gabriel pulled her up by the front of her jacket and pinned her to a bulkhead. "She's gotta know something."

"Vic!"

The big man drove the point of the blade into the thigh of her suit, and her eyes suddenly found focus. He twisted, and her head banged against the metal bulkhead as she screeched.

"Ho-ho!" Gabriel twisted around, waving the bloody knife at Rai. "See? Huh? Someone tipped them off, Dev. Someone fucked us over, and now we lost our charter!"

Rai took a step toward the bigger man. "You can't know that."

"Can too! You think about it. Just think about it. They couldn't know what we were doing. This ship, the contract we signed, the years of service." Gabriel wiped spittle on the arm of his suit. He giggled. "We get the perfect plan, and they somehow figure it out? I don't think so. Not without help. No-no-no!"

He turned back to the ensign and drove the knife into her thigh again. "And this one—I can tell from her voice—she's gonna talk."

He released his grip and let her slide to the floor.

Rai's hand drifted toward his gun.

But he couldn't pull it.

Gabriel was right. It didn't make sense they'd been figured out. Not unless someone had sold them out.

But would an ensign know?

31

GABRIEL WIPED THE BLOODY BLADE OF THE KNIFE ON THE ENSIGN'S JACKET. Rai clenched his jaw, biting back the urge to call the big oaf off. Saliva tendrils stretched between the ensign's twisted lips, and tears tracked down her bright red cheeks. When Gabriel swatted aside her hands and tore open her jacket, he revealed a body that hadn't even been rid of its youthful softness yet.

Rai didn't see an Azoren officer, he saw a kid, no older than that Marine kid Chung had executed.

The big brute snorted. "Ho-ho! Lookit that! Skin white like snow, huh? And soft! You ever even seen a man, sweetie?"

He pressed the tip of the blade against her gut, and she whimpered. "Please. I just graduated." It was a strange accent, soft and subtle.

"But you know something." He pressed his lips against her cheeks. "Oh-ho-ho! You know something! Don't make me cut you any more."

Penn gasped and squeezed Rai's leg. "What the fuck is wrong with him?"

It was a question that could be answered with hours of pointless discussion about the broken, hopeless society that shat out hollow, ruthless monsters like Gabriel. Or it could be answered more directly, with a blast to the back of the head.

That would cost them the potential answers the ensign might have.

Rai finally shrugged. "He's fucked up, like you and me."

"Not like me." Penn shook his head. "He enjoys that shit."

The big thug *was* taking pleasure from the torture. His hands were all over the ensign, and it wasn't just to break her spirit. Her cheeks and neck glistened where he'd licked her, and he was grinding against her wounded leg and making animal noises.

That was going too far for Rai. "Vic, cut it the fuck out. You wouldn't be doing that if that was a guy." It should've been a guy. The Azoren had no use for women, and there weren't many in the military.

Gabriel turned around, eyes barely focused. "Huh? What?" He dragged a hand across his mouth. "Oh! Ha-ha! Yeah? Who knows. Fuck. It's been a while. Ha-ha-ho!"

"Yeah, either way, stop it. Get the information from her, and we're done."

"I am, I am!"

Rai needed to check the systems out. Supposedly, the Azoren techs had fixed everything up, but *had* they? It was technically an Azoren vessel since their money had purchased it and they'd installed the weapons system, but they could just as easily blast it to pieces and leave the debris spinning through the DMZ for all eternity.

What mattered most, though, was knowing what the Azoren knew. Chung's charter was dead, done, but there was still money on the table if the Carone deal could be salvaged without interference.

The big man shook his head like an animal trying to rid itself of a stupor. "You heard the little guy, sweetie. All business. For now."

He pushed the tip of the knife in between two of her lower ribs before the fear could even settle on her face. The ensign let out a sigh that must have come from deep inside, then sucked in air and shrieked loud enough to shatter glass.

It only fed Gabriel's need. "Oh-oh-oh! Yes!" He scraped the knife along the bone, then swiped a knuckle through the blood and drew it across her face. "That almost makes you pretty. Ha! Ha!"

Penn grunted. "He's useless, Dev. You'd get more help from a butcher."

Rai swallowed. Torture had its uses, but this wasn't an act. The woman couldn't be more terrified than she already was. If she was going to talk, it was now. "Vic, ask her what she knows."

"In a minute."

"Ask her now."

"I'm busy!" The big man cut away more of her uniform. "Man's gotta have some fun. All work, no play. Heh-heh. This is fun, right?"

The ensign screamed again and slapped him across his wounded cheek. She shouted a string of words and sounds that didn't make any sense, the sort of desperate noise someone would make while fighting for their life.

And she was.

Gabriel curled up as if he were afraid of her wild blows. "Ho! Ho-ho! This one, oh, this one! Yipe!"

She'd gone from wild slaps to clawing, scratching at his exposed hands and dragging her hooked fingers across his scalp.

He laughed. "Ow! Oh-ho-ho! Ow! You minx!"

Then her fingers locked onto his ears, and she pulled.

"Hey! Ow!"

One of Gabriel's ears came away with a ripping sound, and he backpedaled, hand covering the wound. "Wha—?"

She threw the chunk of flesh to the deck and spat on it, then stomped it into the unforgiving surface with a booted heel. "Animal!"

"My ear! Ho! Oh-ho-no!" Gabriel's hand was slick with blood—his own for once.

The ensign seemed to find courage from that. She charged him, arms flailing.

And then his knife hand shot out, and she froze.

She fell back, fingers clasped now over her belly. Blood seeped from beneath them. A strange, weak moan slipped from her lips as she bumped into the bulkhead and slid down.

Gabriel came over to her. "Oh-ho. Oh-ho-ho-ho! No! You know how much it's gonna cost me to get that regrown? Huh?"

He brought a huge booted foot up and stomped on one of her knees. Bone cracked beneath the blow, and she shivered but apparently couldn't make another sound to express her pain.

Penn held a hand up to Rai. "Give me your gun, dammit."

"No." Rai gritted his teeth. "We need to know."

"He's not asking, Dev! He's just getting his rocks off torturing her!"

"I know." Rai stepped closer as the big man shattered the ensign's other leg. "Vic, you're done."

Gabriel spun around, gory knife raised. "Done? Oh-ho-ho! No. I'm not!"

Rai's gun was in his hand before he knew it. "You are."

The young woman's eyes were blurry. Her hands had fallen away from the knife wound in her gut.

Shock was setting in.

Gabriel didn't seem to notice. He pointed the knife at her. "She's ready to talk. Huh? Huh? See?"

He grabbed her by her uniform belt and hauled her upright, using his knife hand to keep her straight. When her head slumped forward, he shoved it against the bulkhead, then put the knife point against her throat.

Rai aimed his pistol at the back of the brute's head. "Let her go."

"No! Uh-uh! No-ho-ho! My little songbird's about to sing!" The knife slid under her skin until the tip came out behind her jaw, just below the ear. It was a shallow wound that would produce more blood than pain, but there was clarity in her eyes now. "I won't ask you to stand on your own—ho-ho-ho! No-no! But you need to talk. See the dark man with the gun? Huh? Yeah. Well. He wants to know how you got here so fast. Right, Dev?" Gabriel turned, his bloody face twisted into a hideous mask of fury. He resented someone encroaching on his little game, and he wasn't ashamed to show that. "Right?"

Rai forced his eyes to the wounded woman. "I'm sorry about this. Just tell us what you know."

She shook her head. Barely. "I...don't..."

"How did you get to our ship so quick? Why were you in this area?" Rai's stomach twisted at the ruin of this kid, this young woman who should have been just tasting the first thrills of life instead of experiencing the very worst of it. When he looked at her, he saw the pain that had been in Benson's eyes when he'd failed to protect her from Gabriel. "Tell us and this stops."

Gabriel chuckled. "He-he-he! It'll be all better, sweetie."

A single blast would have torn the top of the monster's head off, but Rai had to know. He had to know now. "You don't need to feel any more pain, Ensign."

The young woman nodded. "Diverted. We...were...diverted."

Rai moved closer. "To the DMZ?"

When she nodded again, the wounded flesh along her jaw turned into a bloody flap. "Headquarters. A priority message. To...patrol...DMZ."

"And you never patrolled here normally?"

A howl rolled out from Gabriel. "A destroyer? Don't make no sense! They'd be patrolling light years out if they did. Huh, girl?"

Her tear-glistening eyes tracked to him. She nodded again. "Smaller... patrol...ships."

"See?" Gabriel kissed her hard. "Oh, yes! We are going to *dance!*"

Rai's hand squeezed the pistol grip until he was sure it would leave an impression on his skin forever. "Vic, stop."

"What? Ho-ho! Can't you see? Huh? They were tipped off, just like I said. Had to be someone in the gang. Wasn't you. Wasn't me. Wasn't Quentin." He drove the knife into the woman's shoulder. "Who was it, huh? Who-who-who?"

She shuddered, and Penn shouted, "Stop it! You fucking animal!"

Gabriel twisted the knife around, then released the woman, who collapsed to the deck with a high-pitched squeal. The brute stalked toward Penn. "Why you worried about her, huh?"

"I didn't sign on for this barbaric shit! I just want my money!"

"She don't matter!"

Penn held a hand up to ward off the big man's dripping knife. "Everyone fucking matters, you asshole. She was—" He groaned. "She was just doing her job, and you cut her up like a piece of meat."

"Yeah-yeah-yeah!" The big man easily knocked Penn's hands aside and grabbed him by the environment suit. "But you're the only one that makes sense to be our little sellout, aren't you? Huh? Huh?" Gabriel waved the gory weapon in front of the new target of his attention.

It took some effort for Rai to twist away from the writhing ensign and to face the beast who had ruined her. "Put him down, Vic."

"No! No-no-no! Ha! I found him! I found the guy who got Quentin killed, now I'm—"

"Trying to fuck the Azoren out of a nice target got Quentin killed. Now put him down."

"Don't think so, Devvy-Dev-Dev. No." Gabriel pressed Penn against the bulkhead, and sliced open the front of his environment suit.

Penn grabbed the brute's wrist, but it didn't seem to have any effect. "Dev—"

"I think we're gonna toss this little pig into the airlock, and—"

A blaster bolt tore through the air.

Bits of the big thug's brains and smoking chunks of hair sprayed the bulkhead around Penn, then Gabriel's fingers went limp, and the wounded one-time security man fell to the deck. The larger man's body fell on top, a terrible weight made worse by the stench of his blasted, singed head.

Penn howled. "Dev! Can't breathe!"

The slender, dark-skinned man was there, pulling Gabriel's corpse aside, almost whispering. "It's okay. It's okay, all right? I'm sorry it took me so long."

"Yeah, yeah." Penn sucked in air. "He was gonna space me!"

"I know. Hold on."

Rai strode over to the ensign, who was making a hideous, sobbing sound that was almost a drone. Shoulders slumped, he raised his pistol and put a shot into her head. Her body relaxed, and the terrible noise stopped immediately.

Penn squeezed his eyes shut. "Fuck. Fuck!"

Rai squatted next to the young man and pulled aside the slit environment suit. He chortled. "Well, at least it'll be easier to get you out of this now, right?"

"I'm fucked up."

"I know. I let him go too far. It was just this thing, this whole idea we were sold out."

"I get it, sure."

Rai peeled the environment suit away, then hooked an arm around Penn and got him to his feet. "Sometimes, you get obsessed with an idea, you lose track of things, like basic human decency."

"It happens, I—unh! I know."

"Well, you're gonna be okay, hear me? We'll get you patched up, get some painkillers and stims into you, and we'll be outta here before that destroyer knows what's going on."

"Thanks, Dev. Thanks. Really."

They swung into the infirmary, and Rai set his pistol down on a bed and helped Penn up onto it. Rai slid a drawer open. "Get that shirt off. We'll seal the wounds up."

"Okay." Penn pulled his shirt off with some effort, biting back a hiss. He tossed the bloody thing to the floor and probed the wounds. "Fucking pellets are still in there."

"Yeah. We'll get them dug out when we get to port. You won't even feel them after a bit." Rai set an injector and a bottle of skin sealant on the bed.

"How the hell did you ever work with that guy?"

"Vic? He had his uses. Quentin treated him like an adopted son." Rai sprayed disinfectant over the wounds.

Penn couldn't suppress the hiss. "They were crazy. All of them."

"Not crazy. Desperate." Rai seemed to think about that, then nodded. "Yeah. Crazy."

The sealant was cold, soothing. It had its own anesthetic, but the injection was a full-blown painkiller that made Penn's toes tingle after a couple seconds. "Better. Thanks."

Rai nodded, but he seemed a little distracted as he pulled a gray pair of thermals from another drawer and set them down next to Penn. "I've been thinking, though."

"What about?" Penn tugged the thermal shirt on, then pulled his old pants off. He was looking forward to a shower.

"What Vic said. About there being someone who sold us out. I've been thinking about it, trying to track back who that could've been."

"You think someone did? Sell us out?"

Rai nodded. "Makes sense." He turned around. "Doesn't—"

Penn whipped the pistol off the bed just as Rai flashed a scalpel. "Don't, Dev."

"It was you?"

"It's my job." A cold grimace settled on Penn's face as he sighted on Rai's chest.

"Your job? What kind of job is that?"

"You know."

Rai smiled. "I guess I do. And you know that blaster doesn't have a charge left to it."

"Fuck." Penn hurled the weapon at Rai and rolled off the bed just ahead of the inevitable slash.

But Rai was fast. He hopped over the bed and landed beside Penn as he rolled into the corner. "Tell me why, Eli. Tell me who."

Penn raised his hands. "I'm sorry, Dev." He flexed, and a patch of skin tore away from his wrist, and a small sliver of a gun slapped into his palm. "Honestly."

Rai's eyes widened, and he lunged.

But Penn had the pistol. He fired, and the small slug struck Rai in the chest before exploding.

He staggered back, grunting as if he'd never considered it possible he could be shot by someone. His back slammed into a wall, then his feet gave way. The scalpel slipped from his fingers and clattered off the floor as he dropped onto his butt.

Rai blinked, and his dark eyes fluttered. He pulled a necklace from inside his shirt and clutched the chain. "The...great...con..."

"No con. Just the job."

"The...great..." Rai's eyes closed. "Con."

Penn grabbed the scalpel with a bloody hand, stepped on the other man's wrist, then checked his pulse. It was fading fast; slashing the carotid finished the process. As Rai bled out, Penn tended the wound caused by his pop-out weapon. He saluted the fallen man, then limped back to the cargo hold, where he took Gabriel's environment suit and headed to the airlock.

The job wasn't quite done just yet.

32

As the Kedraalian petty officer headed across the umbilical, Captain Ulrich Keller headed up to the bridge of the *Hammer of Heaven*. His shoes tapped smartly against the dimly lit gray steps of the central stairs. When he reached the bridge, he hesitated at the hatch long enough to study the device the young woman had left with him. It was the sort of engineering marvel he would expect from one of the assorted research and development centers back on Heimatwelt, the Federation home world. Well, minus the eye toward the accepted aesthetic.

He sighed. There were scapegoats enough to save his career, but that wouldn't undo the losses suffered. Good officers and Marines had died. The ship had been damaged. And in any debacle, there was no true escape for a commanding officer.

Unless he survived what was almost certainly a conspiracy.

That was the idea the Kedraalian woman had painted: the image of a twisted plot.

Her hand had been so warm and gentle against his, her clothes and flesh passing along her heat. He sniffed—yes, perfume. Delicate, flowery.

Preminger had joked of his captain forcing himself upon the woman, but Keller wondered: What if she had actually been interested in spending some time with him? What if she had offered to stay with him to become a prisoner to the Federation? Would he have found pleasure in her? Surely she was too beautiful to have been—

He squeezed his eyes shut and chuckled. They had been in space too long, and his mind had started to lose its edge. And the stress. Yes, the stress of teetering so close to war. How else could he have found himself drawn to someone inferior? And to think of lying with her?

The hatch opened, and a young man froze halfway through, long face drawn and pale. "Captain Keller!" The lieutenant backpedaled and stood at attention, his eyes staring straight ahead. "Captain on the bridge!"

Keller breezed past, device clenched in his fist once more. "Status, please."

Commander Foster spun around at his position behind the helm. He was an older man, older even than his captain, with white hair and pockmarked skin that seemed to hang loosely from an unpleasantly blockish skull. "Captain. Sergeant Preminger has Marines gathered in the hangar bay. He requests permission to take them across to the *Rakshasa*."

The idea of Preminger squeezing his chubby body into an environment suit to relive his glory days as an assault Marine almost brought a smile to Keller's face. "How long before we have power?"

"Fifteen minutes at worst."

"Send them across. And have them perform a more thorough search of the ship."

"As you command, sir."

The old sergeant had been something once, more than a decade ago. Let him enjoy himself.

Keller took up a position behind the command console and listened to the unnatural calm. Without the ventilation system and the hum of systems, the bridge sounded like a mausoleum. When the officers spoke, it was in hushed whispers that gave away their discomfort and confusion. In a battle, they would have *something* to do. There would be the intensity born of a desperate struggle for survival. For now, they were dead in space, waiting, and the only way to strike against the enemy was to send troops across and engage them.

But when they were done with the traitors, the *Hammer of Heaven* could dispose of the ships with warheads from the missile arsenal. With or without power, the enemies would be erased.

Until then, Keller had to find something to keep his mind off what the pretty Kedraalian woman had suggested.

Who would be behind using him and his crew—his ship!—for this?

Rivals, of course, but which ones?

He would have to dig deep, call upon allies and those who owed him a debt. Once he was safely back in Federation space, that was exactly what he would do, but for the moment, he studied the device. It seemed an intriguing part of the little mystery he'd been hurled into.

As he rolled the thing around in his hand, he wondered about the rationale for sending the *Hammer of Heaven* to the DMZ in the first place. There were ships that could have arrived to the same point for patrol much quicker, and a destroyer seemed far too much to deal with threats of this nature. After seven months on patrol along the Gulmar-facing planetary holdings, his crew was overdue for rest.

Another question to be answered—he would have to call in more favors.

Lights flickered, then the consoles all around the bridge flared to life. A chorus of relieved laughs replaced the silence.

Foster smiled at Keller. "Power restored, Captain."

"Thank you, Commander. I noticed."

Foster chuckled. "We should be able to connect with the Marines now."

Keller pocketed the device. "Do so, please."

With a slight bow, Foster returned to the bank of consoles at the helm. He muttered something to the pale-faced junior officer running the communications system, and the young man spoke earnestly into the headset he'd just slipped on.

"Sergeant Preminger, this is the *Hammer of Heaven*, do you read? Over."

The young man squinted in concentration, then repeated himself. A moment later, he whispered something to Foster, who turned to Keller. "They have found corpses on the ship, Captain."

"Corpses?"

"Two of the privateers and...one of our ensigns. Wallot. Engineering."

Keller grunted. He felt like collapsing in on himself. Ensign Wallot had been a competent and in fact promising officer. The Wallot family had enough connections to get their daughter into the prestigious Federation Naval Academy, and then onto the *Hammer of Heaven*. And they would no doubt destroy the career of the captain who let her be killed.

Finally, Keller found a little strength. "Did she kill them?"

Foster checked with the young officer, who was still chattering with Preminger. "Apparently not, Captain." Foster brushed at his white hair. "She was...treated unkindly from the look of it."

Keller looked away. A medical examination would be called for. Inquiries. Shame.

It was exactly as young Miss Stiles had said: The privateers were animals.

Foster cleared his throat. "Sergeant Preminger says there is still one privateer unaccounted for."

"Which?" Keller hoped it might be the brutish one. Unleashing an interrogator on the man would provide at least a small sense of justice.

"The one who disappeared, apparently. There is some confusion."

"Who has gathered the dead aboard the *Hammer*?"

"Lieutenant Holmann. He should have them in the infirmary." Foster seemed to realize what was expected of him. He stepped away from the console and started speaking into his private radio.

While Foster gathered the most current information, Keller tapped his toes. It seemed an ideal solution would be to evacuate the privateer vessel and blast it to pieces, but there were questions unanswered. Any one of those answers might make sense of the madness and maybe even salvage his career.

And then Foster was there, face knotted in a way that said he didn't have such answers. "Sergeant Preminger says there is another body, this one in a hidden cold sleep area off the infirmary."

"The missing privateer?"

"No, Captain. A woman. He has no idea who she is."

Keller slammed a fist against the command console deck. "We need answers, not more questions!"

"Yes, you are right, Captain. And there is good news." Foster smiled broadly. "The giant is among the dead on the *Rakshasa*. So is the dark-skinned man."

"How is that good news?"

"Lieutenant Holmann has confirmed the dead in the infirmary: the old man and the young boy. That leaves only the one reported missing earlier."

"Then he could easily still be aboard the *Hammer*."

Foster's smile withered. "Y-yes, Captain."

"Alert the crew, please, Commander. Promptly."

Rattled, it took Foster a second, but he turned back to the helm and passed the command along.

It was obviously time to start removing variables. Keller had long ago grown tired of all the crazy, ridiculous unknowns. He rapped the console with his right hand. "Commander, please bring up the video of the Kedraalian search-and-rescue vessel."

Foster passed the command along to the officer running sensors, and the image of the *Pandora* filled the main display. The ship was a dull gray against the backdrop of space. The *Hammer's* lights showed an old vessel, unassuming, probably not even functional enough to be a tender ship in the lowest of the Azoren fleets. There was a faint, blue glow around it: deflector shields. The petty officer was in the process of getting the ship running, at least.

And nothing remained in the small vessel but the pretty, young petty officer.

And the dead crew.

Keller set his jaw and leaned forward. "Both ships are to be destroyed. Recall the Marine detachment. Start with this one. A missile barrage."

"As you command, Captain." Foster's voice shook as he relayed the command.

Would the strike be quick enough to prevent Stiles from suffering? It should. Even just one of the *Hammer's* missiles could tear apart a ship twice as large as the Kedraalian vessel. At worst, the young woman would be hurtled into space and would die almost instantly from exposure. If she had an environment suit on still, she would pass out once her oxygen was depleted.

It was almost merciful.

Yet Keller's hands shook. The order seemed almost petty, but he had been handed a mystery to unravel with no clues that made any sense.

He drew the device from his pocket and was surprised to see a red light blinking. The light was perfectly flush with the skin of the thing and in between blinks looked exactly like the rest of the skin.

How strange.

"Captain?" Foster sounded almost frightened.

Keller squeezed the device. "Yes?"

"Weapons crews report something is wrong with the missiles. The warheads are already armed."

"Armed? How is this possible?"

"Something has accessed our systems. The launch codes are compromised!"

"But—" Keller opened his palm. The flashing was more persistent. Could the device...? "Eject the missiles! Now!"

The flashing turned to a steady, bright, red glow.

Rumbling began from deep in the warship's bowels, and warning lights flared on every console on the master helm deck. The young officers gasped and twisted around, looking to their commanders for guidance.

Then Keller had the answer to how quickly Stiles would have died from the missile strike as the force of the simultaneously detonated warheads tore the *Hammer of Heavens* into fiery pieces that flew apart and spun until all oxygen had been depleted. But Keller felt only an instant of crushing pressure, which pulverized him long before the fireball washed over his bloody flesh.

Stiles pulled her environment suit helmet off. The corpses of the *Pandora*'s crew lay in a horizontal line near the base of the stairs leading to the upper deck. They hadn't been abused in any way, which would have surprised them if they'd lived. It didn't surprise her; she knew a great deal more about Azoren behavior and culture than most.

In theory, she reminded herself. Training was one thing. *Living* an experience was something else.

Now she had lived through an encounter with the enemy.

So far. If she didn't act quickly, that might not hold true.

It was cool in the cargo bay, the air still thick with the pungent remnant of the boarding weapons. Her breathing was nearly as loud as the circulation system churning away, trying to clean the air. With the cargo bay mostly emptied, it felt cavernous and lonely.

No time for loneliness.

There was so much to do and so little time. She had to start with the most important item, and that was getting everything online again. She hurried up the steps and let herself onto the bridge, where she queued up diagnostic runs and launch prep. If everything checked out, the deflector shields would power on, followed by the engines. She unzipped her environment suit, then her flight suit, and pulled a small device from the pocket of her shorts. She set that device on the console, and it transmitted coordinates to the command console. Even if something happened to her, the ship had its destination.

She rushed back down the stairs and readied herself for the next part —the worst part. Work from easiest to hardest. That was the only way to get things done.

The smallest of the corpses was Parkinson, the gangly little engineer, but she couldn't bring herself to deal with him first. Instead, she turned to Kohn. Almost as slim and not too much taller, she could manage his weight, and she actually cared about him. Some.

She dragged him to the forward lift and set him down at the doors, then returned, first for Dietrich, then Benson, then Grier, then Halliwell, then finally for Parkinson.

Once they were all at the lift, she opened the door and dragged them in, using Parkinson's body to hold the door open. What were a few post-mortem bruises?

On the upper deck, she repeated the process, dragging Parkinson out to block the door, then dragging the others over him. This time, she got them to the infirmary hatch before setting them down. And from there, she got them into the surgical bay.

It got harder at that point. She was soaked with sweat from exertion, and her muscles ached.

But work remained.

Stripping the bodies was the worst of it. The gore, the ruined flesh, the dead faces. She washed them down quickly, checked that they were all still viable—no head wounds, no hearts destroyed before the resuscitation medication could have shut them down—then moved them to the cold sleep chamber.

She slid a drawer out for each one, lowering them into the protective gel, then buckling them into place. Then she pampered herself and showered, washing away the gel and gore and grime from the exertion.

When she stepped out of the shower, she gasped. "How—?"

Penn set Rai's pistol on the counter of a sink. "One of their Marines got me. Help me out of this suit."

She wrapped her towel around her and undid his environment suit. "Are they dead?"

"All of them."

"The infiltrator module worked. And your explosives placement was perfect."

"Six months of nonstop training. It paid off."

She helped him to a toilet stall. "The deck plans were still accurate?"

"Mostly." He groaned as she pulled the thermal top off. "Watch it."

Her fingers traced over the slick sealant covering his wounds. "Are the pellets still inside?"

"Every single one. And I can feel them, even with painkillers."

"You're lucky you didn't bleed out."

"I know. It was the big idiot. He nearly got everyone killed." Penn grabbed her by the fold of the towel. "Wouldn't you have liked that?"

"We're on the same team, Agent Penn."

"Sure. Same team. Everyone's on the same team."

She glanced down at his hand and cocked her head. "Is this going to be like the privateers now?"

He let go. "I don't know who to trust anymore. Undercover for all this time—"

"You'd think the Directorate would take better care of one of its most valuable assets."

"We're all expendable in Security and Intelligence."

"That's a terrible attitude."

Penn snorted. "You think it's any different in GSA?"

"Of course not. Everyone in the military accepts that they could die in the line of duty." She studied the sealant covering his bloody wrist. "You had to use your gun?"

"Rai was smart. He figured something was up. He nearly got me."

"I can do a better job patching that up, if you'd like?"

"Maybe later. We've got days before we arrive." He playfully tugged at the knot in the towel. "You got any ideas about how to pass the time?"

Her cool stare seemed to get through to him. "We're not out of here yet."

"Group for Strategic Assessment." He chuckled. "They teach you to sleep around and get in the heads of your targets, but they don't teach you to sleep with SAID agents?"

She stepped away as he dragged his underwear down. "I told you, we're on the same team."

"So show a teammate some love, Brianna."

"Clean up first."

He smiled and stepped into the shower she'd abandoned. "Isn't this great? GSA and SAID working together? The Republic can't lose when civilians and military all have the same objective."

"Just keep your perspective."

"I always do." He turned the water on. "Maybe you could wash my back for me."

"Or not."

"So testy."

She picked the pistol up. It was a Graynard LP-7, the same model the dark-skinned privateer had used. "That Rai, he was fast. How'd you get the drop on him?"

"I almost didn't. He left that out for me to grab, and I fell for it. No charges left. He came close to getting me with a scalpel."

"But you got him with your snap-pistol?"

"Last second."

"Seriously?"

"Why would I lie?"

"You *are* SAID."

"Sure. But I thought we were buddies."

"It would still be something to see. You catch it on your recording device?"

He poked his head out of the shower and tapped his left eye, chuckling. "I caught it all."

"Left eye camera?"

Penn's chuckle died as she sighted on the right side of his face, then smiled evilly. "No charge. Remember?" He pushed the door open and stepped toward her.

"Did you bother to check?" She calmly pulled the trigger, and his head rocked back from the blast, then he crashed to the shower floor. She walked to the infirmary with the same calm, retrieved a scalpel, and returned to the shower to cut out his recording device.

Everything the GSA needed to know about Penn's mission was embedded in that cybernetic eye.

It was a messy struggle getting him back into his thermals and environment suit, which she stuffed a few critical storage devices into before blasting a matching hole in the helmet. She almost enjoyed dragging him to the lift, then through the cargo bay. Debris rattled off the *Pandora's* deflector shields and moved the vessel away from the *Rakshasa* as Stiles stuffed the SAID agent's body inside the airlock. She waited a few minutes while the destroyer's debris cleared the area, then evacuated the air from the airlock, expelling Penn's corpse. She counted to ten, then remotely triggered the *Rakshasa's* SOS beacon again, this time letting it run continuously.

Everything was in place now: the blasted husk of the Azoren destroyer, the unregistered Union privateer ship with a key Haidakura executive in cold sleep, and the body of Eli Penn, complete with evidence of his work as an Azoren spy.

All floating in the DMZ.

She changed into a fresh uniform, cleaned up the mess in the bathroom, then returned to the bridge just in time to strap in for acceleration. It would be several hours before she could jump to Fold Space. She typed in a message and studied it: *Mission Accomplished.*

That looked right. Short and to the point. She encrypted it and transmitted it to the predetermined coordinates.

Then she relaxed and drifted off to sleep.

Her work had just begun.

THE END

ACKNOWLEDGMENTS

Shadow Moves is the first chapter of **The War in Shadow**. The series explores a combination of space opera and military science fiction in a way that I hope will entertain readers of multiple genres.

I drew on numerous influences to put this story and the series together. First and foremost, I wanted to give a nod to our history and to current events. In a world where nuclear weapons are still only a button press away from use, we should be listening, watching, and planning, all with an eye toward avoiding war wherever possible. But when war is called for, we should be ready to execute it effectively. And where our security and survival is at stake, we need to be merciless.

It's a lesson we oftentimes don't seem to have learned.

For the setting, I drew on the various materials, including those I recall from games I played in the 1970s and 1980s, in particular *Space Opera* and *Traveller*.

This particular tale gives a nod to Quentin Tarantino's "Reservoir Dogs" and Bryan Singer's "The Usual Suspects."

If you enjoyed *Shadow Moves*, I hope you'll pick up the rest of the series. Also, please consider posting a review and letting friends know about the series. Word of mouth and reviews are pure gold.

For updates on new releases and news on other series, please visit my website and sign up for my mailing list at:

http://www.p-r-adams.com

ABOUT THE AUTHOR

I was born and raised in Tampa, Florida. I joined the Air Force, and my career took me from coast to coast before depositing me in the St. Louis, Missouri area for several years. After a tour in Korea and a short return to the St. Louis area, I retired and moved to the greater Denver, Colorado metropolitan area.

I write speculative fiction, mostly science fiction and fantasy. My favorite writers over the years have been Robert E. Howard, Philip K. Dick, Roger Zelazny, and Michael Crichton.

Social Media:
www.p-r-adams.com
pradams_author@comcast.net

Printed in Great Britain
by Amazon

38105881R00175